NIÑA HUANCA

NIÑA HUANCA

Faustino Gonzalez-Aller

Translated from the Spanish by Margaret Sayers Peden

A RICHARD SEAVER BOOK

The Viking Press   New York

A Richard Seaver Book / The Viking Press
First published in 1977 by The Viking Press
625 Madison Avenue, New York, N.Y. 10022
Published simultaneously in Canada by
The Macmillan Company of Canada Limited

Printed in the United States of America
Set in phototype Palatino

LIBRARY OF CONGRESS CATALOGING IN PUBLICATION DATA
Gonzalez-Aller, Faustino.
  Niña Huanca.
  "A Richard Seaver book."
  I. Title.
PZ4.G64935Ni3   [PQ6657.05113]   863'.6'4   76-46525
ISBN 0-670-51338-5

Logbook of the brigantine *La Belotte*, written in the maternal blood of a bastard who wanted to be president of a Caribbean republic.

A NOTE ON THE COLONEL'S "WALKERS"

In 1855 an American adventurer named William Walker took advantage of a dispute between Nicaragua's Liberal and Conservative parties to promote himself from Commander in Chief of the army to President of the country. In the process, he captured a ship owned by Commodore Cornelius Vanderbilt, who promptly mobilized the neighboring Central American nations to oust Walker.

Walker then tried to find another presidential vacancy in Central America but was unsuccessful, and finally, in 1860, in Honduras, he was caught and shot. In Colonel Arruza's nation, Walker's name has been immortalized to signify the hired guns of his personal guard.

—THE EDITOR

NIÑA HUANCA

"Grab 'im, grab 'im!" The man selling sweet-potato candies should have been shouting "Get your sweets here!" but his pocket was as light as a good man's conscience and he was yelling "Grab 'im" to distract the official who was checking peddlers' permits. The sonofabitch. That many candies, made every night in Cholita's kitchen, meant that many centavos for the tax man. "Grab 'im, grab 'im!" His cry was barely audible in the plaza surrounded by colonial columns, with canvas awnings and fly netting baking beneath the sun. Screeching parrots, people cursing, begging, and quarreling, and everywhere a stench like blood coming as much from sweat-darkened clothes as from the hanging slabs of meat or the peel of the wild plum. "Wanted: Trinidad de los Santos, guerrilla or bandit." "Can you read this for me, buddy? What are the authorities saying here? Pretty soon food prices will be coming down, a break for the poor. A good day to you, sir!"

"Candles, candles and votive lamps for the saints!" "Shoe polish and shoelaces!" "The federal officers made a raid last night. Brave men. Fine, upstanding men, do a lot of good. Don't laugh, I mean it. Our honorable President and his good lady . . . God bless 'em! His wife's pregnant, it's that season." "That green blouse with the lace trim, would you put it aside for me, honey, until I get back from the café?"

"Thirtyonethousandeighthundredandtwentyfour!"

"Hey, *chola*, baby, are you coming with me to the café?" "Do you always get your way, huh? And so fresh!" You'll never see teeth like these, or a smile as sweet. "Long live Trinidad de los Santos!" "Who said that? You talk very big, and it's all hot air." "You're right. The people are nothing but trash." They crawled up the steps of the cathedral on their knees, clutching candles.

There's a little of everything in the plaza with the columns. Behind the cathedral, the Presidential Palace. Right now he's probably in his office with his ministers and the Chief of Police. The Indian soldiers in his guard never laugh. Neither do the Indians crawling up the steps of the cathedral. It's the others who smile: buyers and sellers, the men pissing against the columns, and the ones selling parrots, and herbs to cure lumbago. "Hey, beautiful, why're you walking like that? Because you're such hot stuff?" *"You'll* never know." "Long live the President!" "I am a cavalry soldier, I wear a special uniform because I'm in the cavalry. . . ." Trinidad de los Santos doesn't have a horse. The Spaniards brought the horse. Trinidad de los Santos goes on foot, wearing boots he stole from the engineer at Shelter Limited.

The Spaniards also brought the burro, the best thing that ever happened to the poor. "Then why doesn't Trinidad de los Santos have a burro?" "He has one, but Gloria and his three kids are using it to follow him through the mountains. They say Gloria's expecting, too, like the President's wife." It's the mating season for everyone and everything. And why not? The dealer in prints and secondhand books was an educated man, and it was a pleasure to listen to him.

"My uncle, the choirmaster of Santa Engracia, taught me to love Bach. When I was a young boy like you—all illiterates are boys—I used to dream about music. To me, everything was music: the wind, the streams, the moans of the Indian women. I was a very primitive child, I think. Wouldn't you say so? It took my uncle's arrival at my parents' house to pro-

2

duce a real transformation in me. In three summers he taught me solfeggio, harmony, and counterpoint. As I learned, I ceased to notice the sound of the streams and the wind. What memories! One day the sacristan came to tell us that my uncle had jumped from the choirloft to the baptistery."

"Your fine uncle? But the church wasn't meant for people to commit suicide in, to kill themselves in—hell, that goes against God's law. Don't it? Well, don't it? Don't give me a lot of crap about how holy he was, my friend. He jumped, and that's that." "A coin, sir, for the love o' God." He was blind. But he was truly blind, one of those men who draw a curtain across the window of their sight. "I wish I'd seen Trinidad de los Santos just once, don't you? Only a good-for-nothing is lucky enough to get a break like that. Give me a peso's worth of *chicha* for my friend here. A man can't keep going without a little drink. Isn't that right, my friend?" "*Hey, mister! I know very well the city.*" A wink. The kids are sharp about leading the tourists to places where they sell sombreros and maracas and crocodile handbags, and to the local whorehouses that are sometimes called *quilombos*. "*Very exciting!*" "*Isn't it cute?*"

A man making baskets, a man selling big clay jars. "Jars and jugs, jars and jugs here!" "Give me three soupbones, and don't be stingy." "What can an honorable man do in the face of all these germs and wars? Not to mention taxes, and a featherbrained, ungrateful daughter. It's a good thing my oldest son is in the Common Market. A great thing, yes sir." "What do you suppose the President is saying at this moment to the French Ambassador?" "The worst thing about our times is the lack of respect for life. I remember my emotions during my last days in the maternal womb. You can't? Well, these are things we inherited from the Maya. No one understands us."

Pale and blond as a German, little bastard. "I wanted to see the light, I remember that, and I was crying because my blood still wasn't whole. I was in France twice during that period. There in the womb I could hear my dear mother's voice when she saw the Eiffel Tower. God Almighty! That was a great event for me, hearing my poor mother's cry announcing me to my people. Poor mother, a victim of the September Revolution! And not one of us will ever see the end of it."

"Doesn't it make you sad?" The Ambassador knew how to talk for the sake of talking, and he could listen to anything at all, for hours, for years, on end. "I wouldn't like to die before the first day of the twenty-first century." "Yes, it's beautiful to see the beginning of something: a day, a century, a civilization, freedom. I was born on the day they opened the Panama Canal. They started a savings account for me with twenty-five pesos." Colonel Arruza's car drove into the plaza with the columns. Even the parrots stopped screeching. He began to walk, flanked by four soldiers with machine guns. He patted the heads of children and haunches of the burros. A man with a flute took a deep breath and started playing again. The Colonel liked it. Someone smiled at him. You'd never find smiles like those, not even in China. The whole plaza began to smile.

"Whenever I hear the flute I have premonitions. Perhaps today I will hear the voice of Abraham. What profound mystery, Lord, what profound mystery there is in all your creations. My heart, at moments like these, has no greatness, it has nothing. Don't you ever, my sons, long to put your hand inside your breast, pluck out your heart, kiss it, and put it back in its place again?"

Smiles. Fixed. Smiles. And suddenly "Long live the Colonel!" It was a loud *viva* that echoed until Don Félix Arruza Villalba disappeared in his bulletproof limousine. And Trinidad de los Santos was in the mountains. Mountains everywhere. They said that Trinidad de los Santos was the Colonel's man. "Who said that? I'll spit on the bastard!" "Shoe polish and shoelaces!" "*Mister, mister, you want to see the show?*" "You see? The price of food's gone down three centavos. You just have to have patience and hope." The first rays of the sun parch the peddlers' brains. The idiot was still catching flies. "You mean to tell me this money is no good?" Ibrahím Obregón heard everything. He was a spy for the Chief of Police. It was better not to say anything around Ibrahím. Trinidad de los Santos had marked him for death; still, every day, there was Ibrahím, lively as the butterflies. At night, Ibrahím disappeared in Rampart Street. Trinidad was wrong. You'd have to kill a lot more like Ibrahím who had their own spies. "I like my little *chola* but we only talked about the kind of thing you have to talk about at times like that. You never know who the little bitches are going to spill everything to." "Candles, candles for the saints!" "My kids don't drink milk, but they like powdered milk. They get it at school." "Long live the First Lady! She's expecting, like the wife of Trinidad de los Santos."

"Officer of the guard!"

"Colonel Arruza!"

At exactly one o'clock he had a conference with the President. Officer of the guard! Every day they shook hands, cordially. They drank scotch and soda. The President's office was air-conditioned. A photograph inscribed by Billy Graham. "Trinidad de los Santos. How can it be, Colonel?" The President's second son came in for a minute to accuse his brother Efraím of trying to poison him. His father gave him a kiss and a hundred-peso note. "Trinidad de los Santos. Why hasn't that man been caught yet, Colonel?" The Colonel drank, his eyes half-closed. He was very softhearted that day.

"It will all work out, Mr. President, it will all work out."

From the marketplace, through the closed windows, they could hear only faint sounds of Indian men and women, children and parrots. And the soft notes of a flute that made the Colonel's heart skip a beat—as if it were a fucking quetzal.

After the roots, we will eat the leaves. Our filthy bodies are wrapped in rags. When will the tears in the eyes of the poor be dried?

—*Sinkiang folksong (before the Revolution)*

They came from every direction. Did you see them? They walked swiftly with their cartridge belts hidden beneath their shirts. Product of Central America. Dacron and rayon. 12 ½. Where's your gun, Silverio? My gun's in the banana tree, God knows. The Colonel knows too, but *they* don't know that. The boss of the rich guys knows everything. Obregón must have told him. There are Obregóns in all the cornfields, dressed in burlap and straw like the scarecrows. What do you see, buddy? Nothing. The burros are loaded with vegetables and big clay pots. Is there contraband hidden in them? Just innocent-looking goods poking through the holes, that's all. Will they unload everybody's burro to see if it's carrying anything else? Obregón said they should. They ought to—we don't want any surprises, right, counselor? But the guards roll their eyes as if their only mission were to show off their black pupils. Go on, go on by. I knew that's what they'd do. It's raining so hard you'd think it was the day of Noah's flood. Burros are swimming in the valley beds, with Indians hanging onto their tails. They have to be in Potchilango before midnight. There someone will tell them where to go next. Trinidad de los Santos had sent word three days before. Come, and bring everything with you, even if you're struck by lightning. God will be with me! What side are you on? Me? Right where I've always been—behind an empty table. My woman and kids—they're so small I could carry them in the packs on my burros—stayed behind in the hut with our hen that lays an egg a day that we save for little Lito, who's been on the cot, with fever, for three months. Sandals aren't much use against that dark water, thick mud, stones, drowned livestock. White pants stick to thin legs. Over the shirt, a rubberized poncho, the kind you can buy in the American supermarket. And the big hat with the wide brim that rolls up on the sides like gutters. Can you make it, brother? Sure, I'll make it. I have to make it. Trinidad de los Santos asked me to make it.

Trinidad de los Santos is sipping his pulque, very slowly, as if he didn't enjoy it. He's at the Maryknoll Mission near Potchilango. The missionary's name is Father Richard Godfrey. Blond and thin. From Massachusetts. The two are smoking cheap black cigars. Hidden around the grounds of the mission are Trinidad de los Santos's most trusted men. See if you can find them, Obregón. The priest is trying to convince Trinidad de los Santos not to attack the barracks. Something stinks. That's the way the American priest talks. Trinidad de los Santos's woman stayed behind in Santa Cruz to have their fourth child. The other three and the hen are with her and the friend who is looking after them all until Trinidad de los Santos can finish what he's doing. God grant it turn out well! Trinidad de los Santos is small and neat. His thick hair is as black as his eyes, which are like two pieces of night. Why do you hate me, Trinidad? The guerrilla doesn't hate anybody. He doesn't hate the night, either. Those eyes will change at the dawn of the day everyone's waiting for. Amen. Trinidad listens without moving his eyes. Not because he dismisses what the priest, who is his friend, says, but because there's very little to say once the dogs have been untied, isn't that right? I'm with you, Trinidad de los Santos, and I'll march beside you to the barracks. We'll die together, if necessary, but this—it's too easy, it stinks of a trap. A swine's trap, my friend. It mus' be done, Padre. I know it is a trap; do you think I'm still wet behind the ears? But I'll use their trap to spring my own. The priest draws on the strong cigar. The guerrilla hands him his handmade lighter and peers out the door. Men are arriving, drenched with rain. The Peace of God, Trinidad! Men emerge from the bushes and show the new men where to unload the clay pots from their burros. See? They're coming now, Padre. This time I'll have more than a thousan'. The Colonel needs to trump Trinidad de los Santos's trick. That doesn't mean that Trinidad de los Santos is going to *let* him do it. There's the trace of a smile on the guerrilla's face. The priest doesn't completely understand. At one o'clock the rain stops. Why so many fires when it's so hot? Hot as blazes. To dry their pants, mister. To get their cartridge belts back in shape. You'd expect a lot of noise, but there isn't any. Where are the women? There are no women this time. And no children. They've taken the guns down from the trees. They're rifles, not shotguns. They oil them with mineral oil.

What are those lights? They're the black-light traps from Dr. Cortez's hacienda. The banana trees around here are bein' attacked by black fruit flies. Black light, black hair, black eyes, black flies. What do you want, Trinidad de los Santos? To govern the country? No, not me. We have all kinds of sprays and killers for plants and animals. We'd be better off if the Snipe Commander that flies over to kill the horn flies that feed on the cattle would wipe out the bloodsuckin' insects that light on the backs of the Indians to suck *their* blood. Ah, yessss! It's nothin' to do with governin'—God knows I don' know nothin' about that—what we need is jus' to kill off all the human pests. Why not? After a revolution the same thing always happens. You go back and one by one you run into the losers. Some threaten, some beg. But in the end everything's the same: more tortillas and more measles. I was born here. A good land? Bad people? A little of everything, Padre. I had a father, but after one of the revolutions, they shot him. Zósimo's father was born a coward, and they shot him, too. Maybe Zósimo's grandfather picked a bad night to make a son. Or a bad woman. Though she was an Indian. Anyway, Zósimo weeps for his father, in spite of everything. And he's my lieutenant. You know what I tell him? That he mus' be lookin' for a chance to be filled with bullet holes. How can I hold back that flood? Zósimo dug down and buried that chicken-hearted father very deep so there wouldn' be no ghosts to scare his mother at night. When they execute someone, either military or civilian, Zósimo's father turns over in his grave, because he knows what it's all about. He should've turned over a little while he was alive, it's no good once you're dead. I don' know what the gringos think of my people's ways, but that's how we are and that's how we will be as long as the sun shines on the land of those who have owners' papers. Not for me. Even though I'm hungry and I'm thirsty. You can see, there's enough land for everybody. You're afraid, Padre. Don't worry. Things that begin bad end right. The worst thing is to worry about it before the lead turns cold in your body. And he poured more pulque. The two men drank. Zósimo came to tell them that everybody had come except Enrique the Cripple and Amado Suárez. It was two in the morning. And now, Padre, bless my troops before we start out for the capital. Where are they? The trees are looking at us with the eyes of brothers. Ready? Well, spit to the east and hope that we travel the road of God. They left the burros in the corral that they had rigged for them, along with the packs under the sheds. Zósimo! The priest was walking alongside the lieutenant. Do you have children, Zósimo? I had one but I los' him. You lose everything in this thievin' land. But I'll have another if I get the chance. A son would never be too much to feed, don't you think?

They formed a white line in the clear night.

Colonel Don Félix Arruza lived in a French-style mansion on the Country Club grounds, because this exclusive development, where VIPs paid a lot of money to play golf, also belonged to him. But between the Colonel's feudal estate and the golf course stood a line of guarumo trees (whose leaves are a good tonic for the heart) and ten soldiers, who, because of the color of their uniforms and their stolidity, resembled eucalyptus trees. People called them "Walkers." Things that hang on from past history. The terraces behind the mansion led down to the shore and a small private dock for the Colonel's yacht and motorboats. In the two towers of the house were machine gunners, fingers always on the trigger. The swishing petticoats of lusty servant girls were forbidden there. "And where do you think you're going?" The Colonel awoke very early, as the mockingbirds were beginning to sing, and completely naked went for a swim in the transparent water. Then he visited his greenhouses, and his tigers and owls in their cages. He liked these nocturnal birds that cry when they smell a woman's flesh. At eight o'clock he breakfasted English style—kidneys, bacon, sausage, eggs, and tea— while he read the newspaper in the company of his secretary, the lawyer Don Cleto. What interested him most were the obituaries, both national and foreign. He relished the news of Trujillo's demise and of Tacho Somoza's. . . . The third *T*, Tiburcio Carías, was still missing. The Colonel was getting older, but he was a better man now than he'd been when he was young, when he had fathered a son on Niña Huanca. He was fifty-five, as trim as the Indians who cinch their belt buckles at twenty inches. Oh, baby, this is the life! But although he was in great shape, the Colonel was a cuckold, and had been for many years. His wife was named Virginia, like the light, blond tobacco. Virginia Pfandl, daughter of a rich German coffee planter, who still knew how to wield the sickle and the machete. Virginia Pfandl Andrade, educated in France, in Germany, in the United States. Virginia Pfandl Andrade de Arruza, of the Red Cross, the National Commission on the Social and Legal Status of Women, the Protective Association for Native Children . . .

"Virginia-the-cunt!"

She usually slept until eleven in a round bed, protected by mosquito netting like the meat in the market in the colonial plaza. Two Indian girls, dressed like the maids in a vaudeville sketch, scurried silently about the room, which had a reputation as a stable for illiterate studs and was a monument to the pricks of the upper classes, the lower classes, soldiers, film stars, and the imposing pillar of Porfirio Rubirosa, may he rest in glory. The señora slept in the raw; her flesh was young and firm, with the rich, fruity odor of the mammee apple. The Colonel liked to wake her early with an insult. Then he would get into his bulletproof limousine, followed by his escort of Walkers. His wife, awakened by that "Virginia-the-cunt," ate papayas and mangoes peeled by the servants, enjoying the honey-sweet juice that dribbled down her breasts and traveled the furrows of her belly. Then she went immediately to the pink-tiled bathroom, where she took pleasure in her easy bowel movement. She lay for half an hour in a foamy bath, singing silly songs and talking on the telephone with the lover she had chosen for the day. And the Indian girls giggled with embarrassment as the cockatoo, Toña, screeched a wild atonal "Whore!" "You're the thorn of a rose buried deep in my heart, la la la."

"What did you say your name is?" Don Cleto inquired of the man bearing a letter of recommendation to admit him to the hospital.

"Pantaleón de Rivas, at your service."

And Don Cleto sent him to the hospital with a second letter, primarily to be rid of the stench of the ragged shirt that reeked of pus and seborrhea. And he offered him a few coins from his pocket. "Doesn't the gentleman have any ol' clothes?"

Old clothes, very old clothes, the country has its fill of them. But the Colonel was unaware of such trivia as his limousine sped along the dusty road lined on either side by interminable rows of banana trees. As they watched him pass by, the laborers respectfully removed their wide-brimmed hats, although in various dialects each was shitting on Don Félix Arruza's sonofabitch of a grandmother. These were cinnamon-colored men dried by hunger and the heat that came from the sea. Heavy oxcarts with brightly painted wheels. Could Trinidad de los Santos be somewhere nearby? As the road climbed into the mountains, the Colonel began to smell the perfume of the white flowers of the coffee plantations. Can't you see it's the Colonel? He saw, but he was more interested in drinking from his water gourd. Or shouldn't Juan Nepomuceno, a peon who has coughed since Christmas, even pour *water* into his empty belly? Red initials on the front of a small ranch house: Revolutionary Party of Democratic Unification. Scattered scrawny hens. Women weaving bright blankets beneath thatched roofs. Chickens running through the wild cane. Stone slabs for shaping tortillas pick up shadows from black tresses. Grandpa's as old and stiff and gnarled as jungle vines. How old are you, grandpa? Forty-eight but bent beneath the dead weight of the yokes, he looks double his years. Stones to keep the wind from carrying him away. Oxen ruminating. Poor devils, they're castrated, but at least they have something to chew on. The Colonel's cattle are Holsteins, and he also has Rambouillet sheep. Sheep with Basque shepherds. No one knows the origin of the Indians who ride herd on the cattle through green canyons. They're a different kind of Indian who speak Spanish, like white men; because of that they call them Ladinos instead of Indians. And they eat well and wear good clothes they like to show off in the capital on Sundays. Still, they call Don Eloy and the schoolteacher Ramírez Indians, because they're so poor, to make a distinction in class. Even though the teacher worked for a while in the OAS and speaks English. The man who has the red initials of the party on the front of his little ranch house tries to cover them with tar during the night so the Colonel won't see them when he drives by; that would be disagreeable. Good day to you! The Colonel doesn't even notice. He's thinking about the cattle he's planning to sell to the slaughterhouse in Managua. The stuff is canned and no will know where it came from. Product of Central America. How are you getting along? Gettin' along fine, Colonel. His hacienda is big, beautiful, and right on the border. A hop, skip, and jump and you're across, slick as a whistle. The house sits on a slope, with the volcano in the background. The air is still and balmy, good for the nerves and lungs. Oh, good morning, *patrón*. Her name is Elvirita Parra and she's as pretty as the flowers that bloom at the edge of the snow: tiny white flowers with a blue center. She knelt to greet her *patroncito*, and he gave her his hands to kiss. They had coffee in the pergola with the bellflowers. Elvirita smiled at the *patrón*, revealing the perfect teeth of those who eat tortillas. I love you, Elvirita, but I don't know why. The *patrón* always said pretty things, things that touched the heart. And he brought her presents from the capital. She gazed at them, stroking them with her little cinnamon-colored hands, trying to believe they were hers. The Colonel fell asleep in the rocking chair, lulled by the midday silence. The alarm clock was the airplane from La Taca en route to Guatemala. Elvirita is very happy with the things you brought her, it's like a dream. The Colonel laughs, and strokes the Indian girl's thighs and kisses her firm breasts. Until she, of her own pleasure, legs parted, sits astride the Colonel. The Walkers patrol, hidden by the madrecacao trees, quiet as the macaws. A child makes a boat with a piece of wood. The Colonel picks the cattle that will cross the frontier at sunset and trots Blacky through the meadow. Later he eats roast meat and an avocado salad Elvirita serves him, and goes back to the city to have a few drinks with the President. Trinidad de los Santos. The country has about twenty thousand square miles, almost all jungle. Trinidad slips through them like a rattlesnake. They provide for all his needs in the villages, which they don't do for the government troops. A picture of the guerrilla hangs in every general store in hope that someone will inform on him. Have you seen him? Never, never. How many men did this bandit have with him? Nobody knows how to count above twenty-five. Then there were more. The Colonel knows that Trinidad de los Santos has more than five hundred and fifty riflemen in his band. And they can shoot, yes sir, they shoot to kill. You understand? Today it was so and so. Tomorrow it will be you. And deep inside the Indian laughs because he knows that Trinidad de los Santos, who is like his brother, will never kill him. The Colonel orders his driver to stop at the Governor's house. With great ceremony, the Governor offers him a drink.

"He didn't come through these parts, Colonel. You can be sure of that. If he had, I'd have grabbed him with my men. One way or another, sooner or later, we'll get him. I've baited a trap for him with special cheese, he's like a mouse about cheese. I thought that when they cleaned the brush out of the coffee groves, he might turn up around here, but he's clever, and has a sharp ear. But I'm keeping my eyes peeled, Colonel."

"That's the right idea, Governor; that's the right idea. Otherwise, one of these days you might find another man sitting in that chair. I have one ready for the job. Good-bye."

The streets were patterned with the shadows of people who stared in silence at the bulletproof limousine. Coca-Cola, the drink that refreshes. Tamales, pork tamales! In the outskirts, Maya ruins facing absolute silence. There are still

14

slogans from Cuyamel. In the old days they made presidents. Fruit and heads of state. Fruit is cut while it's still green, and the necks of presidents, too, according to the custom. It's a dangerous profession. Swiss banks are accustomed to paying the widows. Your number? That matters little to the child flying a paper kite. I'm a number, Director. And I'm accompanying her in her grief. Here is your twenty million. Do you want it in greenbacks? Yes, I'm going to live in Miami, in order to be near my beloved homeland. But the President is still alive. So how's everything? Once again, as usual, they are sitting face to face, contemplating each other like gamecocks in separate cages. The Ambassador of the United Fruit Company has presented a complaint. *I got my job through* The New York Times. The President twists restlessly in his easy chair. His wife is pregnant. At any moment, he will have another child. The President lectures on administrative law at the university. He is Dr. Juan Elgidio Báez. He belongs to the Liberal Party. In the party they call him Professor Báez. His wife inherited extensive landholdings on the Pacific coast along the Pan-American Highway. Dr. Báez speaks Harvard English. The Colonel speaks it like a Brooklyn taxi driver. *We feel strongly about the plight of our people.* They have burned a banana grove; they have stolen three trucks from the fruit company; they have kidnaped the captain of the *Peter Townley. Our government has a responsibility toward the UF and must discharge it despite our people's continued defiance of international law. Son of a gun! Our life . . .* those lousy rebels don't understand . . . depends on foreign investments. Parliament is in session. This afternoon I shall summon the cabinet. Will it be a boy or girl? If it's a boy, I'll call him Lincoln. If it's a girl, Rosa Guadalupe. The Presidential Palace looks like a bank. Across the street there is a fourteen-story building with several American offices. And big automobiles line the street. United Fruit has asked for guarantees, or we'll lose the job, that's what the Ambassador told me. The roast meat lies heavy on the Colonel's stomach. He says good-bye. He feels an urgent need to see his wife. But everything is prepared for a reception. Virginia likes people. She has enjoyed her day. This time it was one of the Walkers. A new one, blond, who speaks Spanish badly. The servants are preparing dinner. Cold turkey *en gelée*, shrimp with cocktail sauce, lobster enchiladas, green peppers stuffed with bananas, bean salad, and chilled champagne, the bottles taken from the galley. Don Cleto places Havana cigars on small sandalwood tables, along with bottles of liqueur brought up from the cellars. French cognac and Dutch *crèmes*. Virginia is going to wear one of her new gowns from Balenciaga. The Colonel wears a white dinner jacket with medals. He smells his wife's perfume. He feels the desire of approaching night. She has not put on her dress yet. Only the black bikini, revealing dimpled buttocks. And a French brassiere. The Colonel hesitates. Virginia teases him with her tongue. A tongue like a guava, red, sweet, and juicy with sweet saliva. The Indian girls run laughing from the room, Virginia is like a mare. Hurry, Colonel, give it to her.

To the Honorable Dean of the School of Theology
University of Maguncia
Germany
(Mainz, Fed. Rep. of Germany)

My well-remembered friend and teacher:
I am not sure whether the term "Honorable" (oh,
ancient Europe!) should be applied to you or to the
Rector. In any case, as this is the seventh letter I've written
you—without response to the six preceding—I use the title to
see whether this way my anxiety and your pride might be better served. Come now, Professor, that's a joke! But, I am
serious when I say I need your good counsel. I am at a
crossroads, here in a fly-filled room in the Hotel Alfonso, on a
public square, with a little mulatto girl who keeps bringing me
highballs. This is the last stage of my voyage in search of
myself. The broad-bladed ceiling fan barely stirs the vapors
emanating from Corín's and my naked bodies. I have already
read all the morning newspapers. The radio is turned on and
so is the television (but only the picture, without the sound).
So on the verge of leaping into a terrifying vacuum, I ask
myself: Should I go ahead in this undertaking, or would it
make more sense to turn back? How I envy you, Professor,
there in our beloved library with the drowsy attendants,
among old books on old theology, most ancient logic (poor
logic!), and prehistoric astronomy! Everything began—do you
remember?—one day when we arrived, as usual, at the university and found it was a holiday. We went for a walk along
one of the boulevards bordering the river and immediately became fast friends, in spite of the difference in our ages.

Maguncia was for scholars. Mainz for sailors. You took me to visit the Archbishop and told His Eminence that I was a young Central American. The prelate stared at me as if I were a parrot, and for a moment he seemed tempted to ask if you had taught me any dirty words. During the last semester of my law studies, our friendship deepened. Together we visited all the printing shops run by master draftsmen, sons of masters in this noble craft, and in one we found a map of Central America. That moment was the first chapter of this story I am now living. Standing before the engraving, you asked, not looking at me: "Why don't you go back?" And I answered, "All right," almost without thinking. For two months, the drowsy attendants propped open their eyes long enough to find all of Humboldt's works on America: maps, maps, maps; treatises on geography, on botany; all the histories of the New World; there was nothing on the shelves that we didn't have dusted off and brought to satisfy our curiosity. I believe that Fritz and the Little One—the two attendants—came to hate us. One evening we established, according to the information available to us, the possible feudal holdings of my father. At that time the only thing we knew about him was what my mother wrote: that I had been sired by an important Central American politico. A red ring, like a sacrificial fire, encircled the jackal. How little we left unstudied within those imagined boundaries! Even though we were feeling our way. After I arrived here, I found that the center of the circle was where we had stuck our pin. We could have placed it in a different spot and it would have been the same. What a business, Professor, what a business! If the Lords of Xibalba had granted Humboldt satanic permission to return once again to America, it is certain he would have chosen to return to the shades before completing his voyage. A short time ago I came across a copy of his *Les vues des Cordillères et monuments des peuples indigènes de l'Amérique*, and I felt terribly sad. It was not the same thing to read the account in the library with the drowsy attendants as it was to be here face to face with a reality transformed into a caricature of what Baron Humboldt had seen. One wonders whether the author of the monumental *Kosmos* was a visionary of rather limited scope, or whether America, unintentionally, is capable of refuting all the laws of natural evolution. The amazing thing is that not only he, but also all the other travelers who fill the bookshelves of all the anthropological and geographical societies of the world, have finally come to appear ridiculous. Like Don Quixote, you and I have read all the books on chivalry, great exploits, and good deeds that were written about this part of the Atlantic between the sixteenth and nineteenth centuries. And I tell you we have let ourselves be misled, as if we had lived before the discovery of photography, by things that could not be contradicted with more convincing proof at the time they were written. And finally, Professor, I am mounted upon, and I shall not dismount from, the battered steed of my madness. America does not grant many opportunities for a timely return. Perhaps that is the secret of its continued existence. Its life, nevertheless, is precarious, absurd, and what is worse, tends to bend with every wind. I think this is because it is inhabited by people (not the natives or those of mixed blood) who are spiritually uprooted from the land. They live in this land but their eyes constantly scan other lands whose pasts or futures are ruled by sycophantic love or schizophrenic hatred. They never see themselves as a part of the national reality that surrounds them. And it is worse when they do, as in the case of the United States. Do these imported peoples have a true national or continental coherence, even with many native-born generations behind them? They say they do. And what they say and do is genuine, if they swear it's so, but to those of us who come from outside, even though we were once one of them, they seem only a bad imitation of what they secretly admire or fiercely despise. Here one can expect that the most incomprehensible things will happen. The best and the worst. But neither reaction has any meaning. And here I am in the midst of them, not knowing exactly where to plunge my knife into the ripe *sandía,* which is what they call watermelon here, for no particular reason. My father (rubber latex drips from my tongue as I write this word) is a white Creole product for white Creoles. As others have been. There is no lack of dictators, unfortunately, in America. Still, I believe that Colonel Arruza is the most astute of them all. He has always hidden behind someone he can hoist up or pull down as he pleases. And the country belongs to him. A small number of men of flesh and blood are easily controlled with money, position, decorations, or threats. The others don't count. The "men of corn," men of the land, resign themselves to oblivion. "I gave my back to the smiters" (Isa. 50: 6). Hundreds of years ago their own gods resolved to shroud their eyes with mist. And they do not see. Their backs are better. If a man turns his back, then there is no longer any reason to smite him, right? Among those hundreds of thousands who *have* turned their backs, there are a few who rebel and hide in the mountains. Days and nights I have been here without shutting an eye, exhausted by heat and humidity, with my brandy and soda, and my tidbits of ham and tamales, but how have the accompanying relaxations of my body (and let me tell you, those of the libido are not so frequent here as the books say) served my plans? Certainly not well, neither in the health of body and soul, nor in making our dreams reality. Save whom, Professor? There are men here who by inheritance get to pick the low-hanging mangoes; then there is the enormous majority (Indians, whites, blacks, or mixed breeds, whose code is "So, wrap 'er up in a tamale, what the hell do I care"), and a couple of thousand rebels with a stout stem but little flower who appear in about equal numbers on university campuses and in the banana groves. The university students yell a little, print their pamphlets, and occasionally spend some time in jail, sleeping on linen sheets and eating food from hotels until the pleas of the relatives of the guy who is in the soup have an effect on Colonel Arruza. The peasants are a different matter, a very different matter.

There is a man leading them now, an Indian, I would like to meet. His name is Trinidad de los Santos, and every day he gets his knife into the government and its army, as well as my father (yechhh!), Colonel Arruza. Trinidad de los Santos; a man named Zósimo, his second in command; his third-ranking man, a gringo priest; and the six hundred men who follow them, they really interest me, but how do I get in touch with them? I think about it all the time. Highball. I am going to think about it some more. Relieve my tensions. The more I think about it, the more the idea appeals to me. Write to me, Professor, for it would be better for two to make the decision than just one. There is another way to sneak up on the capon and wring his neck before he gets any warning, and that is to change some of the main pieces his political party is playing chess with at the moment. This is only a rumor that nobody believes at all, but I get a kick out of thinking it might be something more than mere gossip, and the idea that I might be able to make it a reality amuses me enormously. Can you imagine Arruza running the risk of soiling his fingers as he reaches out to move certain pieces on his board? Black or white? White or black? I would laugh like a madman. Highball. Trinidad de los Santos. Ham. Corín! Every week, ever since I've been here, I take a walk through the outskirts of the capital. I pretend that any one of the Indians I meet might be Trinidad or Zósimo. Yesterday I came across one riding a burro, his bare feet dangling against the beast's flanks. A bulky mass wearing a vividly colored poncho and a wide-brimmed sombrero. Could it be he? Zechariah prophesied: He "cometh lowly, and riding upon an ass. And I will cut off the chariot from Ephraim and the war horse from Jerusalem." I had to slap myself. Anyone who believes that a social messiah will come to America one day is dreaming. The Indian rode off (dreaming?) on his burro. I stood quietly (awake?). The chariots of war are the state carriages of those who ride along the royal highway. And horses pull them. Stallions that kick out at foul-smelling men. And we have come to the point where I seek an answer. What is my connection with all this? Is the fact that I may be the bastard of the man who commands here sufficient reason to be dancing this *merengue?* A few days ago I saw him walking surrounded by Walkers with machine guns (his personal guard). My guts turned over when I saw the person who begat me and so many others. Hey! How would it be if I formed an army made up of all my brothers. Joke, joke, highball. The dead eye I left buried behind in Maguncia on the shores of the Rhine shouted to me, even from that distance, how painful it was to look upon the face of that exhausted old stud. Corín had to clamp her hand over my mouth to keep me from shouting, you can imagine what, from the balcony. And since the open sore of anger is burning red hot, it will be an effort to wait three weeks for your answer. After that, I shall rush to do battle with that sonofabitch who dishonored my dear mother (I'm not terribly sure about the latter, but the tropics turn one into a sentimental liar). Your letter, whatever your response, will be welcome. Mine will be mailed from the Belize post office. Around here there are Obregóns who sniff and pry into everything. Send your reply to Box 324 in the capital city of British Honduras.

My greetings to the Little One and Fritz, as well as to the Archbishop and Professor Ormayer. And please accept the warm affection of your disciple, friend, and apprentice hero.

MIGUEL ANGEL

P.S.: The Obregóns also spill their gossip into alien ears. Arruza has had his fill of President Juan Elgidio Báez and is looking for an excuse to kick him out. It seems that early tomorrow morning Trinidad de los Santos plans to attack the infantry barracks in the capital. The Colonel knows about it. Are he and Trinidad in cahoots? I don't believe so, although there's so much filth about one never knows. I have decided to do two things. To warn the President, I don't know why, and to take advantage of the coup to make contact with Trinidad de los Santos. It cost me a hundred pesos to find this out. Since then my fever's risen two or three degrees. *Vale.* Again, warm affection.

The first automobile enters the Country Club grounds and comes to a stop before the line of guarumo trees. Two Walkers step in front of the headlights and lead the way for the first guest—Dr. Ernesto Lavalle—a man who watches his money grow in a country where the majority seem to have eyes blinded to that possibility. Footsteps on the gravel. Wheels following the footsteps, slowly, slowly, very slowly, so as not to awaken the tigers, I say.

From the enclosed wooden porch Don Cleto, wearing a spotless *guayabera* shirt and a black cord tie, observes the automobile headlights and the Walkers' flashlights. Don Cleto, tiny and neat, is the kind of a man who talks to himself. "Whose man am I? The world is full of contradictions. This country! What good did it do me to study the humanities? People say that I'm one of the lucky ones who pick the mangoes from the low branches. Suppose *they* had to put up with that dark, grudging, vengeful spleen. Of course, they do have to put up with it, but in a different kind of way. I, a man born to be a scholar, nothing but an asskisser. Caught in the whirlpool where the tides of the sea meet the current of the river. That's my lot. A canoe in the waves, lashed by gales, sucking up to the *patrón* and the *patroncita* all the day long."

Lights reflect among the royal plams. Don Cleto kisses his own hand.

"What's become of you, my son? Always hanging onto

the shirttails of that idol they say does not—but I know does—
have his touch of the tar brush. For if not, to what does he
owe the ingratitude of that perfidious soul?" Don Cleto falls
silent. He hears voices from upstairs: sheep in rut; ram and
ewe. Don Cleto assumes a sad face when he hears the sound of
a slap, and a woman's weeping.

"You're worse than a Jew, the way you treat your baby."

"Who's the macho in this country, I'd like to know?"

"You may be a macho to everyone else, but not under this
roof!"

"Well, then, on my knees, I beg your favors, my lady."

The weeping becomes bleating and bellowing. Don Cleto
pours himself a drink.

"And now God, in his infinite innocence, believes that a
new embryro is making its way to a womb. Ignominious and
perfidious life. How lucky the nobodies are in their little huts,
spared the docility of this bird with his wings clipped. And
she, *perinde ac cadaver*, as St. Ignatius sought of obedience.
Christ! As scatterbrained and deceitful as the iguanassss. And
I, here, acting the part of the dentist, administering the chloro-
form and novocain, drawing the curtain before this animal
coupling. You've got to stay soused to take it, God knows.
Why don't they go off in the hay, like decent beasts? And eat
mutton scraps, like all bastards. Ah, the fucking luck!"

The Walkers open the door of the wealthy landowner's automobile and stand at attention on the porch as he passes.

"Go to the door, Eustaquio," Don Cleto orders the majordomo, who is wearing gold-trimmed livery, knee breeches,
red stockings, and a wig like that of English magistrates, from
beneath which run streams of sweat.

The majordomo announces:

"His Excellency, Don Ernesto Lavalle!"

And a tiny Don Cleto steps forward to serve as intermedi-
ary in delivering the guest's panama hat to Eustaquio.

"Doctor Cleto Espinosa, at your service. The Colonel will
be down in a few minutes. May I offer you a drink?" The land-

owner asked for tamarind juice, which Eustaquio served him. Señor Lavalle has a healthy color, especially on his broad, taut-skinned, bald pate. He is vain about the seventy-six he shoots in golf. Vigorous and resolute, he is always in good humor, because he always talks about himself.

"You are the most punctual."

"We businessmen are always conscious of the clock."

"It must be wonderful to be so rich."

Don Cleto approached devotedly, almost tenderly, close to the landowner. We rich men! Don Cleto felt a sweet tingling in his anus. It was different with Don Ernesto, he didn't feel choked up the way he always did around the Colonel.

"My grandparents were also extremely wealthy. They had gold and silver mines in Copiapó. From there they came to this country, but the mines still belong to us. They began in Potosí, where in order to mine the ore, they had to buy all the mules in San Antonio del Vallenar, Papioso, and Coquimbo. In Copiapó they installed mine cars pulled by burros. How times change! Just like Commodore Vanderbilt, who dug out the channel of the San Juan River in order to reach the Pacific. Nevertheless, we Lavalles now have a fleet of more than a hundred trucks. What does the Colonel want? I was going to leave for New York today. These goddamn ideas always occur to him at the most inconvenient times. Everybody's afraid of him. I don't know why. One day I had to say to him: Just cool it, friend. They can't kick me around the way they do the President. I shit on United Fruit. In front of Mr. Wrightson, everybody turns to putty. . . ."

"But you're very powerful. The rest of us are just ordinary men."

Lieutenant General Armenteros's automobile entered the park. Warm blue moonlight fell on the crickets in the road and on the tops of green eucalyptus trees. Lieutenant General Armenteros, National Hero, is wearing a white cape over his flashy uniform and, above a sallow face, a gold-braided red Spanish shako. He steps from his automobile among the

Walkers, who stand at attention along the wrought-iron fence.

"Lieutenant General Don Eladio Armenteros!" announces Eustaquio in a quavery voice.

"The Hero of Eternal Peace," adds the landowner, coming forward to greet the soldier. He embraces him warmly. "Did you come on horseback, old friend?"

"By tank," the Lieutenant General replies, prolonging the joke.

"One with a bidet, no doubt."

Both laugh boisterously. Don Cleto knows that the General drinks nothing but pear juice and vodka, and he himself prepares it. The two guests walk out to the enclosed porch.

"You're looking good, General."

"Did you know that a plaster cast of my genital apparatus is being sent to the Museum of Historical Reproductions in Brasília?"

"It's a damn shame that a man like you has no enemy army to destroy."

"There is no enemy today. Only enemies. Little shits like Trinidad de los Santos. Do you see what's happening in Vietnam? A bunch of dwarfs with a little rice strutting like banty roosters before the greatest army in the world. What do you think of that? Everyone knows I have a Prussian sense of strategy. I wish to hell they'd give me somebody worth fighting; I'd blast them off the map. But all I get is Trinidad de los Santos and his gang of motherfuckers, who are only in the mountains for nuisance' sake, nothing more. . . ."

"You need a war, Eladio. The country owes you one."

"Yes, but . . . who the fuck against? Central Americans have become a bunch of old ladies . . . freaking debutantes! Now it's the bourgeoisie, the proletariat, and that blessed cult of Che Guevara, they're the ones in control. How do you move artillery and tanks and planes against that, tell me?"

"I don't know. My business doesn't give me time to think about such things. When I'm not in New York, I'm in London, and if I'm not in London, then I'm in Copiapó. You know, where my family's mines are. And the chicle plantations. What do I know about what's going on! Then there's my brother, Martin. The only thing he knows anything about is spending money, and he gets his kicks from dope and grass. And my wife, you know about that. I have too much on my mind to be able to worry about politics. Do you have any idea what the Colonel wants?"

And with that, ex-President Oruro arrived. Huge, strong, sensational. The Constitution of 1940, the Constitution of 1935, the Statutes of 1937. The Pan-American Conference. The status quo of the unions. Yes, please. And that sweetheart of a songbird, his Chiquita Banana. The *Clarín del Caribe*, the *Estrella de las Antillas*, whose editorials destroyed the political career of this same Don Valentín.

Traitor, traitor a thousand times over! Exiled. Up to his elbows in dirty money, in deals with foreign companies. Don Valentín, the swindler. Oh yes. Such a big man with the poor, a real hot shot when it came to rounding up votes in the tiny village stores and peasant communities. What did the Colonel want? Was he planning to make a tasty, spicy broth with these three and force the country to swallow it? Putting *these* three together could really fuck things up. What business did a political has-been have in this parade? Only the Colonel knows. Perhaps he can put some life back in him. Say whatever you want. Reticence. We helped you make those deals. *Fides servanda est.* How is Chiquita Banana? *Fidem qui perdit nihil ultra perdere potest.*

Why don't you fuck off? *Fides non habet meritum ubi humana ratio praebet experimentum.* And he's upstairs, screwing. Don't you hear them?

"The people don't know what they're talking about. It's very easy to point an accusing finger at those of us who came out against a dangerous tolerance of competition. But one newspaperman, one word in print, and you're out. They did me in. All right, so I'm a rich man, but can anyone tell me what element of external competition could curb the possible monopolistic tendencies that result from a policy of unification and reciprocal understanding among industries with similar production in the other countries of our isthmus?"

"It's difficult for me to consider a question of honor as mere mathematics or economics. I'm a man trained for war, but if I had to choose between a campaign without honor and an honorable peace, I would hesitate a long time . . . a *very* long time!"

"My position when I was, first, Minister of the Economy and then President was that our basic national product can only be protected by an international regulatory center. And for saying that, they called me a traitor. A traitor to whom? To our country, or to the vested interests of those who divided up the land in 1828?"

"You don't deny that with that policy you were playing into the hands of our competitors on other continents. . . ."

"Ridiculous! The Colonel launched that campaign to discredit me and then replaced me with that idiot Báez. But I, old man, I hung onto my machete and I'm getting along fine with my Chiquita. I know why he did it, but here we are, and I come *close* to getting angry, but nothing ever comes of it. I don't pretend to be something I never was. We've never died of hunger, what with our bananas and coffee and tobacco, and as long as we get all the ass we want, we seem to be content. I was in the Presidential Palace for three years—not so hot, but not too bad either. One little school to make things look good, and three fucking big highways so we could ask for credit from the World Bank. And our bananas, and coffee, and tobacco, and asskissing. Screwed, but content! What no one knew was that Valentín Oruro was planning for the future. What our oxen haul means wealth for outsiders and poverty for our country. And because I wanted to change things, and that's the *only* reason, he kicked me out. And now he summons me, the bastard. He didn't like the fact that banana buyers wouldn't buy from private growers. I know your cocks are straining to hear everything I say. So go ahead. You'll see where you stand when the minute hands stop at twelve and nobody knows whether it's noon or midnight."

"Shit! That *is* serious." Lieutenant General Armenteros was truly alarmed.

"You bet it's serious," the landowner agreed.

"That isn't a soreheaded politician talking now. That's the patriot."

The Lieutenant General was livid with rage, staring at the waving treetops outlined against the starry sky. Suddenly he shouted: "One day they'll come knocking at my door and ask me to save the country from the invader, but it will be too late. I swore that oath at the tomb of General Aldama, and when a soldier swears such a thing before a revered tomb, it isn't just the liquor talking. It will be too late! Look at these medals on my chest. Do you know anything about military decorations? This one isn't a joke; you don't win *these* for riding a bicycle."

Lavalle was also deeply irritated, but he expressed himself more moderately.

"The Dutch, masters of commerce and good sense, say: *'Hij beoordeelt een ieder naar zichzelf.'* . . ."

But the other two, preoccupied with the march of history, were not listening to him.

"Someday they'll appreciate the guardians who looked out for this country, and then, as they stand awaiting the invader, the civilians will realize what cold and snow are!"

"Thanks to my watchful care, the country was at the point of converting to a modern economic life, and with a clear awareness. If it hadn't been for that animal, we'd have made the leap from underdevelopment to technological salvation maturely and scientifically. But when a president is about to sign an important decree in this land of cutthroats and petty clerks, he has to think twice."

Buttoning the tunic of his uniform, the Colonel descended the stairway. He had had two women that day, and he was looking his best. Don Cleto was waiting for him with a pisco sour. Here, Your Excellency. So how's everything going, gentlemen? They admired him; they had to admire him, because he was like a great palm in its prime. Firm, strong hands, the right hand pocked by a bullet. Seven times they had tried to assassinate him. People said that in one attempt they'd blown off one ball and that's why he was a cuckold. Many believed he was an old man who tottered off to bed with a glass of milk. Why say anything more? But some also said he was a sorcerer who painted his one remaining ball with white lead. How does that grab you, brother? Only fools maintain that one swallow does not a summer make, or that crows don't flock when the weather threatens. What degree of consideration, of health, good manners, respect, what proteins does the man merit who can piss the farthest? You're saying . . .? Prurience and blood: the two terms in Pérez's binomial. He embraces the Lieutenant General and calls him Scourge-of-Virgins and Scatter-Tits. He kisses him on each cheek, as they do heroes in France. The invader, the invader! He wished that one of these three apes would draw his revolver. He feels like dying tonight. Just one good shot, and it would be all over, forever, and he'd be lying beneath a shovelful of sterile earth. Wearing a different Paris gown, his wife enters. They kiss her hand. Eustaquio passes among the guests, carrying an enormous silver tray. Oh, Copiapó, Copiapó! As beautiful as ever, madam. Does that sound a little hollow? He also hands Doña Virginia a pisco sour. Where are the ladies? None has come. That doesn't ruffle the señora. Such things amuse her. Señora Pfandl Andrade de Arruza is happier when hers is the only body to excite the men. An hors d'oeuvre? At every opportunity Señor Lavalle brushes the señora's arm with his hand . . . delicious. The cursing cockatoo has been taken to the loft for the night. Hors d'oeuvres come, hors d'oeuvres go, and pisco courses through the veins. That chili pepper bites! And dinner. The señora does not stay to dine. Dinner is for the men. Doña Virginia prefers the Country Club, where there's dancing and young meat! Go with God . . . and with six Walkers. One of them is blond and can barely speak Spanish. The Colonel doesn't give a damn. But the other three men are jealous. The Colonel won't need Doña Virginia until the next evening. And then he'll have her, open and ready. The others? What do the others matter in this festival of the bed? The Colonel always enters through the rear door of monologues. The impassive honor of his subordinates' wives is fabricated of Christmas ornaments and tinsel. More lobster, General? We had an oriole in our ceiba tree that was crazy about our cuckoo clock. You will be President again, Oruro. The Hero of the Fatherland will execute the *coup d'état* while Professor Báez is dreaming of his herds and his smudge pots. And you, Lavalle, will be the Director of the National Bank and Minister of the Economy and Finance, but you have to put up a million to get the new phase going. Afterward, you can do whatever you like. I want no martyrs. Not a single additional death on my shoulders. You, General, when I tell you, will send your troops into the streets, and at exactly four-twenty-three you will take the Presidential Palace. Then you will call me on the telephone. That's it. Pisco sour, pisco sour . . . Rocked on the warm night air the music comes from the Country Club. And the poor sleeping in puddles of sweat. Hey, little shrimp, shut up, will you? Don't you know your daddy's got to get up early, with the roosters?

Miguel Ángel Matalax Yanama, just arrived. Where is your father? My father is everywhere. You have an important father and you don't want to see him? Don't you have any family feeling? Besides, you don't even have a roof over your head. At least go see him, tonight. The mulatto girl stays behind on the hotel bed while the man wanders from one end of the city to another. Give me the newspaper. Limes, peeled limes! President Báez, the Colonel, Trinidad de los Santos, the General, the other General, the First Lady, the Second, the Third, the Charitable House, the Fatherland, the Country Club, the distinguished señorita, golden wedding anniversary, diamond wedding anniversary, man sets himself on fire, man dead after drinking shoe dye, Fidel Castro, Central America, school festival, stabbing, the Fatherland, coffee prices, chicle prices, the murderer, bananas, left for the north, left for the continent, the wealthy señor . . . , her debutante party, the Jaripeo trio, the Fatherland, a reception in the palace, a new American brassiere, enhance your bustline, the bizarre captain and the distinguished lady, the Colonel, the Minister, the Director General, the wealthy landowner, has given birth, the President, the limousine, time payments, the Fatherland, the Children's Bank, lost French poodle, the OAS and Don Galo, a new loan, Fidel Castro, nonintervention, culottes in the latest fashion, young executive (graduate of the University of Wisconsin), business administration, the Fatherland, holdup on Twenty-third Street, national disgrace, ban-

anas, the banana plantation, the banana grove, 2, 4-D weed-killer, 800 bushels of grain per acre, caterpillar, the Minister of the Economy, Señor Delgado's zebu bulls, the Fatherland, the Southern Cattlemen's herds of Brahmans, deodorant, mass for Doña Enriqueta (RIP), what to use against gnawing, chewing insects? Azodron; gasoline coupons, sweeten your breath, sweetheart, double guarantee, suppositories for hemorrhoids, the Colonel, the new Stock Exchange Building, the Fatherland, guaranteed, guaranteed, Dr. Sivares's truss, the tourist is a source of national income, be friendly, obituary, engagement, the handsome young Sánchez Correa couple, in business; the Senate session, the lottery, Puchito Rodríguez blanks the Stars, nonintervention, Duvalier, the Fatherland, the Senate, the Republic, the Masonic Center, sandals for the young student, shoe dye, elderly lady falls from balcony, first communion, Trinidad de los Santos, stabilize the economy, order, Fatherland, law, El Gallo shirts, Fidel Castro, the Colonel, Revlon nail polish; the Grace Line, in special boxcars, protect your coffee from humidity and other dangers common to the bean, be patriotic, Aztec wheat, the latest hairstyles at La Dorita, the President, harrows and graders with hydraulic systems, the Fatherland, lose weight in Weight Worriers, Inc. gyms, Adalmiro Fuentes tonight on TV, Turb dehydrators for your forage, Dr. Zorrilla is gravely ill, vote! the stud bull of the Senior herd, Ankonian Gay Jingo, specially prepared for the tropical climate, Fidel Castro, Senator Fulbright, the Yankees beat the Orioles, the Fatherland, heat wave in the north, His Holiness's Ambassador, a Snipe Commander for landowners, tour Central America, frozen bull sperm and storage equipment, the Colonel, a new heart transplant, the President inaugurates the School of Agriculture, printed in Central America.
. . . Thursday afternoon, he reached the conclusion that he should pay the President a visit. Why not your father, my darling? What do you know, my dark beauty, what do you know about it? Men don't discuss these things with women. But, his hunch . . . Corín lies eating the bonbons her lover

34

had brought her. Newspapers are scattered about the floor. Tell the President that Miguel Ángel Matalax Yanama of the Chase Manhattan Bank is calling. Very urgent, very important. He wasn't from Chase, but that always opens the door. The President receives him with outstretched hand. They look one another in the eye, the President slightly disconcerted, since it is not easy to meet the gaze of a man who has only one eye. My name is Miguel Ángel Matalax Yanama. They are my mother's names. That told the President everything. My mother is a boat captain. Balls! Mr. President, would you be embarrassed if I told you how my mother gave birth to me? I'm not embarrassed by anything. I believe it's best to speak out clearly. I'd be a fine President if I didn't know the things a man hides inside him. Are you sure? Sure you know everything? Do you know everything I know? I know you're an impostor. You're not from Chase. Get out of here before I call my guard. They will attack the palace before dawn. The President is speechless. My mother delivered me in the taverns of the port, drinking rum with cloves and betting whether the baby would be a boy or a girl. You should frighten me with that glass eye, but you don't. Why? Because that's the eye that doesn't belong to my father. Who is your father, you bastard? Mr. President, you should know that no man who bears his mother's name is in any position to deny that his father was the hangman of Quebec or the night guard at the Cirque Médrano or . . . Colonel Arruza. This terrible doubt has the advantage of ingenuous variety. "To be or not to be." Why have you come to warn me? Why are you not taking your father's side? Who is my father? Can you swear it isn't *you*? Tonight, Trinidad de los Santos will attack the infantry barracks, and then the National Hero will send his troops into the streets. At four-twenty-three they will take the Presidential Palace, and tomorrow ex-President Oruro will again be signing all the decrees. But this is monstrous; this is senseless. Let me think. I have to talk with my wife, with the First Lady. She's pregnant. You can't do that. But you're strong enough to take anything. He was trembling. He drank a whiskey. Want one? We still have twelve hours. What can we do to save the republic? I have no men, no power; all I have is my wife. She's pregnant. Exile. I can count on twelve hours to get out of the country. It can't be helped. I have no men, no power, nothing. Suddenly I see myself as a professor of administrative law again. I feel the vertigo one feels seeing the tiger sharks circling around his boat. What can I do? Everything was so tranquil and peaceful. I've just come from my siesta.

At that hour the Presidential Palace dominated the Central American silence and stillness. The birds perching on its eaves are the same as yesterday's, but now they seem to conspire in a sinister fashion. Nevertheless, it is one of the most joyous and most beautiful days of all time. The blazing tropical sun erases the shadow of Anabaptists hanged centuries ago in ancient Europe. Rugs and armor decorate the presidential office. The fountain pen is filled with red ink. The President feels like praying. Why are the people half-asleep? Where are my people? Coca-Cola, the drink that refreshes. Hey now, if you're gonna be that way, I ain't gonna love you no more. I'm a Liberal, my father was a Liberal, my grandmother embroidered the first flag for the Liberals. I feel like weeping. I can't tell my wife anything. She's pregnant. When a man becomes the first officer of the land, he should never make a child with his own wife. Poor little orphan! They drank together. Words poured from the President wildly, as fear streamed from him. At five o'clock in the afternoon, Miguel Ángel offered a solution. I will give you a solution and you will order me to get out of here. Drive out to your estate. All Presidents have an estate. Go there with your wife and children.

Hesitation, glass eye, silence, whiskey, heat, fear, prayer, unborn child, the child who will be called Lincoln if it's a boy, and Rosa Guadalupe if it's a girl. Who is this man? A bastard. Gone now, without any explanation. The President also wishes to leave his office, he wants to see the riotous joy of grain fields, not to see the treachery of the Prime Minister, to see the candor of the butterflies, not to see what he does not wish to see. Had he gone to the psychiatrist when his wife asked him to, to ask to be certified as a paranoiac, he would now be an agriculturist instead of a man on the verge of exile, of death, of national ridicule. They've taught these people to believe that the *coup d'état* is their favorite sport. Thus, the eyes of the dead will never be closed. And no one will ever be freed of death unless he has his head screwed on backward. The truth is that madmen perceive things sane men never see. The automobile raced along Refuge Street and soon was covered with the dust of the highway leading to the Pacific. Seventy million square miles to hide in. The lyrebird. The day is so beautiful that one might believe it is the day America was discovered. There's nothing so demeaning as ingratitude. You want a bite to eat? He's not hungry. His wife eats, the unborn baby needs its calcium. Are you worried about something, Juan Elgidio? The children are riding in the front with the chauffeur. One is always trying to poison the other. That's why their mother is always giving them things. I'm not worried, love. Nevertheless, he feels as if someone is stealthily creeping up behind him, someone whose heart is eaten up with hatred. And among the banana trees he sees flickering lights that look like worms in a glass eye. As a boy, Juan Elgidio had learned to talk with horses and to awaken the lark with a reed flute. They are driving along the river. It looks like the Lindo, but it isn't. As a youth in Paris he had affected an elegant beard, like Toulouse-Lautrec. River, river, black current, black as the heart of man. The trees are filled with birds. A little wine, Juan Elgidio? He drinks, he needs a drink. A small airplane is spraying the banana groves. Beyond lie tropical pastures thick with Pará grass, and Pangola, and Guinea, and Napier. Grass as high as a man's head. The President thinks of the calves that have beeen suffering from dysentery. He had not held his cabinet meeting last week because of them. But his foreman had given them Furanterol. The Welcome herd was now frolicking in the pasture. And feeding on

Leucaena. Why is there so much evil in the world, Natalia? He looks out at the fields so she won't see his tears. Rid your groves of weeds with Du Pont Karmex, says a billboard. At one small hut several young turkeys are gathered awaiting the last word. The Reynolds Sugar Company's cane fields lie along one side of the road. Smoke rises from the refinery, scarcely moving in the still evening air. Revolutionary Party of Democratic Unification. Several children are playing along the riverbank. His two children are locked in battle. You two, be quiet! Tree stumps in the jungle. Rakes and caterpillar tractors are clearing them away. Several acres of sorghum are ready for harvesting. Beautiful land! Oh, my beautiful country, but such scum in it. Happier than the President is his double, whose name is Catareo and who lives in peace. A President must always have a double. Little good he's done him. From that attempt when he visited Tegucigalpa, he received only a little nick in his shoulder. And tranquilly he continues collecting his pension. Ah, there are the lowlands of his property, bordering the Pacific shore. It's the right time to come. During the rainy season, from El Pulido on it's pure mud, more than eighty inches of rainfall in six months. But this is the other six. Thank God! Good cotton land. Cotton for his brother-in-law's textile mills. Good evenin', *patróncito*. Everything is calm and peaceful. Everyone is smiling. Are we getting rid of the insects, Raúl? Raúl is the foreman, a man who knows what he's about. Well, you will see, *patrón*, wit' the night traps you brought, we are trappin' all the moths of those worms, and everything's goin' great.

The President's family enters the house. The high notes of a flute sound outside. The young cotton plants, whispering and warm, feel the first air sweeping down off the barren hill pelted by a torrential rain they call the "baby waterfall." And the servant girls go to fetch water for dinner. Want me to help you, baby?

Don Juan Elgidio contemplates a luminous night borne on the cedar-and-gorse-scented air.

The calling card seemed to be a joke.

"What the fuck is this?" exclaimed Colonel Arruza, ready to strike the maître. He was alone, in a restaurant called La Criolla, eating roast suckling pig, yams, and taro root seasoned with peppers. Alone, at one o'clock in the morning. Alone, at his reserved table, a candle in the center, a bird cage above it. On other tables, champagne glasses. *"If you touch my bottom again, I'm going to relieve my-self* on your whoring mother, you fucking gringo." Bubbles dribbling between breasts and in the corners of smiling lips. *"Shut up!"* The Walkers at the bar took in every move at the tables near the Colonel's. The maître stood rigidly attentive, awaiting the Colonel's orders. "Soooo, who gave you this card?" The maître pointed to Miguel Ángel Matalax, dressed in white, leaning against the bar, a lighted cigar in his hand. The Colonel signaled to a Walker who skillfully ran his hands over the stranger's clothing. Another sign, and the Walker pushed Miguel Ángel toward the Colonel's table. Are you the one whose name's on here? Sit down. You almost upset my digestion. What kind of shit is this about *ab ovo*, you'll forgive the expression, when a man's eating? Don't you know I can have you killed? Drink. Speak. You know what? I'd always have the consolation that Mozart died younger than I. Don't be afraid. I was joking. There's a touch of humor in every-body. Help yourself, stranger. Who are you, really, and what the devil do you want from me? "I am a bastard, Colonel.

39

Doesn't my name mean anything to you?" "Let me think. Matalax? No. It's a strange name, sounds like something written with tar. Who the fuck can be sure he's not a bastard? Do you want suckling pig or kid? Grab whatever you like. Like the gringos grab the butts of our señoritas. This is sweet wine. I'll serve you. I like sweet wine. It's something honest that defends a man against the bitterness and bile he has to suffer in this world. Do you know what my punishment is? Tell me. Do you?"

The Colonel had drunk a half gallon of sherry. He was weeping and he hid the tears behind his napkin. Don't be ashamed. Weep, fall in a faint if you wish. If you knew how many years, how many centuries, one can dedicate to revenge. The blood of others is the blood that flows. Memory evaporates with tears, never knowing what is tearing and ripping inside another. Men who can only communicate with one another on battlefield telephones, who know nothing but how to try the patience of the weak, and seek the blessing of their mother's photograph. I bless you, fruit of my mad misspent youth. I bless you, although you are of cowardly and sickly blood. (Ah, yes, dear mama.) Always be candid and chaste as a heathen. (That's all he has to tell me?) Although you owe me no obedience now, there is a maternal-filial relationship between adults that is founded on the umbilical cord linking the history of the world. You will never repent of your good intentions toward your fellows. (Oh, yes, old lady.) Try to see that your fits of anger, of weakness, of cowardice, affect no one but your horse. (So, you've been listening to the old lady, maybe?) In short, my son, considering everything I have given you and all you have taken from me, let's call it even, with my blessing. (Soooooo.) The Colonel had stopped weeping and was looking at him with the eyes of a guard dog. What do dogs guard? Are there also guards who are dogs? The Walkers, for example. Miquel Ángel looked at him as if he had just seen a frozen child. Possibly the Colonel was convinced that he was a creator of eternity. The fathers of Zósimo and of Trinidad de los Santos had been dispatched for eternity. The difference between the two men who sat staring at one another was that Miguel Ángel had one eye and the Colonel had two. But at times one eye is more powerful than a pair. And that eye was dancing with the pleasure of the hunt, like the miserable son of the wandering dreamer. You're hopelessly mad, comrade. He washed the eye in the sweet wine. Don't you remember anything about my name, Colonel? *Dansons la carmagnole! Vive le son du canon!* Does the tree-that-walks have access to the sea? The breadfruit tree, stupid. The bartender is thinking about his tiny son who pissed through a tube. He serves a Bloody Mary. The tiny son who had died. The Colonel says he feels something like a serpent of betrayal slithering up his spine. The bartender buttons up his heart. *May I help you, sir?* The Colonel asks his guest if he has ever been in love. And Miguel Ángel lies. He says he came to know love between two cavalry charges, listening to the death rattle of the dying. That goddess died in my arms with part of her head blown away by a mortar. One is nothing but armor and a piece of cannon. The Colonel is so drunk that he confesses that he indulges in coups only to entertain himself. Matalax Yanama. An important man must not occupy himself with trifles. Suddenly, a planter shouts that he thinks better when he can sleep with his head resting on a saddle. His friends laugh when he puts his feet where his head ought to be. Ah, yes. The Colonel confesses other things. That once someone prophesied that the ultimate betrayal would come from one of his bastards. My people love me. When I go for a walk, children could throw stones on me from the mountains, but they don't do it. I am a sinner, but they love me. Sometimes I speak Castilian, and sometimes I talk just the way they talk around here. Sometimes I speak very formally, but sometimes I call everyone my buddy. I belong here. Only the people who grew up here know how to prepare a proper broth, tasty and well mixed. Even my *wife* loves me. Don Cleto kissed my shoe tonight. The mothers of the children who live on the dumps could stick out their tongues at me when I walk past the public washtubs, but they don't. And yet, I don't know why I feel disturbed before you. Nobility? That isn't why, friend. You see those men drinking so quietly? At one sign from me they would hang you upside down until your soul drained from your pants legs. And I am disturbed, Matalax Yanama, because I have a hunch that behind that fucking glass eye of yours you're hiding something that belongs to me. Do you know what I have to say to you? That I could urinate in that empty socket until your beautiful body was flooding over. I read murder in your one good eye. Tell me, my young pigeon, have you come to kill me? I'll give you a medal. "Niña Huanca" was breathed like a whisper. What time is it? Twenty after two. They're about to close. You will close, bartender, when they drag me out of here by my balls! More wine! Niña Huanca? Why do we have to adjust the date of our deaths? I'm alive. Two o'clock in the morning. Three. And any Indians who are not sleeping at the bottom of a Maya jar will be dead at dawn for being too big for their britches. Don't you hear them walking around? They're close by, stranger. Get those gringos and their pigs out of here! Amid cries of protest the Walkers emptied the room. *You sonofabitch!* For many, the clock will stop tomorrow. Who are you? Niña Huanca? Have you ever eaten pompano from the Gulf Stream? Get that bartender out of here, too! Get the whole crummy bunch out of here! And you stay outside and leave me alone with this jackal who blew in from God knows where. They emptied the room. The dimly lighted bar of La Criolla resembled a cockpit with one one-eyed and one two-eyed fighting cock. We're alone now, which is how I like to be when I talk turkey. When I was young, I not only ate birds that don't fly, but those that don't sing, as well. How do you like that? Niña Huanca! I've asked myself many times whether I committed sodomy with that boat captain. Was she a woman or a man? I don't know. I think she told me her name was Huancavélica. I was riding along the bay on horseback. I had her, and later she fed me a pompano baked in palm leaves.

What have you come for, my fine little shitass? Are you my bastard? Are you what I left sowed beside that bay? A poison seed, no less. There are some who get up early to get to the revolution. And some who never even go to bed. Do you think it's easy to make the puppets obey in this show? Do you think because you're my sperm you're the same as I am? No, you're not the same. The drinks have to be drunk on the march, with courage and with care. If one contains poison, you're right back in your mother's cunt. Do you know why I'm drinking so much? Because I don't want to be calm when they kill them. I'm a sentimentalist. So you went to see Professor Báez? You think I don't know that? He grabbed Matalax by the lapels. You've come to be the crown prince, but I'm me and the game ends with me. Understand? I'm fed up with all of you who come to me to be recognized. You're too big for such nonsense. What do you want? My money? My power? You're number twenty-three on the list. And you hoped to sneak in here, acting the smartass! Sergeant *ab ovo!* I swear to God, I'm going to knock the shit out of you. Come on, if you're a man, defend yourself. What did you think? That you get to run a country by pure luck, or by praying to the Virgin? The Colonel cursed as he punched Matalax into a corner. I don't need dogs or rope or a revolver to pound your cowardly guts to a pulp. He pinned Matalax against a column and with his finger tore out the glass eye. Do you want me to tear out the other so you won't have to look at your sonofabitching face when you shave? Do you want to know what total night is like? He continued to pound Matalax's face and ribs. So someone told you I'm a cuckold? Say it. Call me a cuckold and I'll spare your life. Miguel Ángel fell senseless to the floor. The Colonel emptied a pitcher of ice water over his head and Miguel Ángel struggled to sit up. You're my bastard? I don't want to be even your bastard, mister. You son of a *bitch!* He had no strength for further words. The Colonel kicked him in the face again and again. You'll never look at the sky again, you stinking little worm! You'll never curse again, and now I'm going to piss in that beeootiful socket. And may God protect me!

Then he walked out onto Sixth Avenue, where the shoe-shine boys were all asleep. Shine, Colonel, sir? Followed by the Walkers, he strode up the street toward the infantry barracks. The clock in the five-and-ten said three-fifteen. Still a little more than an hour before Trinidad de los Santos's attack. Good evening. The air smelled of *iguanita del mar* and amaranths. Carts of flowers were arriving for the new day. Flowers for virgins, for the Virgin, for the dead.

At dawn they extinguished the pine torches, only the torches. Someone had staked them in the ground to mark the rows of dead. Emilio the Kid lay with eyes staring, a bloody black hole in his right cheek. Emilio was not yet fourteen. Wearing a battle helmet, General Armenteros communicated the outcome of the battle to President Oruro by radio. In his hand he held a cup of steaming coffee. Dead: one hundred ninety-three rebels and five soldiers. Our wounded number thirty-two. The rebels have left no wounded. Trinidad de los Santos has escaped, and also his lieutenant, Zósimo, who is so badly wounded that I don't believe he'll be enjoying tamales very long. And we've got two hundred and twenty of the bastards in the dungeons.

The soldiers were given big rations of alcohol, but they would have preferred to go to the cantinas near the barracks and drink free beer with salt. Long live General Armenteros! In the early morning the General, with his two aides, rode through the city in his jeep. Women cheered from their balconies. At noon, the President issued a proclamation from the balcony of the palace. The Constitution of 1940, free elections within three months, strengthening the bonds of friendship and economic ties with the sister countries of Central America. We shall not permit . . . The fathers of the country . . . By his side, General Armenteros, and behind him, Colonel Arruza. The radio announced the new cabinet. Industrialization, national defense, and schools. Above all, literacy for all adults. And Señor Lavalle, Director of the National Bank. Economy, underdevelopment, *skill*, the Fatherland belongs to everyone, *viva, viva!* Trinidad de los Santos will be captured by the forces of the law. Curfew. The army. I say to you. . . . Presidential decree. I solemnly promise from this first office of the nation. . . . New ambassadors have been named to Washington and to the United Nations. A new representative will leave early in the morning to present his credentials to the OAS. *El Heraldo de Centroamérica,* with the latest news! Moderate censorship until order is completely restored in the country. "Poem to the Fatherland," by Dr. Rosela Díaz de López Morales. Bus service will be suspended at eight-thirty P.M. on the tenth, eleventh, and twelfth. Use Upercol on your dairy herds and steers, the broadest-spectrum antihelminthic, with multiple action. The dead will be buried at night in a common grave in Las Angustias. And covered with quicklime because of the heat. Upercol, greater weight gains and more profits for you. Improve your flocks. "Poem to the National Hero," by Dr. Ramón Miguel Soto Rodríguez . . . Oh, you. . .! A mite can immunize itself against an insecticide. Resnais's *La guerre est finie* at the Royal. John Wayne in *The Green Berets*, at the Losada theaters. Cantinflas in *El padrecito.* Fungicides, pesticides, herbicides, defoliants. The President on TV tonight. Citizens! And the poor don't know *nothin'*. Veiled eyes, veiled ears, and veiled mouth. Me, my tamale and cuppa' coffee and bread. Tha's all I wanna know. I'll have a Bloody Mary. What did you say happened? Next morning in the schools they sing the national anthem. Soooooo, nothin' happened here. You mean, this is how it all ends? Tha's how.

Please stay. Don' go when you're like that. This is a miserable, godforsaken hole, but I will look after you until you get well. Miguel Ángel lay naked on Lucinda's bed. His white clothing was no longer white, and his face was as swollen as a boxer's. He washed as well as he could and left the brothel without a word. Purposely, he left a few bills on the night table. For once a dark girl can kiss a blond! He arrived at the station in a taxi flying a white flag to enable it to pass through the troops. A sergeant asked for his papers, and he was able to board the train without further difficulty. He reached Belize at midnight. The following morning he left for the key in a Lebanese brigantine. The crossing gave him a certain serenity, and little by little, his face began to look normal. His mother had not been on the key since Thursday, the Lebanese informed him, and she wouldn't be back for four weeks. He needed the old lady, he didn't know why. They told him she'd set sail for Jean Rabel in Haiti with a cargo of hinges and nails she'd contracted for in Galveston. Miguel Ángel flew to Port-au-Prince. There he read an interview a UP correspondent had had with President Oruro. What had to happen had happened. The country had been headed toward rigged elections that an honorable man free of personal ambition couldn't win, only a swindler who planned to milk the nation of everything, without giving a thought to how it would all be paid for. We must never forget that in our country public opinion doesn't exist, only ranting on street corners in the capital and in an occasional park in the provinces. Under these circumstances, our obligation was to accept this new responsibility of leading—along the road of law and order—a properly oriented campaign to recover our traditional values. Democracy was conceived for the good of all, not just for a member of a certain family or political group. We hope to put an end to the notion that government is a game played by men motivated by self-interest. We shall hold elections, and the man the people elect will be respected by all. But, Mr. President, what about the seventy percent of the population made up of Indians? Well, the Indian is not integrated in the language or in the historic and social events of the country. The native is what we might call the chaotic element in our people. He neither produces nor consumes. That is why we oppose that so-called leader of the indigenous population Trinidad de los Santos, because he cannot be, nor will he in the future be, involved in the political and social processes of the nation. One must have blacks in order to know, to truly *know*, what racial integration is, and one must have Indians to be aware of the consequences of a democratic tally of votes among individuals who can't even understand each other. Schools, schools, schools, that is my theme. And while these masses are being educated for the future, we must have serious scientific planning for our economic reality. I greatly regret what has happened, but it had to be. The early morning of the seventh of March is a great lesson in history. Trinidad de los Santos led hundreds of men to their deaths simply to prevent, through revolution, the democratic evolution of free elections. Crassly foolish. My predecessor, former President Báez, had sold out to a foreign power and the country was on the verge of becoming a quagmire of blood and tears. Trinidad is the product of the discontent of the true people. But fortunately, our National Hero, General Armenteros, has again opened the channels for democratic coexistence. When, Mr. President, do you believe that elections will be held? As soon as the country feels sure of itself again. On the other hand, we must not forget that I still have fifteen months left in office. I was deposed, unconstitutionally, by that shameful *coup d'état* two years ago, fifteen months before the end of my term. I shall try, during these months, to ease the terrible blows to my people's morale, and after that, God will decide. We must work, we must sacrifice. We must turn this people, who spend their lives inventing words, into hard-working and efficient citizens.

In Jean Rabel they told Matalax that Niña Huanca's boat was still in Galveston taking on cargo. The purple bruises on his ribs had disappeared. After three days, there was no further news about what had happened in his father's dominions. He moved into a pension near the port. One night he felt ill and was taken to the hospital. He vomited clots of black blood but after three days was well again, thanks to the efficacy of papaya juice. In the next bed was a black man from the Virgin Islands. His name was Henry and he had served in the Caribbean Legion. He had come to die in a place where they could give him morphine. The black enjoyed talking about his past. According to what he said, he had spent seven months with Colonel Arruza's Walkers. He admired the Colonel. He's a real bastard. If they kill one of his puppets he simply calls in one of their doubles. That man is so cunning he can see the feathers grow on a quetzal bird. In the jail in Enriquillo there's a guy who looks exactly like the President; another, I've heard, is in Tampa or Baton Rouge. He's a Greek and his name is Phineas. Lavalle's double comes cheap, because he's the coward's twin. And so if you search through the Caribbean, you will find all the doubles he has concealed until he needs them. I wouldn't be surprised if this was a different Trinidad de los Santos. All the Indians look alike. A lot they know about Farabundio Martí and Octavio Rodríguez. There you see a sharecropper stuck to his bit of land, or working on communal lands, or paying his percentage for leasing land. One of *them* might be Trinidad de los Santos, and he could be six feet under, sucking arnica roots. Do you know how you could put one over on the Colonel? If I weren't a black man, my God, and if I didn't have this filthy cancer, I'd fix the stew myself; but I'm eaten up and, besides, the color of an old boot. What I'd do would be to round up all the doubles and substitute them overnight. The black said little more. It took him three nights to die. Under the influence of the morphine he sang softly in English, which was his language, "Michael, row the boat ashore, hallelujah!," and left behind him in this world a generous smile. Miguel Ángel had to find those hidden faces. Enriquillo is in the Dominican Republic, on the southern coast. But first, he went to the encounter with Trinidad de los Santos.

With the gangrene and bleeding, Zósimo lasted a little more than a month. He died in the arms of María Candelaria. They placed his body in a clay vessel before he grew stiff, and so he lay drawn up as he had lain in his mother's belly, there to remain forever at the portals of eternity. In his pockets they placed a few coins and between his legs a jug with beans and a gourd containing flour for tortillas, along with hand-written prayers on fine India paper and the photograph of María Candelaria, pregnant and weeping. Good-bye, I loved you well, although you had little advantage from it! Oh, my God! All I have left is this body of your blood! You, sir, will you tell of it? The music sounded good as they climbed the path past the station of Our Most Holy Mother toward the cemetery of Ceibal. You keep alive by breathin' and drinkin', comrade. Don' you know nothin' but that one stinkin' song, Gaudemio? Well, what would you want, man, for a time like this? Almos' anythin' is good enough for the livin', their *comparsita* or their *carrasqueado* . . . but for the deceased, you owe them their Cho-pin or their Hain-del. They drove a wooden cross into the soft earth. María Candelaria lay fainting throughout the elegies. The last to speak was Victoriano. Don' be thinkin' that because Zósimo has lef' us, everythin' has been for nothin'. We all have to die someday, but while we're living' we have to have a challen' in our lives. Do you agree with me? Either we die like Zósimo, like a true macho, for somethin' that's worth it, or we sit and wait to be old men when all we can do with our pricks is piss. Mos' of us die from jus' a cold, or a rupture, or those bad growths, but the man who dies like that isn't a patriot or a revolutionary—he's not even a shit. Swear here on this grave that you will die like that rooster Zósimo, or fizz yourself to death with Alka-Seltzer. Will you swear to answer the call of Trinidad de los Santos whether it be once or a thousan' times? Though slightly discordant, the national anthem sounded beautiful there in the cemetery on the hill, an anthem filled with death, the glorious flag, heroic feats, heroes, sacred soil, our sky, Fatherland, Fatherland, Fatherland, and honor, a great deal about honor. In spite of the volume of the singers and the blatting of the tubas, María Candelaria still lay in a faint. And the bulk of her belly swelled above the earth as if Zósimo himself wished to surge forth to take the place of Trinidad de los Santos. But everything comes to an end, and María Candelaria opened her eyes. From that moment she never again complained or wept. Holding the hand of her cousin María del Sagrario, she left the holy ground. It was almost night, and with their shadows the Ceiba trees were beginning to patrol the fences of fear. Fear, María Candelaria? She walked lightly, aware of the six-months son in her belly. She would never again know fear. María del Sagrario crossed herself frequently. In the distance they could hear the song of drunken patriots. The banana clusters looked like men hanged in the trees where they had been born. Fear? María del Sagrario could hear among the other voices the voice of Arcadio. When they tell you I have a heart of stone, that should not matter to you, because stone and solid rock, my beauty, are the same; they are the same.

Oaths of love and of patriots sworn in a cemetery don't last very long, *Comandante*. Trinidad de los Santos doesn't know how to read, but he has someone who reads for him. Father Godfrey censors some of the things Victoriano's letter says. They're saying around here that one of the political big-shots sold out Zósimo and the men who were machine-gunned that morning. You're hiding something from me, Father. This is the third time the revolutionaries have gone to their deaths while others sit around wiggling their toes. Is that what it says? That's what it says. The writing is labored, difficult to read. Victoriano passes for a man of letters. I made them swear in the cemetery, and I spread the word through the district, that the *comandante* is recruiting men for the last struggle, but the people, I don't know why, are quiet. They swore, but they don't keep their word. But I will be there, Trinidad, whenever you say the word, and with me my brothers, Juan, Narciso, and Epifanio, who have the balls to show up.

Trinidad walks outside to wander through the fields. He wears two pistols at his belt and crossed cartridge belts. There are no bonfires here, or anyone to say "At your orders." Scarcely three dozen guerrillas are still with him, and they're around somewhere begetting children in some girl's bed or in the deep grass. Trinidad doesn't know who Emiliano Zapata was, but he feels the same bitterness. Who goesss there, eh? A little vizcacha that looks at him indifferently. Trinidad kills it with one shot. Too bad the guerrilla's family is in Xiltenango. The kids could eat the vizcacha. Trinidad de los Santos needs someone who is more intelligent than he is and braver than the priest. Not that everything that's thought in anger is craziness. If the men are tired of following him, there must be a reason. But who is it who's just wiggling his toes? Trinidad looks at his feet and sees his own toes wiggling. Who goesss there, eh? This time it is not a vizcacha but a tall blond one-eyed man. Trinidad de los Santos considers shooting him. He wouldn't be the first who wanted to play the hero with the guerrilla. But he doesn't draw his pistol. Father Richard, who is sitting beside a window writing, sees the two men meet but cannot hear them.

Dear Father Flanagan:

I regret to inform you that I shall not be returning. My place is here beside these men who have been forgotten by man's justice. I know that your orders that I return to the monastery are due to intense political pressures and the dishonorable suggestions of those motivated entirely by self-interest. I shall not leave here as long as I feel my presence among these people is necessary. My leader is out walking with someone who just arrived. For an instant I thought Trinidad would kill him, but they shook hands and are talking as if they'd been friends all their lives. The man has a very distinctive personal characteristic that for reasons of security I am not going to describe to you. *Forget it.* That is for the censor. Trinidad needs a man like the one who just arrived. I don't know who he is, but I can see that in only a few minutes the chief's morale has begun to improve. The poor man needs it. Imagine, Your Reverence, they accuse him of conniving with that infamous Colonel Arruza. You met Trinidad de los Santos, and you know that this Indian could not be bought with all the gold in the National Bank, which must be very little by now. The one who left probably took all of his and everyone else's money to Switzerland. And now we have that bandit Lavalle. It looks as if I will be writing this letter in parts. Trinidad de los Santos and his visitor are walking toward the house. The three of us have now dined. Campbell's soup and some tacos prepared by Yili, also known as El Chino, a mute Chinaman who follows the road of revolution with two clay pots in each hand. Do you know what? The man is the bastard son of Colonel Arruza and he wants to destroy his father. That might not be Christian, but the future it would open to the country is beautiful. He has shown us the scars his father inflicted on him in a fight. He has plans that I cannot reveal at the moment. *Forget it,* SIM Chief. My mood has also changed in these few hours. It is a hot and humid night, but it is as if a wind of liberty were blowing from some distant mountain. If there were trumpets in these solitary headquarters, they would sound of their own accord. Trinidad de los Santos is smiling for the first time in many days. They have gone outside again so on the run I can write some letters to our people. I have listened to him. Powder? What good is powder? The fox does not kill hens with a rifle. Only another fox can compete with him in his depredations. I must bid farewell to you, Your Reverence. My greetings to the fathers and brothers of the order.

Devotedly,

FATHER RICHARD

Why do you want more men, Trinidad de los Santos? No one can deny anything you say. You have two or three thousand men with you. Let the colonel come to see whether it's true. We have to wage psychological warfare. You are the enemy, you are *all* the enemy. As long as you live, the revolution will live. You represent the people. Don't ask them to die. That's the way revolutions were fought in the past. No one has to die. Everyone must live, live, live, so they can eat the things they've never eaten and enjoy the things they've never enjoyed. You find yourself alone because you've asked too much.

Oh brother, oh brother, oh brother!

We have to kill number one, you understand? We must destroy the mechanism. We must leave his Walkers turned over on their backs like turtles. Do you remember Batista? When he got home late at night, he always went in through the back door.

Trinidad de los Santos spit.

All right, my friend, spit. But as long as you insist on entering through the front door, they'll kill your men and you'll find yourself cornered here or some other place, if, that is, you manage to escape their search parties. Besides, there's the matter of your reputation. Tell me, how is it that Trinidad de los Santos always escapes alive? That's what they're asking in the capital. Listen to me. A half-dozen men will serve you better than a thousand. The priest is writing letters for the four party chiefs. After they arrive, with them and the priest and El

Chino, you will break up camp and announce that you're at the opposite end of the country. Your footsteps will be heard everywhere. Are they your footsteps, or the footsteps of the people? When you were *someone*, why was it so, my friend? Because you were a threat, a contained fury, a buried shout. When the reality of all that power was uncovered, what remained of Trinidad de los Santos? Nothing, or very little. No one fights any more the way you're fighting. And no one wants to stir during the hunt; don't confuse the man pointing the gun.

Dear Father Flanagan:
　　Our packs are rolled, and I am writing to say good-bye. We are going to a part of the country whose name I have not been told. We have two thousand men with us and they say the number will increase along the way to five thousand. We have received arms in such quantity that we find ourselves forced to bury more than half, which we do not need for the moment. I ask Your Reverence's pardon for my rebellion, but my place is here. Greetings to my brothers, and with a plea for your blessing, I remain always, devotedly, in the hands of your mercy.

FATHER RICHARD

His companions started on their way. It was late afternoon, and a resplendent sun was just beginning to seek shelter behind the mountains. As they crossed the bridge, Miguel Ángel bade farewell to the six men.
　　Don't forget that three thousand men are following you. I would tell everyone that a whole town is following in your footsteps. It was a beautiful hanging bridge, it might have been a swing for a train, or a trapeze for the river. They call it the bridge of San Vidal, in memory of the famous battle. On the shore of the river where the federal troops had been dug in, the vegetation is dominated by eucalyptus and mahogany. On the opposite shore, where the soldiers of former President

Menéndez had camped, scrub stretches as far as the eye can see. Some Central American historians disagree about the exact positions of the two bands. What is clear is that in this place the destinies of two of the young republics were decided. Every fourteenth of August the people who dwell along the banks of the San Vidal River, forgetting ancient quarrels, meet in the middle of the bridge, exchange embraces, throw a lamb into the water, and return to their respective shores with light hearts. May God protect the guerrillas! A trembling of leaves, and a shiver of movement among grazing sheep. Miguel Ángel carries with him Father Richard's letter to be delivered to a certain Sly Juan. Barefoot countrymen returning home along the rugged paths recognize Trinidad de los Santos, but follow at a distance. The cantina at El Mirlo is about a half league away. Miguel Ángel must press on before night overtakes him. In the cantina there are three old men and the serving girl, Asunción. As soon as he enters, she brings him a beer and some jerked beef. . . . Sly Juan? Over there. He joins Miguel Ángel and orders pulque. Has he come from the other side of the river? Bad land and bad people. That's where I came into the world. General Armenteros was born a little farther up the river. He's not from this country, though the bastard's taken plenty from it. I'm a Lutheran and a farmer. A soul in pain, others say. Pulque sits well on the tongue. Give me the letter. Does this one fall into the hands of SIM? Miguel Ángel placed a green bill in the old man's hands. It does. Satisfied, Matalax returned to Belize, where he had already taken Corín.

"Virginia-the-Cunt!"

Finally the Colonel had surprised her in the act of adultery. He fired at the student seven times. Virginia screamed hysterically. Don Cleto came with two of the guards to carry away the dead man. The terrified Indian girls came in to scrub the red floor. Don Cleto turned on the tape recorder. Virginia's voice. You're a well-built young man, and I like your good manners. I don't want to hear that! You *will* hear it, whore! Are you one of those poor students who has to work his way through college? What are you studying? Economics. And you're healthy enough to bring a son into the world! No, no, I don't want to have children. I had a son; he was blond and wanted to be a bishop. His name was Aristarco. And he already knew Latin and algebra when other children were filling their pants and saying pee-pee. I'm not a virtuoso, and you're none too virtuous. So what the devil are we waiting for? I pray to the air that caresses the church steeples, but I am a sinful woman! Well, wish to heaven and close your eyes, señora. Give me your hand in compassion. Hold out your hand even if the other clutches a rawhide whip. Take off your panties, we're wasting time. I am opposed to anything that is not God's will, but I cannot help myself; it's like a sickness. Heads, the boy; tails, nothing. So be it, so be it. This is the only time I'm happy. It's a mystery I can't explain. Afterward, I will despise you, but it will be too late. My hatred always comes too late. Shut up, baby. I, oh, I can't talk any more. A Walker signaled to Don Cleto. The tape recorder was silent. Someone delivers an envelope to the secretary. Don't try to soften me up with those tears. I have no choice but to slit your throat. Say your prayers and tell me what you want me to tell your father. Don Cleto hands the envelope to the Colonel. A report from SIM. Trinidad de los Santos is moving toward the Pacific coast with five thousand men. The Colonel strides from the bedroom and goes to the private room where he keeps a teletype and a telephone switchboard. Chief of SIM! That can't be. Three days ago he had three dozen scroungy bastards. Didn't you yourself tell me that? I don't know, Colonel. Everything began to change when the guy with a glass eye arrived.

FIRST STAGE OF
THE VOYAGE OF
MIGUEL ÁNGEL MATALAX YANAMA
IN SEARCH OF A DOUBLE

The only men who never feel the desire for revenge are those who have lost their natural dignity and acquired one that is artificial.

From a speech delivered by the Rev. M. R. Kuntz (Methodist Church) at the Congress of Protestant Churches, Uppsala, Sweden

Martin Lavalle's mansion in Belize is a lacustrine dream with indigo-painted walls. Gigantic shells from the Sea of Tasmania filter the jungle air. What are you thinking about? Eh? A vinyl fish hangs from the ceiling. I believe spring's come, don't you? Who ever thinks of seasons in this sun-baked land? The many rooms are filled with castanets, sistrums, and black maracas. Martin wishes he could get it up to make a balloon. Georgiana contemplates her flat belly and accepts the fact that she will never fly. It never swells up. One can buy a balloon, of course, but not the kind that blows up women's bellies. Georgiana, dressed in a green sari, is lying quietly upon a zebra-skin ottoman. You can't judge a book by its cover. Martin will go in search of other bellies, and Georgiana knows it, has known it, will know it. Martin Lavalle is the brother of the millionaire Lavalle. Mines in Copiapó and other things that the poor never know how to find. The dog has died. Its name was Cid. Martin loved him. More than Georgiana? Georgiana, who is beautiful, would be happy if the fury of the wind blasted out the windows. The next hurricane will be called Celia. It is the third storm of the year. And they will have to flee. But it is always summer in this land. Suddenly she screams. Martin tries to make a bark like Cid's, but it doesn't turn out right. And he stares through the picture window at the monkeys. Georgiana tries not to think of her husband, Martin's brother. She cannot be consoled for the

59

death of the dog; she loved it too. She screams. Martin barks again. A servant brings gin and tonic with ice and mint leaves. They live at number 12 Potti Lane. It could just as easily be 13. The air conditioning is turned so high they have to wear scarves. Cold. One can buy winter. It must be beautiful to live in the Andes and have heat. Buy summer. Didn't you say it's spring? Why don't you ever think twice before you say something? Tell me about the world, Martin. Are there still children in the world? Children? There must be. At least there were when I was a boy. Perhaps there aren't any now. How can there be a land or a woman without children? No one has any future. There's no reason we should all be so limited. There must be a future in the depths of the sea or in astral space. The hands of Miguel Ángel Matalax, polished in the current of a river. In the Cauca, or the Jordan. It is important for believers that there be a river. He says he's thinking, he says he's thinking. . . . It's been years since we've done anything, we fill ourselves full of reproaches, and then with morphine. Afterward she wants to drink from someone's, anyone's, hands the water that flows from Mount Hermon. Haven't we met somewhere? In some war, in some shipwreck? Hush! Your pupils were once grooved with untraveled highways. And I? What's to become of me? He had been sure that someday someone would need Martin Lavalle, but time passes and no one calls him. He was like one of those elephants in the circus that balance on a mirrored ball. He never believed that one day the sun might rise in the west. Sadness forces him to say adieu. It's time for the nurse. It's time for the iron lung. The nurse lifts Georgiana and places her in the machine. Indians smile only when they are dead from cold. Martin is afraid of the strips of aluminum and plastic that cage city men. Georgiana! She smiles as she is rolled toward her room. "How could you kiss her hands?" For the first time Martin notices Miguel Ángel Matalax, who has been in the living room for three hours. Come watch the macaques masturbate. Miguel Ángel excuses himself. He does not like the spectacle because of his single eye. He says he's hot, and goes inside. What are you talking about? Only the just can calmly bear cold feet while everyone else feels upon him the warm breath of the daughters of the Maya. Did you hear, Martin? This stranger has come to propose that you be the sole owner of the mines of Copiapó. When did I get my injection? He has to laugh. Thanks, buddy, I'm nobody. My twin brother took everything that belonged to me. All I got from him was Georgiana. And you've seen her. Paralyzed. My brother, Ernesto, is a cuckold, but he has the power and the money; a sad past and a shameful present. Is it incest to have a sister-in-law in your bed? To me it seems only half incest, or civil or political incest. Miguel Ángel speaks of the future. There was gold and silver, my God, was there ever! And Martin accepts the idea that he can be Ernesto. It was all a question of waiting for the sun to rise in the west. Right?

SECOND STAGE OF
THE VOYAGE
OF MIGUEL ÁNGEL MATALAX YANAMA
IN SEARCH OF A SECOND DOUBLE

*If we should publish your theory, Mr. Tannenberg,
that plants weep when they are pruned, then I do not
know what would become of us.*
—Secret files of the Vegetarian Society of Belfast,
Northern Ireland

A cell—cot, washbasin, table, chair, urinal, and a ray of
light—is, at times, an unattainable dream. Sinfonías is
in jail. There are also monastic cells. Once, the prisoner
had a mute woman who kept him and the others happy. Sinfonías is the spitting image of a Latin American president.
That's why he's in jail. So no one will see him. He emerges
only on certain occasions. He is like a twin brother to the Most
Honorable Señor Don Valentín Oruro. Sinfonías has presided
over certain official ceremonies. At one of them, they tried to
kill him. Where have you been?, his woman asked him in sign
language. And Sinfonías answered, in the same sign language,
that he had just come from dedicating a bridge. She died in
the cell where they had lived together for more than three
years. A portion of the Dominican landscape, where a man
had cracked his whip over the red earth for thirty years, could
be glimpsed through the tiny window. *Our* sonofabitch. But
still, there are doves and lambs that although they tremble
with fear before a weaponless hand will allow themselves to
be stroked by barefoot children who dream only of fishing for
shrimp along the shore of the Caribbean. Many Dominicans
still have convulsions because they wished so strongly for the
death of the plunderers who paraded as machos. When they
need Sinfonías in the Presidential Palace, they take him by
small boat from Punta Beata and leave him in Belize. There a

few men wait for him in an automobile and by night drive him through the banana plantations to his destiny. Sometimes they dress him in a frock coat; at others, in a dinner jacket festooned with decorations; and one day they dressed him as the head of the Red Cross.

Sinfonías had been a clerk in an apothecary's shop in Bogotá. He had been in charge of the leeches and snakebite serums. One day a Central American diplomat who had come to the shop to buy some suppositories noticed Sinfonías's resemblance to a certain personage and offered him a post in the country he represented. Sinfonías's dreams had always been a little like Humboldt's. He embarked in Cartagena with Clara and a basket containing Berta, a snake with eyeglasses a belly dancer had sold him at the time of her marriage to a wealthy landowner in Antioquia. Berta died during the crossing. In Belize he had an interview with Colonel Arruza, and after three months of training in the mannerisms of the President, they sent him to Punta Beata and from there to the jail in Enriquillo. This was a matter of mutual convenience between The Benefactor (RIP) and Colonel Arruza. Trujillo's double received the same treatment in the Colonel's territory. At first, the couple from Bogotá did not understand the game. But little by little they became accustomed to it. The jail had a patio and an elderly jailer. Clara roasted reptiles on the barbecue, and from the fat concocted unguents that enjoyed a brisk trade in the village. They were intended for certain female maladies. Sinfonías began to study the antivenom properties of mushrooms. He had read that the peoples of the north merely got drunk on muscarine, but that when the same potion was drunk by Dominicans, they died in a torment of suffering. One day they brought him a woman who had drunk the liquid of a certain herb. He hesitated whether to bleed her or give her atronine. He bled her; she shivered like a quivering aspen, and fell dead. But another day, using tannin, he saved the life of a small boy who had smoked his grandfather's pipe. They allowed him to travel to Santa Marta to bury Clara. While in

Colombia he bought a mockingbird, which with patience he taught to say "Hello," "Good evening," "Did you sleep well?," "Merry Christmas," and "You're right."

From then on he felt less lonely. The jailer kept him company at dusk, when the starlings come out to feed on mosquitoes. Other cells held the doubles of other important men, but they were not allowed to associate. They had never even seen one another. After he was widowed, the jailer asked Sinfonías whether he wanted a woman. No, he didn't want a woman. A little rice, some porgy, an avocado salad, and three ripe mangoes . . . what more could a man want? And coffee. And a cigar. When the first light of day appeared, another mockingbird, in another cell, sang "Guantanamera." The jailer had a sister who was named Manuel because their father wanted a boy. Sinfonías also had a sister, named Sonora. And they talked about them, primarily about their virginity. One day the jailer announced that a stranger had come to see Sinfonías.

There are royal doves, common doves, Tripoli doves that boast a diadem of ruffed feathers. What a great man Garibaldi was! Sinfonías is a family name. Was Garibaldi the one who said, *"La guerra fa i ladri e la pace li impicca"*?

"My name is Miguel Ángel Matalax Yanama. I've come a great distance. . . ."

A soft breeze filters through the tiny window. It makes a man yearn for a smoke. The jailer is brewing coffee. He has an offer. After the coffee. Never spoil the good moments. They say that the hour of a man's death is marked, that he can feel it. A falcon soars overhead with a kid in its talons. The jailer makes the coffee as his mother, a Jamaican medicine woman, had taught him, tossing hot coals into the pot. Night is upon them, and bats hang from the palms. The three red dots of their cigars barely penetrate the shadows.

"One day I shall need you in the presidency . . ."

And this one-eyed Matalax continued:

". . . not to dress you in a frock coat, or a dinner jacket, or any of that fucking nonsense; not to inaugurate little rural schools, or cut the ribbon of a new highway. . . ."

He pulled out a bundle of green bills. These are for you, jailer, and these are for you, Sinfonías. In the light of a match they saw that they were hundreds. You'll have an equal amount when someone comes to get Sinfonías. God be with you! They would have answered *Amen*, but it was so dark they were afraid.

June 23. On board *La Bellotte*.

Longitude 65°. Latitude 17° 45′ N. 60 miles west of Frederiksted, St. Croix. *La Bellotte* wasn't built to sail with ballast. She's dizzied by the winds astern fanned by the eleven thousand Virgins. We've left St. Croix, the last one, behind, and under half sail we're en route to Barahona, where we'll take on the barrels of molasses ordered by Rosky's nephew almost a year ago. He's getting them a little late, so he'll tell me to shove them up my ass, and I'll have to be rough with him. Just because you're a woman, you don't grab your balls and run. God our Savior has spread a beautiful night over this dense, deep sea. Jesus! There are thirty thousand feet beneath me as soon as I get past Puerto Rico. Although—as my dear departed father used to say—give or take a foot, it doesn't matter much as long as you don't run your nose aground. When I was young, that Italian in New Orleans told me no one knows more about the mud of Venice than the gondoliers. That old ass! Too bad I gave it up to him before he said that, because I don't go to bed with ignoramuses. It's a fine night, and we've all got full bellies on board *La Bellotte*. Paulito at the helm. Nimes looking to the sails. Weis sleeping until five. And Cortés preparing my coffee. Eleven-fifteen by the clock and Handel's Largo on the radio. Just a minute. Coffee, and a letter from my son, Miguel Ángel. For a little I'd crack that devil-freaking Cortés's skull, he has no mind for anything but trying to find a name to give the "cocktail" of his blood. He says someone gave him the envelope day before yesterday in Frederiksted. Sure, since he was suckled on manatee's milk, he thinks all mothers are indifferent.

La Bellotte had been sailing the Caribbean for more than a quarter of a century. Originally she was a schooner built by A. D. Story, in Essex, in 1910. She was designed by McManus, the same man who drew the plans for the famous *Elsie*. In 1935, Simón Matalax, a sailor of the Spanish Mediterranean, bought the schooner in the oyster beds of the Bay of Delaware. She was called *Sphyraena II* then, but he changed her name and had her towed to Corpus Christi, Texas. There he installed a motor to make her easier to manage in docking and calms, and conditioned her hold for carrying vegetable oils, molasses, and bales of cured tobacco. Simón Matalax Vives was a native of Castelldefels and had begun his American career at the age of fourteen. From Pensacola to Gibraltar, from Galveston to Barcelona, from Havana to Bilbao. In 1922 he sighted land on one of the many inlets along the Texas coast, and built his house on a key between Santa Isabel and Matagorda. For years he had sailed the hundred miles of warm quiet water of the sound in a catboat. She accommodated four, and carried her cargo on the deck. He paid a hundred pesos and a lottery ticket in Campeche for the small ship with tall sails, and sailed her up the coast toward his key. Between 1920 and 1925 Matalax contracted as a pilot with the Gran Panameña Company to save his house and his catboat from the approaching economic crisis. He not only saved them, but also saved enough to buy the key, and to marry, in Callao, Huancavélica Yanama, a young Indian girl with eyes so moist and sad, so beautiful and enigmatic, that Simón Matalax dared possess her but three times. Niña Huancavélica was the fruit of their last mating. It was later that he bought *La Bellotte*.

In the letter my son calls me Niña Huanca. Juancita called me "Baby" Huanca to set me apart from my mother. There isn't much left about me that's "baby," and nothing's left of Juancita. She was the family bible. She could remember things that had happened twenty years before as if she could still see them. She even remembered the color of the flowers they placed in my dear mother's hands. They were blue bellflowers, my child. It was from Juancita I learned my mother had been buried in an earthen vessel, sitting up and wearing a pretty dress, beneath the ceiba tree on the key. My father wept then, and I believe he wept his widowhood through all the taverns of Corpus Christi, Texas City, La Porte, Anahuac, and Baytown. Until one day he got a man by the balls in Jacksonville and they packed him back dead to the key in the hold of *La Bellotte*, which Nimes commanded in those days. I was fourteen then, and I saw that he was buried beside my mother. But Papá was buried lying down. When he died, the key already had a dock and more than two dozen houses scattered around ours. People from all over lived there. Some earned their living fishing, and some from smuggling. But these things don't have any bearing now. Juancita died two years ago. My son tells me he was in Belize to find Lavalle's twin brother. Now he wants another man from the jail in Enriquillo. Enriquillo is right next to Barahona. I won't even need to change course. I'll simply load on the prisoner with Rosky's molasses. And may God be with all of us. Good night.

On February 23, 1937, Nimes had been very surprised when he saw Niña Huanca, wearing men's clothing and with a seabag over her shoulder, climbing up the ship's ladder. She was seventeen, with skin the color of cinammon and a voice as clear as crystal. There began the story of the captain of *La Bellotte*. A logbook was the girl's diary. Winds and latitudes, mingled with dreams and names. For many years there was no more beautiful or freer woman in the pot wherein the Antilles boil. A trail of lovers left behind. And one affair not entered in the logbook of the winds and satisfied desires. The man of the bay, of the stormy cape, of the fury of the tropics, the infidelity of the man on horseback. Only after insistent pleas had Miguel Ángel Matalax succeeded, three years before, in learning his father's name. Colonel Arruza, father of bastards and parricide of dictators. Niña Huanca sent Miguel away. Far from ceiba trees, royal palms, and caimans. A French preparatory school and a German university. Far, far away, where the long shadows of his father and mother would not fall on him. Because there are those who believe that the sparrow in the poor man's hut is somehow less virtuous than the parrot in the bishop's bird cage. But for those people, there are eyes that see the rum before the cane is cut.

When Niña Huanca took command of the schooner, she already knew all the marine terms and positions. Some because she had heard them, others by hunch. Brought up among the shoals of the reefs, she knew depths by the color of the water and winds by the cry of the gulls. No one could explain how Niña Huanca had learned all those things by instinct. Or why everyone—from Nimes, the old mate, to the dwarf Paulito—respected her without muttering and mumbling. Paulito was a dwarf from Barbados; he loved rum and the sea. He would swim among sharks and crocodiles without the least fear, and it would take a circus artist to rival him at scrambling up and down rigging. Nimes spoke very little. Even less after Juancita, who had been his woman, died. Now he refused to leave the ship when they returned to the key. From shipboard he gazed numb with melancholy at the shore where Juancita lay buried. And he believed he saw her through a mist pierced by the glimmer of mussel shells. Cortés was a Honduran of three racial stocks, given to fighting any man who looked like him. Weis, too, was a Honduran, muscular and calm, and when it came to balls, he could beat any sailor going.

And she, shouting:

"Prepare to dock, Weis!" "The port cathead!" "Luff to fucking starboard!" *La Bellotte* was like a floating house, green, with a white stripe beneath her black upperworks. Pots of geraniums and parsley poked through the portholes when they were at anchor. Women's clothes were strung from the rigging, pretty garments she wore to make the rounds of the cabarets in New Orleans, Tampico, and Galveston.

June 24. On board *La Bellotte.*

Longitude 68°. Latitude 17°50′ N. Yesterday we skirted the coast of Puerto Rico some twenty miles offshore. We are headed toward the Dominican Republic; Mona Island lies to starboard. A warm wind is blowing from the Bay of Yuma, filling our jib. We must take advantage of it until we pass Saona Island. My son's letter:

Dear Niña Huanca:
    I hope this letter reaches you in time in St. Croix. I need a man whose name is Sinfonías; he is in the jail in Enriquillo. He's one of the men I need to carry out my plans. Ernesto Lavalle's twin found no difficulty in leaving the woman he stole from his brother—a beautiful woman, paralyzed, whose name is Georgiana—to return to his country and slip into his brother's pajamas. I pointed out to him that one day Ernesto could be Martin, and Martin, Ernesto Lavalle, Minister of the Economy and Director of the National Bank. And I will capitalize on that situation. My next letter will reach you in Galveston. I believe that the third man I need lives either in New Orleans or in Baton Rouge. I haven't yet been able to find out. I'm very grateful for the money you deposited in my name in Belize. That's plenty for now. I was quite taken with Georgiana. By now, Colonel Arruza has heard of big One-Eye. I believe that with my one eye I shall see him hanged. Did you know that we'd met? He insulted me, he beat me to bloody Jesus, and he said that he remembered you, but that he wasn't sure whether you were a woman or a sailor—which didn't seem to bother him too much. I assure you, my dearest mother, that the way he treated me was not the way a natural father treats a bastard who is pestering him but the way a filthy swine treats an asshole son. I must destroy him, Niña Huanca. He went too far. You must have loved him very much, mother, and I know you still have a warm feeling when you hear his name, but he is one holy son of a bitch! I send you my deepest respect and sincere affection. Your son,

MIGUEL

Give the jailer at Enriquillo five hundred dollars so that he can get away.

The fog has descended. It's always the same when we sail along the Dominican coast. It is a dark, heavy, fat-assed fog. By daybreak it will be gone and we'll be able to see the algae that the gulls nest on. The Dominican Republic is a beautiful island; King Fucker's aides gave her *marrons glacés* to lie with her by night. That's why she has the fog and stink, which she never had before. I remember once they tried to take *me* to The Benefactor's bed; some sport, he was lying in bed waiting for me in his undershorts, drinking rum from a hollowed-out pineapple. Then, although no one believes me, I grabbed him hard where he had the most pride and I said to him: "Either you come to me on my schooner, you hardheaded old bastard, or I swear to God I'll yank this beauty off!" So they drove him to the schooner in his official car and he climbed aboard, and only after we had the motor revved up fast did we toss him overboard. For three years, until he was killed, he kept sending his most trusted men to the ports to knock me off. But he still wanted me; first he wanted to hump me, and then hustle me off to the next world. Every time I sail past here I remember that story. On the radio, the "Blue Danube." I'm glad my son needs me. The father knows that someone of his own blood is sawing the floor out from under him. I'll give my last dollar to Miguel Ángel. I love that man as much as the day he made me a mother by the bay, but if his son can knock him off his throne and I see him come crawling one day to beg for protection—creator and lord of presidents—oh, by my cunt, that will be the happiest day of my life! I might hang him from the fore-and-aft, I could do it. But if he tells me where I have a birthmark, I'll forgive him. Yes, I'll forgive him even if Miguel Ángel has a fit. He turned me on. Good night.

She had delivered her son on the key one hot night during a hurricane. Juancita kept placing wads of cotton between her legs while Nimes tried to light an oil lamp. Two other sailors, now dead, tried to hold onto the roof of the shed to keep the wind from blowing it away. When they showed her the child, she could see in that yellowish light that although he would never be as handsome as the father—Colonel Arruza, cockster and adviser to presidents—her son was comely. When Nimes circumcised him, he neither cried nor cried out. It was a good augury.

As the air turned cool, the wind died down. Sunlight fell upon her bare breasts and Miguel Ángel suckled for the first time. The captain said tenderly, "my son." Words which were so often repeated that even the iguanas of the key came to know them.

My darling June:

Belize! Who the hell could be writing me from Belize? You will look at the signature. Oh, Miguel Ángel, Handsome One-Eye. That's what your friends used to call me. Possibly you did too. Pity me! Much more fortunate than I is the cripple; if he's lacking a foot, he can be called a Uniped. Of course, if it's merely a question of being lame, then he's stuck with "gimpy." I wish there were for me—a creature lacking half of one of his pairs—a word as sonorous and fabulous as "unicorn." Miguel Ángel, Unicorn. Of course, that would be as absurd as calling you Junie Uni-pussy, and I know what I've been telling myself ever since I came to these parts. Through an Englishman who knows you—Mr. Reginald Moors, CMG, MVO, MC, I read on his card—I learned that in your nomadic life as a European millionairess you are now in Tossa de Mar. That was always a very picturesque place. Pickled fish and champagne. I wish I could be there with you, but Mr. Moors told me, before he fell off the barstool in the bar where we met, that you are now accompanied by a young Romanian whom exile has turned into a courier of automobiles, an ambivalent gigolo, and an addict of the lesser drugs. As he told me these things, our Englishman smiled and stammered; he hoped to hide his humiliation: a CMG, MVO, and MC with horns as big as a moose! Several times he made a gesture as if to withdraw your letter—your famous farewell

73

letter—from his jacket pocket. He was annoying me so about how unique he had been in your life that I pointed to his pocket and told him that the Romanian would in turn receive a similar note, as I had received one, and the Greek who sold plastic flowers, and the steward on the *Queen Mary*, and the French movie director, and the German baron, and the Spanish dancer. I continued the list until he ordered me to stop. Mr. Moors confessed that the only part of your past that truly mortified him was that you had also given that uni(que) pussy to a lowborn deckhand out of Liverpool. For more than an hour Mr. Moors sat clutching his head in his hands and asking himself *Why?* Since we had time to kill, I invented a story. We poured enormous quantities of gin into our glasses. *For the British Empire!* The barman said, *Shit*, pretending to sneeze. I toasted the deckhand's health, and Mr. Moors blubbered, *God bless you.* Who was it deflowered the flesh and mien of our June when she was barely fourteen? No one knows his name or nationality or occupation. She searches for him in each of us, Mr. Moors, in each of us. In a deckhand from Liverpool, *too?* He sobbed. June's mystery is the voice of a man who enters Echo's caverns to lose his voice among all the others. Blessed be He who in this whirlpool of life gave her to us for a few hours, a few days. Mr. Moors confessed that he had lived with you for three months in Capri. So why is he complaining? My record is longer, but I didn't tell him that. Four months, two weeks, three days, seven hours, and twenty-three minutes. A hotel facing the Adriatic. Albergo Masciangelo. Bari delle Puglie. Only after you left—leaving a wake of letters—did I find out that there in Bari, only three doors beyond our inn, Urban II had presided over a Council of Bishops in the eleventh century. I was tempted to ask Mr. Moors whether in his letter, as in mine, you had said: "I am leaving, my love, to continue my search." Tossa de Mar! Just about now the midday sun would be shining on waves and sand. A flat sun, reflecting off you and off the binoculars of a dirty old man on the terrace. You are not completely naked, although you are nearly so. A body as shining and sleek as that of the dolphin's mate. The Romanian is attempting to shield you from the sun with his stupid hands. That artful hophead! Cocoa-butter lotion on your skin. Dark glasses behind which you hide what you are really looking at. Mr. Moors wants to know who the man was who broke you. I tell him you are searching for him this very minute in Tossa de Mar. Let's drink a toast, Mr. Moors, that our June may find him someday. My English friend tries to appear civilized, but he does not succeed. It is as if his shoes were too tight and he needed to take a leak at the same time. To end the story: they dragged him away after he fell off the barstool. And why the devil am I writing all this to you? Possibly my psychiatrist would explain it with the eloquence given to those who speculate about things they cannot feel. I am critical because I am lost. I am insulting because I am afraid. I forgive in Olympian fashion because I am preparing to show no mercy. And the sun, my beauty, will continue to play over your skin in the same way that my confession will slide off your soul into the pit where all the victims of your indifference come to rest. I wish the Romanian could read this so he could begin to get the drift. It's true, June; in this bar your name has served me as a window through which to shout at the top of my lungs that I am a coward, that I don't know where I'm going, but that remorselessly I must go where my hatred drags me. A tremendous adventure that I believed had begun two years ago in Mainz but that in reality had its beginnings only a few days ago in a place where humbly I had to retrieve my glass eye from the floor. No, no, the sea with all its salt and winds cannot erase it. It can, of course, erase one image in order to create another. So here I am, tranquil and impassive in Belize. *For the British Empire!* The barman sneezes again. *God bless you!* I have met a woman. A blue mystery who as she leaves looks at you in a mirror. She was interested in my hands. Have you ever heard of Copiapó? I don't believe so. The Southern Hemisphere is so rich that you, you of the north, keep it underdeveloped. Two twin brothers—north and south—have split Georgiana's spinal column in half. That's what I say. It can't be anything else. Two brothers repeatedly signify betrayal in the uterus of America. I too shall be a betrayal, but—I found the word!—I shall be only-begotten, thanks to my mother. Miguel Ángel, the Only-Begotten. You always wanted to know who I was. The bastard of a petty king of a minor republic. *Made in Central America.* The black patch over my eye augured that you, on behalf of England, were destined to yield your body to a buccaneer of the routes of gold. That's how the highways of the sea appear in these latitudes, perhaps because the dawns are so diaphanous and the sun sleeps late with a tiny blue lamp above its bed, as rich children do. I am sad. In love—no, not with you, not any more—and trying to save the feeling that has been born in my heart, in a ship without a compass, the keel full of holes, the rudder without a tiller. I should tell Georgiana that I know the road that would lead us to Mount Hermón. I would gladly run the entire distance if I could have her forever in my arms. But instead of doing the sensible thing, one day very soon she and I will plunge into the tropical green labyrinth where, without ever finding them, one seeks the shadows of a cosmic race and the spoils of suddenly impoverished riches. I am infected with the sadness of the tropics. Nowhere else does one feel as one does here. People who don't know where they're going, always halfway between the ice-cream parlor and orange-juice and rum stands. These are creatures who seem to have asked permission not to report to work that day. Here every day seems an eternal stone-broke Sunday. I don't know who's to blame, but that impression becomes fixed in us, as much in the Spanish-speaking countries as in this, one of the last of Britain's colonies. You lie, you bastard! I don't want to go on because I know that my eyeglass is out of focus. I know I'm lying, but that's the way I want it to be. My psychiatrist would say I'm preparing the ground so I can justify what I have to do. I suppose that if you saw me with various poultices on my still-tender and unhealed scars, you would feel pity for me. And if I explained in what battle I earned those bloody laurels, you would understand my bitterness and my hatred. But I shall tell you nothing. I believe that I love Georgiana and despise all other beings, including you. I also place my mother in that ark. Perhaps this letter should be for her. But I prefer to vent my anger on you, on your indifference. Right now you are probably inscribing in the sand *merde*, the elegant way to express what that word says in other languages. Yes, *merde, mierda*, shit! But read these next few lines with close attention. With attention, I say! Like Mr. Moors, I am drunk. In a short while they will carry me away, too, drag me to my room. Don't worry. I've addressed the envelope, and that barman, the one who says "shit" every time we toast the British Empire, has orders to put this letter in the mail. Miss June McLean, Hotel Levante. Tossa de Mar. Spain. Special delivery. Registered mail. Everything. This letter must reach you. I want it to be as if I myself strode into your bedroom when you are seeing your little lights—that's what you used to tell me, what did you dream up for the Romanian?—and I myself spit on them one by one and extinguished them. Read it with attention, June. A moment ago I got down from the barstool and crawled on my knees to the center of the bar to ask pardon of all those I insulted several lines above. Are they sad or are they better? They see themselves facing a slovenly drunk babbling nonsense who asks their pardon and offers them a drink, and they neither laugh nor accept the invitation. I try to convince them that I am Judas, and that I'm going to betray them. Do you know what they did? They picked me up off the floor, and put me on the barstool again. I tell you all this, which you will not believe, in order to tell you (I can scarcely see the paper) that they are good, that I am a piss-poor excuse for a man, that my beloved mother is good, good, good—how can I describe her to you?—it is as if the heavens had burst one day and spilled the cream of the Milky Way into a saucer called *La Bellotte*. But what do you know about that? You, your bikinis, your man-

hattans, and your little lights that light up down there . . .
You knew so well how to make me believe I was worth a
hundred men! And then one morning, the letter. Urban II. I
believe I walked back to Mainz. My friend Professor Eerkens
saved me from despair. Why? Here I am now, lost. It would
have been better if I'd committed suicide in Lausanne, as I
first intended. But there's always some charitable imbecile
who grabs you by the lapels just as you're about to jump. I
stood there in the middle of that beautiful bridge over the
Flon . . . everything would have been better. I was thinking,
in those moments that precede the fascination of death, about
the ridiculous treaties that had been signed in Lausanne,
among them the Young plan, which ended the reparations of
the First World War. I can barely see. With my right leg over
the railing, I was remembering the equally useless international conferences that had taken place in that beautiful and
cultured city and I was overcome by the strong desire to end
my own useless existence. But it wasn't to be. *Merde!*

Sincerely,

MIGUEL ÁNGEL

Niña Huanca was reading a copy of the *Nautical Almanac* for the year 1812. *La Bellotte* was en route to Punta Beata on a clear night with a calm sea. Nimes was at the helm, his eyes on the stars. Paulito was curled up asleep in a coil of rope at the stern. Cortés and Weis were tending the sail, which was swollen with wind; everything was normal. The two Bears were there to tell Nimes the hour and the latitude. Niña Huanca's drunken voice rose from the hatchway. And the heavy smoke of tobacco. Would you know anything, Nimes, you little shrimp, if during your watch as pilot there wasn't any sun to tell you where you were, or if at night you couldn't find the Pleiades and the Bears in the heavens? Always afraid, with no sun in the sky, to wait for the night, and at night, eh? . . . what if in the greatest sky in the universe, right here in the tropics, you couldn't find a single fucking star? Eh? That's what Blundeville said, centuries ago, and he had no fear of the infinite. And so speak I, the Great Cunt of the Ocean. The dwarf's snoring did not reach the captain's cabin. A captain wearing metal-rimmed bifocals. An oil lamp. An English commodore's room, with geraniums and parsley at the portholes. Rum on a mahogany table. Rum from Martinique. The bottle is encased in straw. On the walls, portraits of Nelson, Mercator, and Ortelius. A map from the secret atlas of the Dutch West India Company. Another of the English Channel with the chain of great triangles between the meridians of Greenwich and Paris drawn under the supervision of General William Roy. And many books crowded into mahogany shelves. *Astrolabium*, by Ritter, *Catalogue de l'Exposition Internationale de la Cartographie Officielle*, Leiden, 1938; *Die Philosophie der Griechen*, by Zeller; *The Origin of the Medieval Italian Nautical Charts*, by Wagner . . . More than three hundred volumes, all on geography, cartography, astronomy, and philosophy. Drunk or not, she read Plato. Before or after thousands of orgasms, she read Smith on *The Art of Painting in Oil, To Which Is Added the Whole Art and Mystery of Colouring Maps*, London, 1769.

Huanca Matalax Yanama, mother of many unborn sons and one brought into the world; captain of all the winds. On her table, also mahogany, and like all the rest of the furniture in the cabin, screwed to the floor, was a sextant she had been given in Roxborough by a captain of the Swedish navy, retired, in Tobago. In a drawer, a logbook that resembled a pornographic volume more than a navigational journal. In truth, it was a prudent mixture of both. At dawn Paulito awakened and prepared coffee for the crew. Every time he served the captain's coffee, the dwarf wanted to sight through the telescope of the sextant. Jean Picard's is a good one for you, Paulito. The sextant was rarely used on board *La Bellotte*. Everything was done by sight, even though the captain was deeply knowledgeable about seamanship. Perhaps that's why she had no need of instruments. But Paulito adored the instrument that measures the latitudes. Arbalest, Jacob's staff, cross-staff, *virga visoria, radius astronomicus*. Paulito knew all those names, as well as the stories that accompanied them told by the captain to the little man with homicidal eyes. Sometimes Niña Huanca talked to him about Regiomontanus's astrolabe. When the sun peered above the curve of the sea, the captain took a turn about the deck. If the wind held, they would reach Barahona the following night. Let out the lugsail and take up the jib! And she went to bed. She slept until noon. At that hour she emerged naked upon the deck, and

Paulito drew pails of water from the sea and poured them over her body. Then he served her a plate of bacon and eggs and an enormous cup of black coffee. Are we making good time? Out of the corner of her eye, she glanced at the sky. We're farting along like the wind. A Danish transatlantic ship loaded with tourists passed to starboard less than a mile away. Cortés took the helm. Nimes slept, and Weis, after several hours' rest, tended the sails. Huancavélica dressed and came on deck. Paulito brought a canvas deck chair and a folding table for her. From his pockets he took an inkwell, a pen, and dark-blue paper.

Dear son:
    We are heeling a little before the wind because we are only a few miles from the Bay of Ocoa, the bowl from which the Devil drinks his soup, where it is good to commend yourself to God even when the sea seems smooth and of a good color. From what you write me, my beloved and long-forgotten Colonel is stirring up bad winds for you, but he's going to get more than he gives. Take it from me, my son, it's bad that he didn't recognize you among all his sons, but it's worse that he has no memory of me, for besides love I gave him everything he needed to become so much more than a second lieutenant in his country. But now you are there to collect the bill. What pleasure that gives me! I will deliver the two men you asked for to the coast of Belize, at the point you know. First I will pick up the one in Enriquillo, then continue on to Galveston to find out who the other is. Don't worry about money, my son, for like the buccaneers I have it hidden in all the caves along all the coasts of the Antilles. You already know who my agents are in that. They know my instructions and you have only to tell them how much you want. Don't worry about the amount. You're the only son I have. Everything the winds and seas have given me so generously will be for you. You will be President or Archbishop or Marshal, though I don't know what good they are. In Enriquillo, I will give this letter to a

guy from Trinidad who has his own plane and will deliver it to you by hand. Day after tomorrow you will have it, more or less at the time that we, with your man on board, will be at the headland of the Formigas. Do you know how much it pleases me to help you? Two months ago, when I received your first letter asking me for help, I felt as if someone had said to you in some alleyway somewhere in the world: Does your mother know you're lost, little boy? and that suddenly you'd been stung by the desire to go home. This is my home. They gave me your letter just as the schooner was about to set sail from Pichones Keys. *Keep smiling, baby*. I don't know what your plans are, but everything will work out fine. The swell is getting worse every minute, so I'm going to take the wheel. Maybe there will be another letter from you in Enriquillo. I send a thousand kisses, with all your mother's love.

NIÑA HUANCA

She was sealing the envelope as she shouted to come about with the mizzen and put the hooks into old Nimes and hoist him out to help man the ship. Paulito carried away the chair and table and writing materials. Huancavélica took the wheel. Weis ran to the bow to lend a hand to Cortés, who was swearing at the wind. After three bad hours they found themselves at Martín García Point, and afterward *La Bellotte* continued toward Barahona with a good wind astern. Paulito prepared punch for everyone, and brought a platter of herring and black bread. About one o'clock in the morning the schooner was right on course. Late in the afternoon of the following day, after taking on the barrels of molasses for Rosky, they set course for Enriquillo, and they anchored there that same night.

The jailer was given the five hundred dollars Miguel Ángel had promised him earlier. Go wi' God, brother. Sinfonías came quickly, as soon as he had tied his belongings in a bundle and pressed the hand of his friend in solitude. What shall I tell them when they ask? That's what the five hundred dollars are for. Tomorrow, then, I'm off for St. Kitts. I have family there. He'd have to get out of the Dominican Republic as soon as possible. Sinfonías had no objection to hurrying off with Weis, who was the one who had gone to fetch him. They stopped in an all-night tavern at the port and bought three gallons of Dutch beer. While waiting for Vincent, the man from Trinidad, to arrive, they drank another gallon. They heard his voice: *The rose is red, the violet's blue, pinks are sweet, and so are you.* They handed him the captain's letter and an envelope containing money. Vincent had an artificial leg. While his breakfast was being cooked, he changed socks on both feet. He never spoke; sing, sing, was all he did. And fly. He had a small plane he used for carrying personal messages. He never asked why, only for whom. Ten years before, he had lost his left leg when his Piper Cub stalled over the ocean. It wasn't barracuda or sharks that got him. Why always blame them? It was the propeller, which in a last-gasp effort gave a sudden spin in the water. He ate six eggs fried in the fat of the bacon they broiled for him; he drank a pint of gin and water, and then returned from whence he'd come. *Matthew, Mark, Luke, and John, bless the bed that I lay on. . . .* The owner of the tavern charged an exorbitant price for everything, and then a little more when he produced a letter for the captain from Miguel Ángel.

And again the schooner set out on a calm sea. The lighthouse on El Can was ringing its bell, as if it feared the coming of day. They fixed up a cabin for Sinfonías next to Huancavélica's. Do you get seasick? No. Do you want a drink? No. For the moment, they said little else. Their course was northwest. More than fifteen hundred miles lay ahead of them. The captain didn't like the motor, but there was cause for haste on this occasion, so Weis started up the diesel. At least *La Bellotte* would get past Formigas Bank before she was under sail. And so she did, without mishap, at eighteen knots. She took on supplies in Montego, on Grand Cayman, and in Cozumel. She sailed through the Yucatán Channel four and a half days later, and from there all that lay before them was open sea to the north; they made half the trip by power and the other half under sail.

Tampa, July 22

Dear Mother:

    I hope you receive this letter in Enriquillo. Everything is going according to plan. Without your help, of course, I couldn't have done even half of what I set out to do. Mendive and Bárcena gave me all the money I needed. Thanks to that, Obregón ignores me, and the colonel who commands the sector of operations against Trinidad de los Santos is protecting our guerrilla. I need Sinfonías. I am in Tampa, where they have told me I can find the whereabouts of the other man. I am sending this letter to you in Galveston. With those two men and the twin from Belize, plus Trinidad and a few others, I believe I can give my father the scare of a lifetime. I enjoy calling him father, even though it leaves a bad taste in my mouth, because I don't want any conservative or uninformed forces in the country to think that his death is an ordinary political murder. Of course as far as killing goes, I could have killed him by now, but that's not the only thing I want. In any event, this is a hell of a fight between two good gamecocks, as they say around here. The old man is looking for the one-eyed man, and I am looking for the old man, to trim his spurs a little. I will continue to make use of the generous assistance you offer me. I am neither lying, nor fooling myself, when I tell you that I love you. Receive a warm kiss from your son,

MIGUEL ÁNGEL

Junker, in German, means a reactionary and aristocratic
youth. What does that mean to me? Junker planes piloted
by men with monocles and long white scarves. In English they call the person who collects scrap a junkman. The
German makes scrap, and the Englishman (or his descendants)
sells it. Or the reverse. Peanuts. To Chilito, a poor Chilean, a
shattered man from Punta Arenas now making meat pies in
Tampa, everything was shit. Chicken shit, horse shit, and bull
shit. There was no way to get any other word from him. There
are all kinds of shit, some with bigger lumps than others. But
that's a different matter. Chilito lived in a smoky little shack in
front of Joe's junkyard. Streets near the port lined with steep
walls of junk. Automobile graveyards. Pure shit. Of course,
that's how that guy from the south made a living. *Junkyards,
junkmen, Junkers.* Are there any left? Take a look, buddy.
North of Ybor Street you can find anything. Nursemaids to
deaf-and-dumbs, prospectors (for Spanish galleons as well as
mines), hard-up tightrope walkers wintering with Ringling
Brothers in Sarasota, tea testers, dog trainers, Junkers, there
must be Junkers (old fags getting along without the consolation of German social security), magicians, poets. Like I told
you, there's a little of everything, and they come from everywhere. Early mornings some Pentecostal preacher and his
skinny daughter serve free coffee in a tent and stand around
making the *V* sign with their fingers—what a crock of shit. If

you don't believe me, friend, go see for yourself. And Chilito, a diminutive of Chile, of chili, hustles his ass around there with his meat pies. He's getting along great. That way no one gets ahead of him. Getting along well in a country where you can go around in your undershirt if you want, why should a person fall apart? Chilito smoked five or six cigars a day, those big fat ones the Cuban cigar makers roll in every storefront. Who knows, perhaps if you could loosen the old guy's tongue, he might spill something. In the evenings the mockingbirds sing and lustful women loosen their clothing. Isn't that right? A beer or two, and some of the bourbon that zaps you right off your feet. What'm I doin' here? I can tell you that right off. For twenty years and one day, first, down there in the south part of Chile—good for sheep—and then later in Valparaíso, I stood waitin' on windy street corners for someone to say hello to me. I mean hello the way it oughta be said, like you're interested, not that crap the old hustlers hand out. But every single bastard went around with his eyes glued to his belly button like he was either goin' to ask for a loan or pay one off. What a shitass way to act. Chilito, that's what they call me here. And you, hey, what do they call you? Miguel Ángel Matalax. My mother never married. Well, don't be ashamed of that, man, 'cause even though my ma was married, and I mean really *married,* my pa was a bachelor like yours. So we're pretty much in the same boat. Do you think all that shit matters? It don't to me. Nosireee, so I tell you, buddy, let's look after ourselves. Down there in the south it was so cold I didn't have enough breath to gripe, but when I got to Valparaíso, I went down to the docks and shouted like a newborn kid: Ya hear me, wind, d'ya give a shit about me, a broken-down old bum, a shadow of hunger, a crock of crummy shit? And I yelled to the sailors on the foreign boats, too: Hey, you there, Admiral, tell me somethin', say somethin' even if it's nothin' but shit! Order me to do something', or toss me your gold braid, or *somethin'!* Nope, not the wind, not a sailor, not the wife of Chief Caupolicán the Brave, not the guy with the treetrunk.

Maybe in some other country, I told myself. Want a smoke? I said to myself that like as not bankers is good folks. I like the *outside* of banks. So I made me a little leather bag and I began to put some money aside.

You been one-eyed since you was born, buddy? I lost my left eye in the Thirty Years' War. War, shit! Those two Germans up on the hill say that the war ain't over. That it never ended. That it's still on. One day, maybe tonight, I'll take you out to their orange grove. Those guys have an orange farm, those two birds. Well, I like banks 'cause there's always palm trees and blond secretaries that rub old Washington and Lincoln's faces like they was lovers. I've got a bank account of my own, yes sir! Do you know anyone named Phineas? The day I opened it, they gave me a calendar with two dates marked on it each month, the fourth and the twenty-eighth. Phineas? And it's got pretty-colored squares on it, but no writin'. What was you saying about Phineas? I asked you whether you know a guy they call Phineas; a guy who lives somewhere around here. Hey, I never heard no one say nothin' about no bastard named Phineas, so les' talk about somethin' else. So one day I grabbed a LAN plane and landed in Miami. I was a whole year lookin' for a place to light, till I set up housekeepin' in these parts. Yes, sir, you know it was still hard to get the gringos to give me a lousy hello. The blond secretary in the bank was the first one uncorked it; she was smilin', too, ya' know. It was the same day—April fourth—the day they killed Martin Luther King, that I felt like I'd just been born. I know if I ever went back to Valparaíso someone'd say, that's why you went away, stupid? You didn't have to go way up there for that. Hello, hello, every damn guy'd be saying hello to make me feel good, but I don't want no shitass sugartit, ya know. I'd rather be here, gettin' a little money out of the pies my ma taught me to make, 'cause that way I got a chance to see that blond secretary every week, ya know. Phineas, ya said. I dunno. I dunno. Tonight les' go out to Al López's stadium. After that we can go on out to where those two German brothers live. They call one

Mr. Junker (the sharp one) and the other one Mr. Junkman (the lazy one). The same thing happens in every family. Maybe those two guys know somethin' about your Phineas. They always know what's going on. They got a radio transmitter out there for kicks. You gotta handle 'em on a loose rein, but if they got somethin' to say, they'll say it. I got nothin' to do 'til morning.

At eleven that night they passed a patch of scrub prickly pear, beyond the Crackerjack factory. Chilito was carrying a rubberized pack with half a pie and a dozen cans of cold beer. Hey, buddy, be careful, 'cause those guys've got a dog that loves to sink its teeth in your ass. They were skirting the edge of a swamp. Tampa was three miles away, but in spite of the distance the red lights of the city glimmered in the greenish water. Kids come here to hunt for frogs. They were pretty far along the path Chilito knew as well as the palm of his hand when the Germans' dog ran out toward them, silent, but baring its teeth. Before the animal could bark its hoarse fury, the Chilean split its skull with the pack of beer cans. I prob'ly crushed the hell out of our pie, but we can toss the bastard in the swamp now. Yes sir, I been wantin' to get him. Into the mud that veiled a saurian mystery splashed that purebred sonofabitch. They continued along the path. Someday, ya know, I'm going to the seashore to listen to the wind sing. The orange blossoms smelled like the breasts of a bride, and in the silence of the nuptial night they opened. Less than a hundred yards ahead was a wooden house, and on the porch, rolls of flesh swaying rhythmically, sat the two Germans, Junker and Junkman. Tropical rockers. Sit down here, buddy, and we'll listen. From this patch of brush we can watch 'em and hear 'em, and drink our beer.

Some shit was playing on the radio. "Over." Where's Tiger? He's out there somewhere, Junker. Dogs've gotta get theirs, too. You know he's a fairy. You made him like that, Junkman. It was you who taught me all about those marvels. Junkman was the one who slobbered when he talked.

That's how those guys spend their nights, putting down everything's that holy. Junker wanted to listen to the monologue of some radio ham in the Philippines. Shut up, you old prick, and let me listen.

"He couldn't. How could an ashy-skinned Jap who stank of fish, who'd lost the power of speech during the war, who wasn't even wearing a hat, be a friend of mine? Do you hear me, do you hear me out there? They say it to destroy me. I am an engineer here in Pinay. Hot as an oven. One Palm Sunday at the entrance to the Lutheran church, this man came up to me and said, 'Cri.' Just 'cri,' like the crickets, like the screw in an organ. He pressed the palms of his hands together, the way Indians do, to greet me, and left me this card: HAKAYAMA (AKIRA), *Seeker of Friends.*"

Shit.

"One must always have a good friend, or, as the American missionaries say, a big brother. Hakayama scrubbed his teeth with a juniper toothbrush, but still he had a gold tooth. 'Cri.' He took me to his house, and for an hour we sat looking at his treasures: a malachite inkwell, a pornographic pipe with two juxtaposed figures, and an enormous coral box containing a certain irresistible aphrodisiac. 'Cri.' I said 'Pi' to him. 'Cri.' That 'cri' was the scream of many maimed ephebi. 'Pi' is science. Do you hear me, friends?"

The creep was a fruit; you don't sweat that out of you with the heat. Chilito was laughing like a maniac, without sound or grimace.

"Because I had the 'pi' of Heidelberg. A minimum expression of wisdom. Let no one maliciously misunderstand the word that sustains buildings and bridges and all superstructures of reinforced concrete. I did not see Hakayama again until Pentecost. He was standing at the door of the church, and that time he was wearing a hat. 'Cri.' 'Pi.' No one can bottle his breath in a broken heart, believe me. He left me a different card that said beneath his name: *Disillusioned Traveler*, and he walked away. From the corner he waved good-bye with his hat. The Lutheran minister's automobile crushed him as if he were a cricket. I swear it! 'Cri,' he said for the last time. May God gather him to his bosom. 'Over.' "

Junker took the microphone and began to shout: "Fruit, fairy, vielle pédale, Caroline, queer, verfluchter Schweinehund, sodomite, leck mich am arsch . . . !"

The night was suddenly so silent there on that point in Florida that Mr. Junker felt he wanted to hear his dog's bark. Shut up, brother. We need the silence so you can hear me. You're bad, Junker, I know that. But we must help each other survive. You humiliate every living creature, except that dog. Don't you realize that the SS doesn't exist any more, and that your uniform and medals are rotting in a bunker somewhere? What are we doing on this peninsula in Florida in this heat? Well, von Braun's doing the same. In Huntsville. *For I come from Alabama with my banjo on my knee!* My contempt is in that music, and the air from this fan will carry it to him. I know what you mean. Do you know that von Braun is a traitor who sold out to the Americans? You sold out to the Americans, too. That's different. We've all sold out to the Americans. You're a yes-man, Junkman. I feel at peace in my heart.

That's all. That's all, ever since they operated on you for cancer of the rectum. All you think about is war, Junker, and revenge. I think about infinite peace. You believe that the rocket ought to blast off from Canaveral with a load big enough to blow up the world. Except for my orange grove and my dog. I dream of rockets that go to seek cargo from other planets. New fruit, new meat, new wheat. Rockets look like phalluses. Astral phalluses. That's what you dream about. They would bring the food of the universe, you understand? You're suffering from delusions. I believe every mother's breasts should always be smeared with butter and marmalade. Oh, tits, tits; they're delicious even without anything. Like all heterosexuals, you have no respect for women. And, deep down, you have an Oedipus complex. Instead of throwing stones in the parks, children should play with sugar balls and throw them to stop the watch that measures useless hours on the belly of the guard. And they'd know who's the richest, because the guard would protect—pay close attention to this, Junkman!—because he would protect the best. Why did the engineer shout "Suck my cock?" Did he shout that to you, too? Don't waste any time calling me names. Don't you care any more? I care whether the sun comes up. That's what matters. A new day. It will rain. The horizon is sticking out a dry tongue to St. Peter. One day I'll be somebody again, with all my rights. Do you still have hope? Hitler lost the war, but I'm still alive. I won't die until I look down once again from my own heights upon the heads of men as small as thumbtacks. Don't go on, don't go on; you crushed innocent skulls from those heights. Who was innocent, Junkman? Momma and Papa were innocent. How were they to blame for being named Sara Rosenzweig and Joseph Schwartzbaum? They were two shit-ass Jews. Don't you realize what I'm saying to you? What? That you're a murderer twenty thousand times over, and that you deserve twenty thousand death sentences and twenty billion years in hell. And who are you to pass judgment on me? The judge at Nuremberg? I am the humble and sinful son of Sara and Joseph, and so are you. I've purged myself of that crime by burning my own kind. Oh, poor mother, darling, beloved mother! If you hadn't killed her, she'd be living in Brooklyn or on Riverside Drive. I should have killed you, too, Junkman, but instead, besides sparing your life and feeding you, you know that I shall make you director of the *Rundfunk*; and all because you are my brother and you like to stick your nose in the radio. That's how you always get me to shut up. It's easier to buy a man than to love him. That has always been so. The belly of our poor dear mother smelled of honey and wheat germ, don't you remember? I don't remember. I always remember her as looking very old. And old people turn my stomach. Always placing their legs close to young travelers to feel their warmth. Do you know that I've purposely filled my bladder to the bursting? And do you know that I'm going to empty it over your big fat boar's head, Junker? And Mr. Junk-man tried to do that, but instead, he tripped and fell in the grass. His brother did not hold out his hand to him. He walked away from the house calling Tiger. Here, pretty Tiger!

Miguel Ángel and the Chilean started back down the path. They were so drunk that they got lost in the tall reeds bordering the swamp. Did they also call the Philippine engineer pederast? Miguel Ángel felt like talking. Shoot! Chilito couldn't keep from laughing, nor did he try. He wanted to go and get his feet wet in the pond. What're you lookin' for, buddy? I don't know. They sat down on some dry prickly grass.

Looking at the stars reminded Miguel Ángel of a crippled child he'd seen running after a ball in an empty lot on Flores Street in Buenos Aires. There was a swamp there, too. Hey, Amíntore, pass me the ball and I'll handle the bitch for you! The cripple used his crutch to kick the ball. The stump of his thigh dangled like a bell clapper as he lurched along swinging his crutch toward the goal. There is nothing more glorious than the triumph of a crippled child. Are you tellin' me, buddy? I had a little brother who was blind. He died. The social worker was the only person who was sorry. They ate the crumbs of the pie and drank the last two cans of beer. It was getting light, and clouds were blowing in from the sea.

It was easy now to find the path. Suddenly balls of fire cut the air. Chilito fell on his face at the edge of the swamp. Won't you ever get tired of killing, Junker? The other one, too, will pay for Tiger's death. Isn't a man worth more than a dog? Miguel Ángel slipped into the reeds. And I always go along with you. The voices of the two Germans faded away in the opposite direction. Hey, Chilito, here I am, I'm back, I wasn't going to leave you here. The shattered man lay in Miguel Ángel's arms; his pants might be new, but his breast was truly shattered now. A real crock of shit! Hang onto me, and I'll take you to Tampa. Don' waste your time, buddy. You have to die of somethin'. That's what my brother, the blind kid, always

used to say. Lean close. You wanted to know who that bastard
Phineas was. I can tell you now. I didn't think you deserved a
poor man's trust, but you're a good guy. Man, it hurts! I can't
see. He lives in New Orleans. Near the port there's an alley
where some shit called the Husband of Smyrna has a bar.
They'll tell you about the other guy there. Hey, buddy, it's
about over. Don' let them bury me. Jus' toss me in the swamp.
Good-bye, old pal; glad to've known ya. He sank in ten sec-
onds. Chilito's head had split the water immediately, but
Tiger's floated for several hours. Miguel Ángel ran back to
town, his eye glued to the Budweiser billboard. As he entered
Tampa, a young girl called to him: Come on over, lucky! He
went into the Royal Palm Hotel, which took its name from the
palm before the door. The night watchman was in the kitchen
cooking bacon and eggs and coffee. *Good morning!* Matalax fell
into bed, exhausted and flatulent. He slept ten hours. When
he awoke he could scarcely remember the details of the orange
grove and the swamp. But he dredged up the name of the bar
of the Husband of Smyrna. It was enough. It was everything.
He ate rice and black beans and stew in a tavern run by some
Cubans. Then he went down to the port to look for a cargo
ship leaving for New Orleans as soon as possible. He passed
near the little shack of the shattered man from Punta Arenas.
No smoke; nothing. Miguel Ángel stood for a moment on the
corner, his mind retracing the events of the night before. *Be
still.* But it was not still. Sounds passed in and out of the
mouths of the tomato cans Chilito had used to cook his meat
pies. Chilito was a word. Only a word. Impossible to remember his face. He felt like saying the word. He clamped his
hand across his mouth. Shit, shit, *what a crock of shit!* The life,
the man, his drama, his tragedy, everything; perhaps there
was no better way to express the mystery of his meaningless-
ness. Miguel Ángel fled; he did not want to hear Chilito's
voice, now issuing from every crack and crevice in the rusted
iron. Hey, you ol' bastard, where're you goin'? Matalax had
too many things still to do. Killing his father was one of them.

Man has a puffed-up image of himself. Well, buddy, go find out. He climbed the gangplank. It was a little boat from San Salvador. At eleven-thirty they hoisted anchor and the *Manuel José Arce* began to move away from the dock. On every dock there is always someone dreaming of voyages who waves at the ships. The one in Tampa was a small, dark, wrinkled man perched atop a pile of beams and shouting desperately *Hello*.

THIRD STAGE OF
THE VOYAGE
OF MIGUEL ÁNGEL MATALAX YANAMA
IN SEARCH OF THE LAST DOUBLE

Happy the child whose parents meet their satanic
maker through some natural disaster.
—Secret minutes of the Academy of Psychological
Sciences of Peoria, Ill.

A window overlooking a port—preferably New Orleans—
always permits the person looking out to cherish a
strong hope for infinity. In my view, as the Cubans say,
from any window one can see the eight exterior columns of the
façade of the Parthenon. But at times between us and the
Parthenon there lies a mist of Spanish moss interspersed with
mizzenmasts and doors that open only with keys made of
spikes of wheat.

The Caucasian woman's name is Lavinia, and she is em-
broidering a linen dinner service for a hundred guests. New
Orleans spreads out before her eyes, and from time to time she
looks up. She sighs and says, Jesus. It is time for Phineas to be
arriving from the Husband of Smyrna bar. He should be home
by now, but he is intentionally late, hoping to surprise her in
adultery. Ah, if only one day he'd go off on the *Medea!* But the
boat to Tarpon Springs sails only on Fridays. Lavinia has often
seen Ponchartrain from Chalmette, but she prefers the river. A
red-brick house with a tarred roof. Isn't it beautiful to see the
naked river? In such pure air everything can be seen without
sin. Miguel Ángel Matalax Yanama is waiting. She is aware
that he is watching her. Do I have the breasts of a sinner, sir?
The visitor cannot hear her. Lavinia's voice exists in a bank
vault that only she knows; no one else. Lavinia's father was
named Epicharmis; he came from the mountains. Her father
used to look at her like that, straight at her breasts, but he

berated her for not binding them more securely. It is a beautiful port, New Orleans, with its enormous cranes and rows of shops. When will that damned Phineas arrive? Lavinia knows she cannot resist much longer. Her legs feel cold and stiff. Phineas is the double of a Lieutenant General Armenteros, from some Central American republic. He has a pension. One day the Lieutenant General came to meet his double. He measured Lavinia's breasts with his saber and left in silence. Suddenly Phineas appeared, like a cuckolded vulture, and called her whore. Phineas always believed that something had happened. Lavinia thought that her husband had meant to warn her of the danger of that remarkable resemblance. Miguel Ángel notices that Lavinia has the scent of lime and Spanish leather. She notices that her womb is cracking, and that explains the scent. One afternoon like this one she had opened the door. Was it Phineas? Perhaps a little taller. Lavinia's body was as rosy as the sky. On her breast he pinned a large medal he wore on his lapel. At that hour, devoured by the monster of the late afternoon, she had not remembered that her husband never wore medals. Yes, New Orleans is a beautiful port. Whore! A shop filled with bales of alfalfa where he feels for the first time in many years an adolescent rush of blood. That flesh, warm and ripe, could make a new man of him, a man traveling the royal highway where he needn't step in the excrement left ahead by other bastards. And there is hay in the park. It is beautiful, this hour when the gulls can no longer see the fish. The blue light of the beam from the lighthouse would warn of Phineas's arrival, and the buoy on the sandbar would creak like a proper go-between. But Phineas returns, and Lavinia's legs acquire the warmth and agility natural to all good women. The first thing he asks is whether his visitor has touched his wife's tits. He is drunk on rum. And still he orders more to drink. He calls Lavinia "woman" with tremendous scorn. Phineas! Obedient, the Caucasian woman leaves the room.

"I don't deserve her. Believe me. I am dung. Do you see

that small two-masted vessel? She's the *Medea*. Her sailors are Greeks. Do you know Tarpon Springs? It's in Florida, the best sponges. All Greeks. They speak only Greek. Orthodox Greeks. Greek divers. I was a Greek from Tarpon Springs myself, until some guy came and told me that I looked like a Latin American general. They brought me here. There are Greeks in New Orleans too, but they sell fried fish and shrimp. The General came here one day. Better not to talk about that. Although I'm not ashamed. On three occasions I have worn his pants, and I know that in a few places they're too big for me. You know what I mean. What I want to do is go back to Tarpon Springs and fish for sponges, but I have to stay here. That's what they pay me for. The gods have decided. Here I can't drink the good Corinth wine or dance on the beach in my bare feet. I'm nothing but dung. And she's deceived me. I can't decide whether to kill her or shoot myself. While I'm making up my mind I drink rum with the Husband of Smyrna in his bar. Lavinia! Where's the bottle I brought this morning? Don't you think it would have been better if those pigs of Turks had stuck to the Treaty of Sèvres? Resting in Lavinia's arms and breasts, the bottle and two glasses arrived. She served the men and sat down to her embroidery. She was no longer interested in what they were saying about the General. The monster of the late afternoon had slipped away behind her back, down the river toward the Delta, the path of the Gulf's solitude. Nor did she pay any attention to the money the visitor pressed into Phineas's hands. With this money and the pension there would be enough to buy sponge beds in Tarpon Springs. Nor was she concerned with her husband's laughter, or the kisses he bestowed on the green bills. Her feet were warm now and her mouth dry. She began another flower. It had no scent. Lavinia did. The visitor spoke her name as he left, but she did not hear it. In Marrero, Gretna, and Harvey the harbor lights were flickering on.

Phineas got drunk as he always did, and began to count the columns of the Parthenon on his fingers. Eight exterior columns on each end and fifteen on each side. For . . . for . . . forty . . . siiiiiix.

He stared out the open window. The Parthenon stood there blocking the way of the fruit boats. She turned on the lights and went out of the room to prepare dinner. Olive oil and rice with oregano wrapped in grape leaves. Bread. Wine. Olives. Lavinia! Figs from Zante and almonds from Argostolion. A lie, a lie, they come from California. And the Corinth wine and Anthony Quinn.

Phineas falls to the floor on a sheepskin; he believes the wool is the foam of wine fermenting in casks. And the sponges? The soft skeletons of the sea embrace each other, shouting and laughing. Lavinia sets some plates on the table and rests her elbows on the windowsill. Anthony Quinn! She sighs.

"Lavinia!"

"What?"

He wants to call her whore but he can't.

Sailing north, crossing the Tropic of Cancer, *La Bellotte* began to be buffeted by a strong sea; at the same time, the wind was tearing at her blouse and skirts. Come about with the spanker and the lugsail, birdbrain! The schooner was yawing from port to starboard. Diana was lashing her tail from Yucatán to Florida, sweeping over ships and keys. But it would take more than a hurricane to shrink Niña Huanca's man-size pants. Hey, Nimes, climb the leech rope and secure the sail to the boltrope! Nimes was the oldest, but he could race up a rope like a lecherous monkey. Weis took over the helm. Cortés tied up whatever loose ends he could. And Paulito, with the hatch well secured, was sweltering in the engine room. Haul in the damsel's bitching camisole, for God's sake! Sinfonías was shivering with terror in his cabin, too frightened even to pull up his suspenders. Whenever he attempted to look out the porthole to see what the devil was going on outside, all he saw was foam and dancing, dirty shadows, like the inside of a washing machine. Dear Virgin of Chiquinquirá, we're headed straight for shit! Devoutly, he prayed every prayer he could recall, meanwhile sprinkling his innards with a half bottle of rum. Ay, Holy Mother! It wasn't that he was a coward; no, it was just that the sea was getting on his nerves. By the middle of the storm the alcohol had given his soul a slight Jansenist push toward well-being. Oh, Sweet Mother in Heaven, he prayed, terrified to within an inch of his life. The captain came to get him to help. Try to act like a man, and follow me. She took him to the small cabin where the radio, the medicine kit, and the spirits were kept. Sit yourself down right here, Sinfonías, and listen how the goddam storm is going. We're eighty miles from Cape San Antonio. San Antonio, Cuba? Well, it sure ain't San Antonio, Texas. The little lever goes up and down, like this, you understand me, stud? Huancavélica returned to the deck to continue shouting orders. Take in the jib, too! Every few minutes she came below and tossed down snorts of gin that astonished even Sinfonías, Whewwwwww! What does the Coast Guard say? The man from Bogotá attributed his difficulty of speech to a certain thickening of his tongue, and he stuck his fingers in his mouth to test the extent of the problem.

They say that people from Las Villas to Oriente can sleep calm tonight. . . . Sorry, my tongue seems to be swollen. . . . And from Pinar del Río to Matanzas and Havana they don't need to board up their windows. That's what they said? That's what I thought I heard. Then Diana is passing us to the north. The captain went on deck and Sinfonías slipped gradually from Sweet Mother in Heaven, to Holy Mother, to the Virgin of Chiquinquirá, to Our Lady. . . . By midafternoon all that remained of the storm was a heaving sea and a dark sky that was opening to the sun just when the sun's only wish was to lie down to sleep. And so it did, at seven-forty-three P.M. One bitch of a day, eh? Huancavélica came below to share with Sinfonías her relief that the storm was subsiding. There are still eighteen-foot waves, but this schooner slides over them the way I do over the Sixth Commandment. She called for food and hot coffee. Her men's clothing was soaking wet. My father bought *La Bellotte*, and I inherited her. Other daughters inherit a house with a garden. I'm going to talk with someone now who's been through what we've been through. As she removed her clothes she "shitted" and "goddamned" with the radioman of a Honduran fruit boat. Did you hear that? The sea carried away their rudder and snapped the blade of their pro-

peller in two. In two gulps she downed the two cups of coffee
Cortés brought. She lighted a cigar, and did not seem very
concerned that as she removed her blue pullover she left adrift
two breasts well suited to her energetic and candid character.
Sinfonías fell off his chair. After she dried herself, the *patrona*
covered her naked half with a plaid flannel shirt. Lots of people don't like this life, but I was born for it. As she changed
her trousers, Huancavélica displayed to the apothecary clerk a
pair of legs and a breadth of ass of good shape and heft. Sinfonías, lying on the floor, was reduced to babbling. Don't
crawl around there like a caiman. Sit down here and we'll
share the meal. They ate meat, cheese, and bread with a good
appetite. With a *good* appetite. More coffee, and Cortés uncorked another bottle of rum. You can go to your quarters
now, Cortés, this conversation isn't for you. For one hour, in
the smoke of two Jamaican cigars, the story of Huancavélica
unfolded. My father was an honest Spaniard, one of those who
takes no notice of class when it comes to unzipping the fly.
You understand me? And she leaned over to touch Sinfonías's
organ. He made no comment. The Colombian told a tale of
mortars and leeches. The deaf-and-dumb girl and how much
he'd loved her. The captain took advantage of a pause to place
her tongue in his mouth, and they spent a good twenty minutes exchanging rum. In the meantime Paulito had opened up
the hatch. The sea had grown calm following the flight of the
sun. The engineer set the engine at fifteen knots and fell
asleep. Weis turned over the helm to Nimes and went below
to the galley to ask Cortés for food and coffee. Nimes would
not stir from the helm until the boss relieved him. But La Niña
had something extremely urgent to do at the moment. Patience. That urgent task was performed in the cabin until three
o'clock in the morning. Go and sleep, Nimes. I have nothing
more to ask of my Creator. For tonight, that is. And she sang
the song about "Give me three drinks of rum, and give me
two tamales; the rest of the fun, will come on the run, down
behind the loblollies."

The logbook of *La Bellotte* grouped together the last three days of the month of July:

July 29, 30, and 31.
After the shaking up Diana gave us, we're en route to Galveston. We're averaging sixteen knots. Southeast wind and a slight groundswell. The Colombian isn't a very good sailor, but he follows my orders without grumbling. Now he's sleeping to the sound of the *Pastoral* Symphony. It's hot. We're both mother naked. Paulito never stirs from the engine room. That dwarf's too responsible for his size. He's told me he won't miss a single beat of the engine until he turns it over to the witch doctors from the Growth Company in Galveston. On the thirtieth I relieved Nimes a few hours at the helm, and gave the cock from Colombia a few moments' relief from dancing the *cumbia;* he needed it. Cortés and Weis covered the day and night of the thirty-first since no great danger presented itself for a hundred miles. Nimes is sick. He says it's something to do with his liver. When your skin shrivels with the years, if it isn't the liver, it's either your kidneys or lumbago. He purged himself with senna leaves and every morning hung his ass out over the side. By midday on the thirtieth a little breeze from the northwest was blowing that helped push the schooner along at eighteen knots with less engine. By nightfall a red-hot wind from the Texas coast overtook us; that lasted two hours, and Paulito had to rev up the diesel. After that, calm. Sinfonías gave Nimes the senna leaves. We passed the *Monticello,* a Jamaican cargo ship under sail. Cortés loves nothing better than to climb the mizzen and salute by farting a few blasts. I like talking with the Colombian. Besides, he knows a lot about alchemy and herb medicines. A noble wind is blowing from the east now. Part of the night of the thirtieth Sinfonías and I spent on deck watching the stars. A half a day is missing. I know more about the heavens than he does, but Sinfonías knows about the winds and the phosphorescent fishes that leap from the water and shine in the night. The

only one of the crew awake is Weis, who's at the helm. Off key, he's singing some old ballads he says he learned in some abbey in Mexico where he was a lay brother. One moment. Almost day. I waked Sinfonías because Weis's songs were so romantic. He's gone back to sleep propped portside. The light of the new day is so weak we can barely make out the coastline; we should be seeing it. We're ahead of schedule. We'll be there by eight-thirty. Paulito is asking me from the hatchway whether we're going to hoist the sail. I tell him yes, and he wakes the others for the task. We pass several fishing boats out of Port Bolivar. The gulls are soaring toward us with their beaks on the ready. Cortés is fixing bacon and eggs. I take over the ship. Just before twelve we're moored at Dock Forty-seven.

Three days later they unloaded the belly of *La Bellotte*. The men from the Growth Company overhauled the engine and found no damage. Paulito argued technical matters with the engineers that made them laugh, you can imagine. The dwarf kept only one book in the bookcase beside his hammock: *Theory and Construction of a Rational Heat Motor* by the engineer Rudolf Diesel. Nimes and Cortés had gone to buy provisions in a shop in the city where they also took mail and messages for Huancavélica. Two days later they returned drunk, stretched out on the sacks of provisions the shop had sent in their delivery truck. They had to load them on like the other bales, hanging from a hook. From Nimes's cap the captain extracted an envelope addressed to her and ordered the two sailors to be tossed into the sea. As soon as she read the letter, she shouted that they had to get under way *im*-mediately, and they shoved off as soon as they freed the water and fuel lines.

August 1

Dear Niña Huanca:

The third man's name is Phineas, and your men will find him at 184 Decatur Street. It's near Canal, just around the corner from Dorsière. I've just come from New Orleans. I'm now in what the boys call the general headquarters. This is the last stage before the leap. I have Lavalle with me (the bad one, for having stolen the good one's wife, or the good one, since actually it is the other who's the bad one) and Georgiana. What a beautiful woman, mother! She has to spend most of her time in an iron capsule. Untimely poliomyelitis. She is so beautiful and so fine that I wonder whether God paralyzed her so she would be like her lout of a husband: removed from opportunities. They've built me a magnificent radio station from which I can contact all my people—even Trinidad de los Santos—when necessary. Thanks to your money. That was a lot of dough to have to cough up at one time—besides the trucks, arms, wages for the mercenaries we recruited, the supplies and provisions, and so on. I am sure that without you this undertaking, difficult from the outset, could not even have begun. The first thing tomorrow I'm off for the site of operations where I've been told I can find Trinidad de los Santos. I'm going to reinforce the confidence the guerrilla placed in me some time ago. First I'm going to leave Georgiana in the capital. It is necessary to my plans—I don't really know what plans, to tell the truth—that Ernesto Lavalle's wife return home and ask forgiveness of her wronged husband. That conceited, cuckolded gentleman will allow her to return, and it will be as if nothing ever happened. Besides, he will have a captive listener who can't escape all the crap he spins about his mines in Copiapó. It pains me to take her to him, and I don't know how leaving her with him will sit with me. The fool! He's one of those asses who would like to preside even over his own funeral. I've read the history of this country from beginning to end, and all one finds there is a pompous and tedious review of the "great" men—like Lavalle, Oruro, Báez, and so on—who constitute the brains and heart of the nation. Lives of presidents, party chiefs, generals, ministers, senators, aristocrats, exiles who collect from national funds for the difficult and dangerous task of not exercising any direct opposition, ward heelers who gamble on the candidate, candidates who receive the money for their campaigns from those who bet everything on the turn of a few votes, landowners and cattlemen (agrarian reform over my dead body!), policemen à la Fouché, yellow journalists. . . . And one asks himself: Who made the history of France, or of the United States, or Germany? The people, of course, the people. But damn it to hell, where are the people in the history of these countries? Yes, friend, the same people who are mentioned in the national anthem, in the preamble to the Constitution (oh, the Constitution!) and in the campaign speeches. Where are they? If you search for them, mother, through the annals of history, these people figure only in pre-Columbian times or during the glorious days of Independence. They use the people in order to claim the legitimate rights of the aborigine (?) to the land usurped by the conquistadores. A people that loves, and fights for, liberty. And obtains it. But there their role ends. Then come the aristocrats with their goatees and morning coats, writing poems and sipping chocolate. Through all the pages, revolutions *without* the people, meaningless *coups d'état*, dictatorships, changes of government, elections, pacification, status quo, conventions, national coalitions, guarantees, a constitution, another constitution, another. Anyone not from this country will ask himself a hundred times, Where are the people? Well, I could tell them: Look for them, brother, in the high plains, in the gutters, under the scrub trees; hidden so as not to be seen. Where would you expect people to be in a country where social injustice has been institutionalized? There are two concentric circles. In the inner circle, looking toward the pith, the marrow, the heart of the pineapple, those who live off the country. In the outer circle, looking toward infinity, those who *are* the country, blending into the ceiba trees, the volcanoes, the very earth. People, folk, voices silent, feet bare, with eyes that have never known curiosity. Those facing the hub of the circle know the delights of the privileges and the perquisites (yes, perquisites) forbidden to those in the outer circle: bribery, the pork barrel, the free ride, position, influence, the seal, the signature. Those things have no connection with the small sack of maize, or the pine nut, or beans. What does he know of the subtleties of the Common Market, free enterprise, ninety-nine-year contracts, Central Americanism? His stomach is born to eat wind and his shoulders to tote bananas, coffee, chicle, guano, meat, cotton, wool, tin, phosphate. And walk softly and don't disturb me, you hear? And one day, never knowing the extent of the hunger that devoured him, he dies, and bury him way over there, over the hill, please.

Well, dear Niña Huanca, during the time I was there, I saw so many evils that I almost became a revolutionary myself. But the reality is that I am going to return to a country that is not mine, with the goal of waging a revolution for which I have no feeling, to defend a people who never even look at me as I pass by, though my defect is sufficient to attract their attention. In that land I learned that not even the least objectionable formulas that men have accepted in order to live together can exist in the dominions of my father, and that some, for instance, those derived from the great world revolutionary movements, are nothing but empty words bouncing back and forth from wall to wall, between the two concentric circles. Surely you must think I am mad to enter such a labyrinth. Perhaps I am. In my earlier letter I told you there is unfinished business between Colonel Arruza and me. And I will be the one to finish it, as sure as there's a God in the sky, even if in the process I have to mesh the two circles together and rip them to shreds. I have never believed in machismo, or in vindicating honor with a machete slash on some street corner early in the morning. Now, however, I understand the kind of rage that turns a man livid. It is the glimpse of oneself dead, revoltingly dead, with those who scorned you in life blasting a chorus of farts over your coffin. I'm going to strip his hide off. If I can, I'll do it alone. If I need Trinidad's help, then I'll use Trinidad. If I need the Devil, then I'll place my candle before the Devil himself. And let the swallows be startled by the dust of the storm. Not for the Indians, not for the half-breeds, not for redemption, fuck, no! I'll have him pushing up the daisies before I'm through with him. I'm sorry, mother, because I know you're loyal to him for the pleasure he gave you, but a servant owes such a person nothing but anger and humiliation. Nothing more, remembering these things can make one sick. When you arrive—you, dear, señora, I don't know what to call you any more—my men will collect Phineas and Sinfonías. By then, I shall have crossed the border with Georgiana. I want to take her myself because she needs special care. I wonder if I've fallen in love with her. She's so beautiful and so fragile! She's the kind of woman you will find only in Central America. Tiny Maya goddesses man has the obligation and the pleasure to adore. We'll see whether I'm able to escape her enchantment. Again, I want to thank you for all the lost sleep and generosity, and with filial affection I send thousands of kisses,

MIGUEL ÁNGEL

On the third of August *La Bellotte* lay moored in a narrow slot along the dock bordering the French Quarter, a few yards from Jackson Square. Cortés and the dwarf were given the job of bringing the Greek on board. Paulito knew judo and could deliver a low blow that would leave the toughest man senseless. They had no difficulty finding Decatur Street. Phineas was not home, so they had to wait. They eased that chore by emptying a few bottles of beer. At eleven-thirty at night the Greek appeared at the far end of the street, swaying and spitting filth against his wife. Paulito found such things very offensive to his principles, and he approached Phineas to admonish him for his conduct. They had their controversy, which the dwarf concluded in his fashion. Cortés loaded Phineas across his shoulders, and thus, in the traditional way of returning to his labors a sailor waylaid by women and drink, they carried him to the dock. He was hauled aboard *La*

Bellotte hanging from the hook of a crane skillfully managed by Weis. In the air he looked like something rescued from a shipwreck.

They hoisted anchor at one in the morning. Sirens and harbor lights, down the Mississippi; dawn found them on the wide expanse of the Delta. Through the fog they dodged islets festooned with clay and debris, large ships at anchor awaiting day, and dancing buoys with lights and bells.

The Greek had protested his imprisonment all through the trip down the river, but by four o'clock, more or less, he'd fallen asleep. At five-thirty they left the beacon at Port Eads behind them. When Paulito knocked on the captain's cabin door to announce their position, Huancavélica separated herself from Sinfonías, who was happy as a kid at the tit, covered herself with a burnoose, and went on deck to take over the helm. Silently, she looked all about her, and purely by ear refined the sound of the wind, and after setting the course they would follow for two days' run, she hurried below to continue what had been interrupted.

The stars were growing pale, and, inevitably, soon died. Paulito went below to the engine room and Nimes remained at the helm, his lesson well learned. Straight ahead to Cape Catoche in Quintana Roo, and godspeed. Now they enjoyed better fortune. Between the engine and the sails, they covered the distance in less than the expected two days. When they were only twenty miles from Catoche, they veered to the south, and as they were running before a favorable wind Paulito cut off the engine; their speed was reduced only a couple of knots. On the starboard side they skirted the islands of Contoy, Blanca, Mujeres, and Cancún, arriving the following day at Carmen Beach, where they took on fuel and liquor. They especially needed wine to calm the Greek, who had never stopped weeping and clamoring for his Lavinia. Phineas had laid his plans, and when Cortés relaxed his guard for only a moment, he escaped from the schooner. They lassoed him on those boundless hot flatlands along the edge of a chicle plantation.

The captain signaled by mirror not to strain their patience any further but to flog him on the spot, and without hesitation, Weis executed the order. They turned him to guava jelly, red and soft. He returned to the ship without a complaint. Then they gave him tomatoes they'd bought in the market, and he fixed himself a salad with onion and garlic. He dipped his bread in the dressing of vinegar, oil, and salt, and left his platter as empty as the two bottles of wine the captain offered him. When the ship again set sail, the Greek was fast asleep in the bottom of one the lifeboats. On the port side they passed the sound lying between the island of Cozumel and the coast of Quintana Roo, and when they reached Tulum, they moved offshore some thirty miles to avoid the line of keys and islands that flank the shore to Belize itself. When they sighted the rufflike outlines of the last island, Los Lobos, *La Bellotte* made for the coast. A few green jetties lay to starboard as they entered the port. Corín, the mulatto girl Miguel Ángel kept for the second acts of love, was waiting in Belize, with three men of the ilk who slice smoked fish with the short blade of their knives and wipe the long blade clean on the shirts of the dead. They loaded the Greek—now allowing himself to be led without further resistance—and Sinfonías into a truck. Corín handed Huancavélica a letter from her son and told her that Miguel Ángel had already left with Georgiana. The captain talked by telephone with her representatives and confirmed the fact that Miguel Ángel Matalax had unlimited credit. She slipped the letter in her bosom and went to get drunk. Sinfonías had left without much regret, and that, coupled with the fact that her son obviously had not chosen to stay a couple of days longer to greet her, produced a lump in her heart that never could have passed to her urinary tract had it not first been diluted with alcohol. Which she did, and, by fortune, in midafternoon Ed (Filthy) Bowl wandered into Maggy's bar. He was an American adventurer with whom she'd several times shared board and bed, and now half-drunk, they shared good and bad memories, dirty games and some less dirty, blasphemies, laughter, and weeping. About ten that night, stewed to the gills, they went to a room on the second floor, gave one another a good hiding, cursed each other, and performed the act of love contrary to nature. At dawn, while Filthy lay sleeping, Huancavélica dressed, placed some money on the night table, and went to *La Bellotte* to sleep. She had to sleep before she read the letter.

Miguel Ángel's general headquarters were in a villa on Sylvania Road. Fourteen mercenaries were there, recruited from the taverns of Belize. Three were Honduran, two American, two Cuban, one Venezuelan, two French, two Spanish, and two Jamaican. The garden was a veritable arsenal, the arms and munitions covered with burlap and plastic. The leader of those men was a certain Rufo, who had been a lieutenant in Batista's police force. But in truth, the person in command during One-Eye's absence was Corín, the mulatto girl, whom everyone respected. She had the knack of kicking you in the balls at the very moment she was saying "my love" in a soft, teasing voice. Among the mercenaries was a gay makeup artist who was called Doña Ortive since his sun rose in the west. It was said that with makeup and wigs he could transform a senator of the Republic into his mother or his daughter, whichever was desired. Martin Lavalle's face had already been altered by the time the other two doubles arrived. Apparently it amused him to pass for someone he wasn't, for he would go out into the street and, changing his voice, speak with anyone passing by. Doña Ortive also altered the features of Sinfonías and Phineas. These were rehearsals for the final characterizations. For her part Corín made them repeat the recorded voices of Oruro and Armenteros until they could imitate the two of them to perfection. But still the order hadn't come to disguise themselves and cross the border. When it was time, One-Eye would inform them by radio. Wait—that was the watchword. Wait, and be alert. Blas, a Venezuelan who looked like a Honduran, and Lucas, a Cuban who could pass for a Nicaraguan, kept the two refrigerator trucks at the ready. Any night now they would pass the border posts, carrying meat for the slaughterhouses. But the real cargo would be rifles, machine guns, ammunitions, and three men. That's all. And everything would be carried out in the midst of the terrible solitude of the tropics, with the finger of the ceiba trees signaling the owls to silence. So begin all things.

August 8. On board *La Bellotte.*

Strong wind. I've set a course for anywhere. I am alone. My son's letter tells me nothing. I won't record it. I ordered Nimes to throw it in the sea. I don't even have Sinfonías to tell me about the phosphorescent fish and the poisons of the Borgias. Today I would welcome a storm to end everything. But the wind, my great lover, seems unwilling to give me the final blow. Paulito brings me more coffee and another bottle of rum. I believe we're about two hundred miles off Grand Cayman. Paulito, before he left the cabin, kissed my hand. That little man sometimes makes me cry.

He had to find One-Eye. Those were his orders. It isn't difficult to find someone who's been blinded by a stone or disease, but not that one-eyed man with a European accent. SIM had checked it all out. Frightened and furious, Commander Ibarra counted the days before the deadline the Colonel had set. You find him for me or I'll have you shot. A country with no middle ground. You're either a big-shit commander or you're manure for heliotrope—and though that calms the nerves, it stinks! Six hundred stool pigeons were infiltrating every corner of the nation in search of the foreign eye that caused even the Maya ruins to tremble. One month was the time allotted, and twenty-four days had passed. In the meantime, trying not to think of that pointless "right now," the Colonel was spending more time than ever diddling Virginia, who seemed to have changed her ways since Arruza spared her life. He hadn't killed her because he had yet to find her equal beneath the petticoats. And the confident laughter of the Indian girls was heard again. Do you know how to make a coconut custard? It isn't easy. You have to have had a mother-in-law from the tropics. Stingy. He had to find that sly bastard. He was much more important than any cat in heat. The stool pigeons asked in every dialect, but in each one they got the same answer. No one had seen big One-Eye. The Colonel spent hours on end in the house waiting for news, openly talking to himself like an adolescent as he walked the corridors.

Do you know I'm dishonored, Virginia? I've been dishonored in everything. My father was a fratricide. He killed Uncle Jorge and Aunt Susana. My poor mother died mad, after she had tried to throw me off a balcony. You're unfaithful. I've been unfaithful too. What happens now, Virginia? The hour of the bastards has arrived. They're coming to kill me. Against the Devil, a man can do nothing. The vulture has already scented our dead flesh. Afternoon, soldier. The Colonel rides through the night on a horse from his stables. And every dawn they have to shoot the animal that has been returned half-dead. Death should teach us many things, shouldn't it, Virginia? There is a disgusting fear inside me. Let's hold each other tight beneath the sheets. Even the crickets are terrified before the silence of One-Eye. The struts of the bridge of San Vidal are creaking. They are quivering like the ropes of the hanged. It's the night dew. The sun still hasn't appeared. A child could frighten us now. I feel a little love. Do you want to share it with me?

The law is aroused. Considering, et cetera, et cetera, et cetera . . . Whereas, et cetera, et cetera, et cetera . . . They are prepared to recite the prayer for the dead. And that's all. In the capital of the nation, on such and such a day, in nineteen hundred and such and such. He had promised that if he became President he would see that all workers were treated as well as foreigners. And the Indians were still weaving their bright blankets to sell to the tourists. And making earthen pots. And drinking in their cantinas. And why not? You have to keep the money circulating. And you can't clear the weeds from the coffee groves till they call you. Live? Die? What's the difference? Kill or be killed. Now that's a different matter, eh, mister? Don Cleto was a theosophist, and in his youth he had taught magic formulas to peasants to repeat as they sowed their corn. When he had time, he climbed to the terrace of the palace and placed vials of many colors in the sun, and then sold them as philters to cure cancer, rheumatism, and heart trouble. Don Cleto despised the Colonel. They say he doesn't kill, he doesn't kill, but all those chicken eaters don't know what they're talking about. It's a greater crime to kill a chicken than a man: man is reincarnated but a chicken is not. That's why I despise all those people, yes, despise them. People are like the leaves of the nettle. Beautiful, but poisonous. And following his immanentist beliefs, Don Cleto studied the occult forces of nature and the manifestation of the divine spirit that animates the cosmos to cleanse the Colonel's guts of the coming days of anguish. *Huacan* is possession. The royal palm stands between me and the Pyramid of the Moon. *Sorry. Chitlan, rocas,* rocks, cliffs. Perhaps that is what lies on either side of the way of the dead. *Tepexixitl, roca,* rock. Rock, fucking rock, what else? Is that all you see? *Izcuintli, perro,* dog. Dog, sonofabitch. That's One-Eye. After him, Don Cleto. *Tepetl, monte,* mountain. He's in the mountains. Or maybe he's playing monte. *Yahualli, círculo,* circle. Didn't I tell you? The pizzle's playing games! Look in all the gambling halls, all the casinos, all the gaming houses, all the dens. But Miguel Ángel Matalax was not where the immanentist lawyer had imagined he was. Not for that, brother. You'll have to eat your failure with hot pepper sauce so it'll taste better. And add fat meat and potatoes with saffron and blood sausage and squash. Well, what did you think? That some men behave like your women? That they'll just lie down for you? Well, I'll leave it with you for a while, Colonel.

Who knows, who knows? The worst thing of all is to worry before the lead grows cold in your body. He isn't in the country. That's SIM's conclusion. Commander Ibarra sent that information from the other side of the border. He was beginning to get hungry and thirsty after so many days searching for a dream, as if for a common mortal. He was in the Hotel Mediodía. A plump mulatto girl walked by and he took her to his room. He'd lost everything but his virility.

The Colonel couldn't speak. What have they done to your voice? Virginia still spoke, still talked. Your son's eye is like a thread of your echo. For you, he's man's worst enemy.

Virginia laughs. Her laughter is the song of jurors in the spring. Her laugh seems to surge from a universal, communal, maternal womb. Shut up, Virginia! The Devil left the windows of hell open, and SIM escaped through them. *Ipso jure.* It has to be this way so that the country can move ahead. Those who piss wide spray the street from side to side. In this country the walls have holes. Do you see the staring eyes? The hounds are pursuing the young tyrant but do not find him. Doesn't he have any scent? Where are you going, Virginia? I'm going to the country so he will see me naked beneath the poplar; I shall bring him to you, my love, blind, without the other eye, and everything will be as it was before.

And they helped Virginia onto her mare.

REQUIEM IN THE FORM OF A DIARY
FATHER RICHARD GODFREY

Ayoung boy found the loose pages in the rockrose of the dried-up stream. He stopped his donkey to run after the sheets of paper, which fluttered from his hands like butterflies. He gathered them together and placed them in the big pocket of his cotton pants, and while he was riding toward his little hut, he was wondering how many folds and what kinds it would take to make a boat and a plane. A plane like the one that cuts through the heavens from Taca, and a boat like the one that carries the bananas. Now tell me, don't make trouble for yourself, where did your kid find this pile of papers? But I don' know, Mistuh Lawyer; if I knew, why would I hide it? They sent a search party up the stream bed, but the only thing they found was a grave picked at by coyotes and a cross formed from two crutches. The dead man lay well protected beneath three feet of stones. It was the American priest, with a light beard on his face, his eyes burst open. Ave Maria. Dear God.

May 23. Trinidad has gathered his men together. He shook up a few laggards. They are concerned about a deserter who left us yesterday near the Hacienda Los Corrales. I never liked the way that Agapito acted. Always arguing, and an appetite like a horse. Trinidad trusted him. It was a blow. Today when he spoke, he spoke with his pistol cocked. The no-goods knew that, and never took their eyes off him. It's later now;

we ate tripe canned in Texas mixed with hominy and chili pepper. There was plenty of coffee and cigars that Silverio "borrowed" from the girl in the *cantina*. When everyone except those on watch was sleeping, Trinidad and I talked by radio with One-Eye; he's in the capital preparing for the coup. He ordered us to move on Costales, which is more than twenty-five miles from here. When the chief told him his men were refusing to walk any farther, One-Eye said that in Costales we would have good food for two weeks and all the pulque and cigars we could carry.

May 24. A hard day, on the march, stopping only to cut bananas and chew on our jerked beef. All the do-nothings are in the lead, thinking about the good food and drink awaiting them in Costales. We made camp behind a miserable little farm. They gave us coffee and corn for dinner and a lump of brown sugar apiece for the morning's march. We all celebrated when Pinto, with his single arm, brought a turkey he'd lassoed back to camp. Although we'd already eaten, El Chino and Fermín roasted it so we could polish off half of it tonight— we're hungry!—and save the other half for the road tomorrow.

May 25. Fabián deserted. When we came to a large outcropping of rock he rolled down the cliff through the frostweed. He was sick. He won't betray us. But he didn't have the nerve to face the chief and tell him he wanted to go home. As some leave they are replaced by others. A seventeen-year-old boy named Ignacio joined our party as we were waiting to enter Costales under cover of night. Ignacio is from Costales, and he led us to the house of a friend, where we ate like vultures and drank like cossacks. We spoke by radio with One-Eye. Tomorrow, as soon as night falls, we're to leave for Camino Alto, about a dozen miles from here. Three men will stay behind to explode the bombs that Hugo and El Ratón, guided by Ignacio, are setting tonight.

May 26. We learned by radio that they shot down Ignacio as he was running to meet us after placing the bombs. Hugo and El Ratón managed to escape. I believe it would have been better had it been the other way around, may God forgive me. Ignacio was the son of a wealthy landowner. May he rest in peace . . . the father, if he can. I'm beginning to find it difficult to walk. The wound in my foot gets deeper and larger every day. It's better without my sandals. One of the Macabeo brothers tells me that tonight he will cook a *masacúa* in fern water. He says that the herb and the fat from the snake will take care of everything. Trinidad de los Santos walks in the lead, gloomy, looking for all the world as if he had a toothache. He's scarcely spoken for two days now. He exchanges a few words with me, then I give the orders and talk with One-Eye by radio. We make camp at nightfall. Trinidad and I crawl into a cave with the radio equipment. Large cold drops of water are dripping from the roof of the cave and I put my wounded foot beneath them to ease the pain. Hilario Macabeo returns with a *masacúa* dangling from a pole. His brother gathered the ferns. Over a fire separate from the one where El Chino is preparing everyone's meal, the Macabeos cook the snake. One-Eye speaks on the radio. He tells us the bombs in Costales made a direct hit, and the press and radio are reporting every detail of our attack. He speaks in a mocking tone. Where are the three hundred men they attribute to us? He laughs, and my leg aches. Tomorrow we are to strike in Arenilla de Jaíz, if we arrive in time. Lucas Macabeo spreads the fat on my wound; it stinks. I can't eat supper.

May 27. When I awake, my wound is better. On the march, dangling from my knapsack, I carry a small pot containing the fat. By mid-afternoon, from a small hill dominating the southern section of Arenilla, our men snipe at the military garrison. Within ten minutes the five scroungy uniformed soldiers and their families surrender. They come out with their hands over their heads. I can see them through the binoculars. The people acclaim us as we enter the city. Two thousand inhabitants. The boys sack a small grocery and a shoemaker's shop. The owners of the *pulquerías* choose to meet the rebels in the doorways, with jugs in their hands. I don't like all this.

But the boys are happy. Trinidad de los Santos has to tear El Ratón from between the legs of a weeping, screaming woman. The Macabeos, drunk, are guarding the cellar of the Pediatric Clinic, where we're holding the louts from the military garrison and their families. The doctor at the clinic looks at my leg and gives me an injection of penicillin. He throws the *masacúa* fat out the window. My leg is as big as a piano leg. One-Eye orders us to shoot the head of the garrison. We go to see him, and when Trinidad tells him we're going to shoot him, he throws himself at his feet and cries like a baby. His sons weep as uncontrollably as their father, and his wife curses us in a Maya dialect. Trinidad de los Santos remembers his own children and his slender *chola* woman, and he spares the sergeant's life. I sleep in a clean bed for the first time in seven months. One-Eye again radios and orders us to blow up a section of railroad track and the bridge of the highway from the north so the federal troops can't reach us. The mayor, recently named by Trinidad, tries to stop us from blowing up the bridge. He is a corpulent man who is more stunned than happy. The people who acclaimed us as we entered will curse us as we leave. They've given me two aspirins, and I fall asleep while they argue.

June 3. They've buried the parachutists. I assisted the priest in the funeral ceremonies. From the window of the clinic I watched how the boys, overcome with laughter, picked off those gracelessly falling birds. Had I been able, I would have stopped it. Trinidad did not fire. The chief doesn't like to kill without a fight. Twenty-seven dead, eleven wounded, and one prisoner. Trinidad ordered the prisoner shot; to the end he kept shouting about the Geneva Convention. The wounded are in the clinic. One tried to commit suicide by drinking the permanganate they use here for washing out wounds. My leg is better. Recently Trinidad has seemed to decline considerably. Tomorrow another march awaits us, in the opposite direction, toward Salvatierra. I don't know whether I can walk the twenty-five miles One-Eye ordered by radio while he—as the boys say—sits massaging his balls. Although Trinidad knows he has recovered his lost confidence, he is, at the same time, One-Eye's man, all the way. We're going to begin the march before dawn, perhaps to avoid being pelted with curses and rotten mangoes. For a long time Arenilla del Jaíz will be cursing our mothers. We left them without boots, without food, without pulque, without a bridge, and without a train. Plus other things it's best not to mention.

June 4. Fortunately no one realized that we were leaving. The mayor came with us. A cautious man. Once we were a couple of miles outside of town he left us, and I suspect he plans to leave the country. The boys good-naturedly curse these never-ending treks. While we were in Arenilla, the majority went at their courting in earnest. I rode the little mule that carries the medicine kit and the radio three-quarters of the way to Salvatierra. My leg is inflamed again. In midafternoon, a military plane flew overhead. I believe they saw us, but they didn't fire on us or drop bombs. By eight P.M. we'd eaten up ten miles of the march. The pain from my foot has spread to my hip. We are a few yards from the houses of San Agustín de Alza. Tomorrow we will reach Salvatierra. In San Agustín the Brothers of San Juan de Dios have a leprosarium. By midnight my pain is so great that Trinidad loads me onto the mule and takes me to town. The lay brother at the porter's lodge can't believe that the man he sees before him is a priest, and that the other man, supporting him so he doesn't keel over, is Trinidad de los Santos. Trinidad leaves me in the leprosarium for them to cut off my leg. When we say good-bye we both know that's what's going to happen. If it is God's will.

June 27. Today the lay brother, Jean-Louis (a Belgian), took me out into the garden in a wheel chair. The man who cut off my leg is a Spanish doctor who has also been in the Congo. I write to my superior. I believe I am beginning to agree with him that I have no place with the guerrillas. Trinidad de los Santos has inquired about me from the various parts of the country where he's been operating during the last three weeks. El Ratón came to see me on his behalf and told me that they're marching leagues every day and eating shit. The latter is not necessarily true. I never liked El Ratón. He has a big mouth. It's obvious that One-Eye was right. In the leprosarium they tell me that the army is losing heart. They look everywhere for Trinidad de los Santos but can't find him. Before One-Eye, *they* did the looking, *they* sent out the search parties. Now, using a new technique, Trinidad is the one who searches and strikes. I don't know who it was who said that the French army is always prepared for the previous war. Well then, the army of General Armenteros can now rub elbows with the man who commands the officers of St. Cyr. Trinidad is today's war and tomorrow's. Where will the next strike be? How will it come? Without my leg, I don't think as well as before. Does one think with his extremities?

July 7. My superior sends a nuns' chaplain from Salvatierra to San Agustín de Alza. The good man is charged with getting me out of the country. He talks with me all afternoon. Whatever doubts I may have evaporate every time I, on my crutches, pass in front of the mirror in the Spanish doctor's room, where we are talking. They don't allow mirrors anywhere else in the house. What help would I now be to my friend Trinidad de los Santos? I accept what the chaplain proposes. They will come for me tomorrow. A three-day-old newspaper from the capital says that Trinidad de los Santos has received reinforcements from Belize. They speak of mercenaries. Well-armed men with good equipment and supplies. Yesterday he attacked Fuerte Quitache on the east coast. He lost seven men. Three days ago he was at Playa Curbera on the Pacific coast. The reward for his capture, dead or alive, has risen to ten thousand pesos. In Fuerte Quitache he took time out to shoot two informers in the main square. They will not be sharing the reward.

July 9. We are a dozen miles from the frontier. On the car radio we've heard that Trinidad is cornered somewhere nearby. The chaplain is eager to get me over the border and return to his coconut custards and his shitty sermons. He's afraid. We stop at a *pulquería*. The chaplain is wearing his vestments, and they respect him. While we're eating, I am told that the boy sitting on the floor in a corner who never takes his eyes off us knows exactly where Trinidad can be found; he's seen him early this morning. The waiter reports this with a great air of mystery. I arrange with the boy, whose name is Benito, to take me the next day to Trinidad de los Santos. I take my leave of the chaplain.

July 10. The morning is cloudy, with a strong wind. I still can't manage the crutches. Benito helps me; he is very patient. Benito would like to be a guerrilla but says he's still too young for that kind of life. We have to stop frequently. By noon we come to a spring. There is a dried-up stream nearby. It's a gravel bed flanked by rockrose. They call it frostweed around here. Benito points to it, and speaks of the patch of reeds—this rockrose is reedy—as if it were the valley of death. We can't go much farther today, so we decide to camp until morning. At dusk he lights a fire. Not because we're cold but to keep away the coyotes howling and circling about. From his bedroll Benito takes out some tortillas, which he cooks on stones heated in the fire. He opens a can of refried beans and makes enchiladas. With an enormous knife he chops three jalapeño peppers he carries in a small bottle. I don't eat the hot peppers because of my wound, which still hasn't healed. We drink water. Then, coffee. Benito tells me his story. The worst thing about Benito is that he thinks he's telling me something I haven't heard. Finally he sleeps and I meditate and write in my diary. I am sure that *Ramparts* would pay me its weight in gold. I am tired, but I want to keep on writing, I don't know why. I would like to be in my cell in the Greg. I believed that drinking a scotch before dinner with Father McMahon and Father Ulbritch was like stealing a dollar from some hungry Latin American Indian. Benito is snoring with his belly filled with jalapeño peppers, tortillas, and beans, which is what he likes.

Father Ulbritch will still be studying the new theories of Rahner, Congar, and Küng. I'm missing a leg. I'm cold. Father McMahon, who has already had two heart attacks, will sleep tonight, as every night, thinking he will awaken tomorrow in the kingdom of heaven. And I here alone, facing the night with a snoring Indian and coyotes at my back. Again in the .

He was in the capital, so near the market plaza he could hear the screeching of the parrots. Obregón was sniffing into everything, but the one-eyed devil had escaped to hell. He had learned how to make himself invisible in Jerusalem and Angola. It is an art like any other. Like performing sleight of hand on oneself. You have to know how to change your voice and your accent, even your body odor. But the eye, the eye, brother? When you slip a glass eye in an empty socket, it is difficult, almost impossible, to make it move in concert with the real eye. But Miguel Ángel had learned, not in Macao or in Singapore but in Maguncia, that you spread a paste inside the eyelid and insert an eye that moves with a counterweight behind it, the way they rig dolls. And make-up—a complicated science of which he was a master—plus the skin tint, in addition to a bottomless bag of tricks, allowed Matalax to walk through the capital like any ordinary citizen and even talk with Obregón whenever it pleased him. He looked like a little old lady from Beginhof. Posters of Miguel Ángel Matalax Yanama were plastered on all the columns of the plaza. Passport photo. Five thousand pesos. Dead or alive. Obregón was everywhere. Do you know anything, Juanchito? A little bit of his smell to follow, and you're a hero, Juanchito. Ten percent is five hundred pesos. That's a house, a little shed, a corral. Even so, wha' for you wanna blow the whis'le on some for'ner? *He* gonna pay your doctor bill? *He* gonna put beans on your table? I not gonna be part nothin' dirty like that. My tongue is for the prayer or for the sweet talk with the pretty girl. Not for wha' you wan' me do, Obregón. Miguel Ángel consoled Obregón in an assumed Yucatec accent. Drink up, pal, your mouth must feel like it's full of buzzin' bees. Five thousand pesos, that's what I'm looking for, too. Half? Never! Are you out of your mind? Fifteen percent is all I can go. Well, then, you're stuck here with your ambitions and all the rest of it. Ibarra was going to be extradited. The evening paper said so. Ibarra returned! Ibarra returned! Are you poor, Obregón? Poor as a church mouse. Poverty is when things are out of balance. The President speaks. The day has come when the vindication of honor is not the heritage of the individual alone; now it is equally the heritage of the state. A law that cannot be enforced is valueless. Pretty voice, pretty voice. Miguel Ángel listens to it, records it, and sends it to his general headquarters in Belize. We shall never sign a law unless it is coercive, from the Latin *coercere*. Speak, speak, Dr. Valentín Oruro. For me your voice is a treasure. General Armenteros speaks too. I am not given to endless waiting. The country is in danger and the army is ready. Pretty voice, pretty voice. Miguel Ángel listens to it, records it, and sends it to Belize. National Bank? May I speak to the Director? I am calling from Internal Revenue. Hello, Señor Lavalle. Speak, speak. *Indeed, it may be argued that a reduction or elimination of the primitive sector, accompanied by a large-scale shift of the active population.* . . . Over the telephone Miguel Ángel reads the *Economic Bulletin for Latin America. Yes, yes, the facilities of the Genetics and Radiobiology Program of the National Commission of Nuclear Energy will be available for the performance of the genetic and anthropological studies. In addition to these facilities which will be available at the newly constructed laboratory in the Olympic Village, it is proposed to acquire a mobile unit for the testing of athletes in other places in the Village or outside.* Dr. Lavalle is reading from a magazine lying on the table, the *News Bulletin* of the Mexican Olympics. Matalax has to call Lavalle several times before he succeeds in getting him to answer in Spanish. He reads *La OIT ante el futuro*, which he takes out of the wastebasket. Speak, speak, my love. Miguel Ángel listens, records, and sends the tape to Belize. Twin brothers talk alike. Yes, but it isn't the same. For one Copiapó is an entelechy, for the other it is a reality. Hey, have you seen him? Why no, buddy, no. They found a one-eyed man. But he wasn't the one they were looking for. They clubbed him to death, and he wasn't the one they were looking for. He was someone named Don Fabián, a veterinarian from some province in the interior. Miguel Ángel went almost every night to La Criolla. A Bloody Mary, sir? The blood is what matters. The blood of María la Sanguinaria or that of Colonel Sanguinary? Colonel, at your orders. A Bloody, Colonel? The blood of Zósimo, the blood of the strong, sober student, that of the veterinarian, that of another, another, another. They could water the orange groves with it and create a new fruit. The señora is coming, the señora is coming with the Colonel. Hey, didn't she leave him? Well look, there she is. Why do the Walkers always kick the drunk? And yet, he asks, bold that he is, Colonel, would you rather the orchestra played the national anthem or "La Cucaracha"? They throw him out, kicking him all the way. Discreet kicks, no noise. The drunk always pisses blood the following day. Bloody. The Colonel's table. Caviar and champagne and roast kid. The Colonel loves roast kid, done to a turn. Why did you come back? That was stupid. What can a woman on horseback do in the jungle? The Walkers glance at one another. Hey, you, stand up straight there. In the corner. They frisk Miguel Ángel. Virginia looks at him. Does fear turn men yellow around here? The Walkers look like dragonflies beside the man imprudently winking one eye. A beautiful eye, father sun. Is the other eye just like it? It is. Do you want someone to dance with you? You've come here to dance, not to eat roast kid, you know it doesn't agree with you. *You!* I don't want to, Colonel. I have no obligation to dance with someone who doesn't please me. The Colonel cannot believe it. Who doesn't *please* you? Who do you think you're talking to? He lifts his wife's skirts. Look at that. Doesn't *please* you? The Walkers push Miguel Ángel toward the Colonel's table. Are you going to dance or not? The Colonel is drunk. Is it because he can't stand to be any other way? A little grass, milord? The Colonel applauds and laughs. The orchestra plays "Pérfida." The Walkers latch onto Miguel Ángel. They do not hurt him. Look at those thighs. Kneel down and smell them, you big rat! Virginia is weeping, she wants to leave La Criolla. The Colonel forces her back into her chair, amid harsh laughter. Bloody Colonel. Do you want to dance, señora? And they dance to "Pérfida." Miguel Ángel says: Veirtogen faulk ad ith. And she replies: Werf suertigen alk. And as they whirl by the door, Miguel Ángel seizes the opportunity to run out. The Colonel yells: "One Eye!" And the Walkers fire. Dead men in the streets. Shoeshine boys and beggars filled with lead while they sleep. Bad shot, bloody Colonel!

There are those who don't believe in such things, but one has to believe the man who says he's seen flying saucers. Hell, why not? Worse things have been told than seen, and more than one man has been stung for not believing. How was it possible? Virginia the Cunt, not in bed with her legs spread? But she is; I saw her, friend, unless you believe that these eyes, which are plenty good enough to see you with, are blind to little girls and little girls' mamas, you get me? Virginia the Cunt—oh, what a tongue the people have! They named other first ladies of the Caribbean Paulina Bidet, María of the Happy Twat, Diana Castrator, and so on. Virginia Pfandl Andrade de Arruza was in the garden of a house in the capital, washing undershorts in the water basin for someone I didn't see but I bet you anything wasn't the Colonel. The neighborhood, the street, the number . . . where did you see that? Oh, don't hurt my head, Sir. I'd had a couple of snorts. It was a Saturday. You put on your new pants and go out and never worry how you're going to get back home. My woman tells me that some policemen dragged me back by the heels. But I swear to God, drunk as I was, I saw Virginia the Cunt. And she was singing like a mockingbird. Singing in the tongue of the gringos, something like, uh, one of those cocktail songs.

And she was. And like a madman, the Colonel was searching for her everywhere in the country. And everyone knew it. And you'd have to stick Chinese firecrackers in their mouths before they'd talk. They beat up Chiquito Lima for being a bigmouth. You zip up your lip or your woman will be wearing black. If you can't hold your drinks, stay home and pedal your Singer. It was a pleasure to know the Colonel was suffering. Jealousy, fear, the mange, rage? Suffering, that's all. Hey, pal, give it to her again! The salt was passed from one end of the bar to the other and foam spewed as virgin beer cans were pierced. He suffers, no more, no less, now, later, tomorrow, every day, while somebody else's playing his wife's tune. One-Eye ought to be signing autographs with his prick. Bless him! Trinidad de los Santos is a brave man, but he's a shitass when it comes to women. If Virginia stripped *him*, our guerrilla would pee on the floor. But you see what this guy, this One-Eye's doing, he's using Doña Virginia to screw Colonel Shit-in-his-britches! Sweet Jesus! For him I'd take on the whole army. Search, search, Colonel. The mockingbirds are singing in English these days. Hey, stupid, do you know English? Yes. How do you say banana? *Banana.* You do? Sure. How do you say chicle? *Chicle.* Nah. They say *chingó.* That's what they put on the crates, friend, but that's not the word they use when they're tapping the tree. Sure. Hey, Colonel, that gold braid hurts! The way calluses hurt the Carmelites, the way the endless hours hurt the poor, the way a police dog's snout hurts from so much sniffing. Sweetheart. Someone is calling her sweetheart, and with a solitary eye casting the light of love upon her breasts. The tide comes and goes, Colonel. Comes and goes, Colonel. We needed One-Eye here. We needed a man like him to grease the part that makes the cart move. How did you say she was, señor? Was she easy? Come on, brother, as macho to macho, here, just between the two of us, what do I do to get her to . . . you know? Bang 'er, buddy. Me? Well, screwed, but happy. Because the Colonel is suffering, because the Colonel is weeping. Another beer, friend? Oh, buddy, sock it to 'er!

General Armenteros was standing at attention before an inferior. Colonel is a lower rank than general everywhere except where they pluck the low-hanging mangoes. In the constitutions of the Northern Hemisphere it wasn't foreseen that things run differently in the Southern Hemisphere. And that is related to the way you point. Northerners point with the accusatory finger—the index finger; Southerners use the middle finger—the finger of the heart. The Río Grande isn't a frontier, brother, it's an abyss where millions of scrapped autos lie forever sleeping. They have the Ford and we have a toothpick stuck between our teeth. You're nothing but a pile of guano shit and medals and vanity. Ehhh! Don't open your mouth to me! Ehh! You don't know what dignity is. Eh! And no more of your fucking "eh's." The Colonel's office is filled with maps painted on large panes of glass. Camino Alto, Salvatierra, Paloma, Selactenango, Anchilla, Potilito, elevation 25, elevation 234, elevation 7, elevation 2,349, elevation zero. Zero elevation, the country's navel. The capital. I have a girl there named Noemí. The Colonel had marked each point with a red pencil and a tiny national flag. If you don't find me a one-eyed man at elevation zero, what the hell good are you to me? I'm going to have to kiss you good-bye, General, I'll have to do it no matter how painful it is, and in spite of the regard I hold for you. It won't do that you can't find that rat in a broad-brimmed panama. Yesterday he was in

Anchilla. God knows where the bastard's going to deposit his filth today. Don't be funny. I swear to God, I won't tolerate it any longer. You mean you can't find me a foreign pig in a city where the most honorable man would sell his dear mother's teeth for half a peso? Eh? Shut your mouth, you miserable bastard. I'll give you one week to wind this thing up.

For more than a month the Colonel hadn't slept or swum or mounted a horse or an Indian girl. Don Cleto's cheeks were livid these days from being slapped around, but he was so happy it didn't matter. That was when he wrote the poem "Hatred," which circulated in all the casinos and taverns of the city. Anonymously, like the ancient epics. They will place blind piranhas in your blood; they will swim inside you, not knowing how to reach the marshy lake of Culatepelc. And what will they eat of you, with the madness of hunger—the hunger of piranhas!—what will they eat of you besides your arteries and the piece of vagina you stole from your wife? Perhaps the names of the dead, names buried in the cave of your entrails, Pedro, Alipio, Heriberto, El Caporalito . . . You could make a telephone directory with them and call them in eternity to get you a good heart for a transplant. Hello, hello! By now they would have eaten your heart, and you would need another. You will also need new guts to continue to crush Indians beneath your thumb. Seventy percent. Just a little chance, Colonel? Thumbs down, like the comb of a triumphant fighting cock. But not this time, not this time. This time the piranhas of the dead will triumph—you have said that thus does jealousy gnaw at your heart—and we shall see you toppled at the slightest tap from some poor man's widow. And their children will urinate in your mouth so you won't be able even to say Virginia before you die. And One-Eye with his empty socket will laugh at you.

One-Eye read the poem. He wasn't laughing, because Virginia was weeping, Virginia had to go back to her husband. I love you, I love you. She had to go back. It was an order. Miguel Ángel kissed her with a certain tenderness.

Virginia pulled the green dress over her black petticoat. They had lived together twenty-eight days and seven hours. Tears had made her eyes larger. Ay, mamacita! Virginia filled her handbag with memories of those days. I love you, I love you. Virginia felt a new sadness. She had experienced something similar twenty years ago in New York when she'd been studying at Finch College. Then, too, she had wept and wanted to die. Miguel insisted categorically that it was not over. Virginia wanted to die like Elvira Madigan. Virginia was a devotee of Goethe. Fifty percent Teuton blood. Pfandl. P and F, the beginning of lugubrious Germanic premonitions. PF was always embroidered on her lingerie, like the Italian *piano* and *forte*, soft and loud. That was Virginia. PF. When Miguel Ángel saw the initials, he thought that HF would suit her better but he said nothing. High Fidelity. And now she was leaving. Virginia hadn't told him she planned to change the initials to HF. No one would ever believe it, but her adventures had ended in that small house on an isolated street in the city. Calle del Milagro. Miracle Street, number 35. A miracle is what the Colonel would give to know this address. HF. SIM. PF. NATO. OAS. A.M. P.M. Night? Day? Soft and loud. Loud and soft. Now Virginia felt the tears flowing, softly, softly. Outside, a burning sun. I love you, I love you. Thus, most of the illiterate of the world took their siesta beneath their sombreros. Silence of flies. The road to the stadium, Sir? Flies on guava rinds. Miguel Ángel swallows hard when she asks for the last kiss. They have lived together. They have dreamed of the same places. The world, the whole world, belongs to two beings when the maps of memory are joined. Vendôme, Liberdade, Alvear, La Rotonde, Oriente . . . Farewell, my love. It is the hour of parting. Not at night. In the daytime, exhausted by the sun. Fifty-ninth. My street, with the Plaza and the Navarro. Farewell, my love. To live together twenty-eight days and seven hours and twenty-three minutes, and to die like Elvira Madigan. Beauchamp, Veneto, Insurgentes, Queen Anne. One minute more. Matalax doesn't move from his chair, but stares fixedly at the belly replete with love. She is weeping as much as her belly is quivering. Virginia carries three verbal messages: one for General Armenteros; another for Lavalle; and a third for Valentín Oruro. The rendezvous is set for three nights later, the night of the fourteenth. April 14, the Republic in Spain. July 14, the taking of the Bastille. The fourteenth is a good day. Better at night. In the tropics, the night is for meeting and the day for escape. Farewell, my love. Virginia has lived a half minute longer beside Matalax. She leaves with the promise that they will meet again. That is why she can walk between the sombrero-crowned, stone-still figures without falling and awakening them. Her blond hair shines like strings of garlic. But she smells of lemon. She runs through the street, but no one looks up.

Sanjuanitos, Sanjuanitos! The voice of the flower seller is blind. Taxi! His name is Hernando, but he doesn't want to see. The Walkers are enjoying the shade of the eucalyptus. The señora! The dogs bark with pleasure. She is a dog, a bitch. I'm going to kill you, but first you must tell me where One-Eye is. She pulls out a revolver to kill herself. The Colonel pleads, on his knees. The Colonel, his nose buried in Virginia's belly, curses and shouts. Colonel Arruza rips the green dress and the black petticoat. And she cuts the veins of her wrists with a broken perfume bottle. Virginia! She is no longer Virginia the Cunt; she is Virginia who offers up her life, who unemotionally offers herself to death. Virginia! The Colonel clutches her wrists to halt the flow of blood. When Don Cleto arrives with the doctor, the Colonel, remorseful, is kissing Virginia's pale face. We won't talk about One-Eye for now. She has returned. May all my house and my wealth and my hidden sweetness be for her. The following day the doctor allows visitors. Virginia whispers into Ernesto Lavalle's ear. The economist places a hand over his heart and smiles. Virginia asks the General to approach. Poor thing; she is so weak she can barely raise her voice. A preoccupied General leaves the room with the round bed. The President of the Republic also bends over to hear Virginia's words of gratitude. Miracle Street, number 35, at ten o'clock, the night of the fourteenth. She has returned, and my heart accepts the truth. She doesn't love me, but she needs me. In early morning, when the Colonel and the hatred hidden behind a face are alone, Don Cleto says: You are the country, Colonel. We are you. The señora has redeemed her errors. She is you. Sir Christopher Wren's epitaph in St. Paul's Cathedral in London reads: If you would seek a monument, look about you. The cathedral was built by Wren. You have built this country. More cognac? You're a liar, Cleto. The piranhas you placed in my veins have escaped to the lake of Culatepelc; and they've left without eating my arteries. Don Cleto was a Maya sphinx. Pour me more cognac. A very long silence. The Colonel placed a finger to his lips. Virginia slept. Huddled close beside the round bed, the Indian girls watched over her. How beautiful the moon, how beautiful! There are things they don't understand in the Northern Hemisphere. The Colonel swam, naked, his heart content, while the Bengal tigers, someone's gift to the Colonel, clawed Don Cleto to death. One of the things they don't understand is that the tiger is an animal of the Southern Hemisphere.

Obliquity. In the name of the Father. Against the grain. His mind is shaken from recent fears. So many servants, so many enemies. Seneca. My God! I am he. It isn't the same for Jesus Christ to say as it is for Raphael to sing it. Do me this one piss-ant favor. Where will it all end? Of course we die daily. He would like to be persuasive, reasonable, but can reason, can shit, be communicated in the atmosphere of a country forced to its knees? Who can serve as an example to those who hate? Hatred is a law unto itself. Too many servants, too many slaves, too much compliance to be true. It is true that at his table there were never more than five, as the Sicilian poet dictated. Don Cleto was no longer there. There were, though, more delicious and more abundant foods. Never more than five. In the homes of the poor, everyone got together at the least excuse—who were they all?—over their dried beans and rice and the piglet dead of a goiter. Eat your fill, though, my friend, for fire cleanses everything except sin. Archestratus said that more than five at one table was an assembly. People are an assembly, Sir. Why not? If you don't talk and communicate with other human beings, then eczema breaks out on your skin, and bad stys, and all things like that. Lift your glass, my friend, and let us give to the body what it asks and we seldom give. Do you know what's absurd? What is sustenance for some is poison for others. Look at the fields. There they lie. There must be thousands of things beneath them. God only knows. Minerals. An industry with creative goals. A socialist society. Why the separation of man from his society? When both man and society consider the other ugly, that makes for an unhappy dualism. The earth. The Eucharist, as bread is broken and shared, is the symbol for human community. The truth is mine. The earth, with good guano and bread enough for all. Bread and brotherhood are the same. Five at the table is pure capitalism, and there's a fat chance I'd ever go for that, pal. Not five. Only two, sitting face to face. Virginia and the Colonel, with a candelabrum in the middle of the long table and two servants in knee breeches serving from the left and removing from the right. Asparagus, caviar, lobster, *poulet au port*. And the sea and the air.

A red land covered with a tender blanket where children walk barefoot. Forest strawberries. Virginia is sad, and the children are laughing. Can you hate with your feet? Betrayal is evil—even when the one betrayed is a swine. Serene night. Miracle Street. The moon bathes the sea's skin. Fishing boats lie waiting for porgy to bite. The air belongs to everyone. The Colonel read once that the economy should be at the service of man. He has to think about these things so Virginia's silence doesn't make him cry. He can't lift Virginia's skirts as he used to, without permission. Not even with permission. Virginia's skirts lie undisturbed, like the slopes of dead volcanoes. The world is radically divided into poor and rich, possessors and dispossessed. I love you Virginia, but to avoid your mockery I don't say it out loud. The world is sick. It isn't that there isn't any bread. There isn't any love. But I love you, Virginia. A table for two. Never more than five. Anything more is an assembly. There lies the sea, placid beneath the splendor of the moon. Tears trickle down Virginia's cheeks. The Indian girls watch her from a dark corner; they are weeping, too. Theirs is not the same grief, but it is shared grief. Obliquity. Paradox of contradictions. The Colonel would like to create a new world for Virginia. A happy world so small that there would be no room in it for anything but the two of them. Such riches! A world without contradictions. The night is outside upon the sea and in the hollow of the air. Good night. He kisses Virginia's hands. Madam! He is so alone that he's afraid to go out into the naked night. Good night. The Indian girls follow Virginia upstairs. The Walkers surround the Colonel. Where? As a gull lets itself be carried by the current of the tidewater, so the Colonel walks through the dark streets, with sleeping trees and hidden lights. Seventh and Diagonal. Those who see the band of men from a distance turn at the first corner. Or step into the shelter of a doorway, or fade into the blackness of a garden. Everything is in order. Five at the table. The Colonel walks. A distant shot. Someone must have done away with himself. Palm trees, ceibas, and poincianas. And the aroma of magnolias. He stops on Bolívar Street. *El Heraldo del Pueblo.* Linotypes. Someone asks about the pairing of the day's parlay. Cockroach and nanny. The Colonel lights a cigar, and they bring him the galleys. Israel, Vietnam, South Africa, Security Council, West Berlin . . . The editor brings a chair out to the street. The Colonel does not sit down. East Berlin, Bertrand Russell, Jordan, and Syria, Tom Jones, Trinidad de los Santos, Tiatenango, three dead . . . Ring, ring, ring. Will you excuse me? The editor returns with the news that the shot wasn't important. Some man killed his wife. The country is tranquil. Gimme back the rosary of my dear mother. . . . A beautiful, sad voice, it has always been said. The Commons, the Senate, the senator. Of the seven shots only the last was fatal. He was in luck. The Colonel continued his walk. A happy world for Virginia. A child cries. It's bad never to have held a child of your own in your arms. He comes to the outskirts of the city. A ragged line of adobe houses. They're the last. These are the houses of the Chinese, with their gardens behind. Water must be drawn from the well night and day. At night the old people in the family replace the old horse, round and round on the deeply worn path. The Colonel walks directly to one of the gardens. Good evening. The horse-Chinese-horse cannot answer. Near him stands an oil lamp. The rest of the family is sleeping. Early in the morning, in a light cart pulled by two Chinese, they will take their vegetables to the market in the capital. Do you know who Mao is? The Chinese removes the band from his forehead. He smiles. Like the night. Like glow-worms. The Colonel peers through a window into the house. Everyone is sleeping together, and it smells bad. The horse lives separately. Do you know Spanish? Yes, he knows, al-though his pronunciation is bad. What do you take for heart trouble? Ginger. They laugh. You're a Communist, you bad Chinaman. The Chinese laughs again. His lips do not move, but Confucius comes out his eyes. *Ueixiao sh dui uchun wenti weide daan.* One-Eye would have read the Cantonese in the air and with a karate chop ruptured his carotid artery. But the son is not the same thing as the father, even if many believe they resemble one another. In the Yangtze basin they cultivate a grain the Indians of the Andes call *quinua*, and in Canada, oats. Barley. The Chinese is a man who has always seen the arrival of day, not its departure, since he goes to bed before the chickens. He works for a daily wage, every day of the week. A rambler on a round and endless road. Liu Yi is his name. The owner of the house, who is younger, has awak-ened, and serves the visitor a beverage of fermented rice he makes in his own storeroom. Mao. The Colonel wants to laugh, but he can't. A green and purple shadow lies at the back of his heart. The old Chinese returns to his task at the waterwheel. The young Chinese watches, unspeaking. The Walkers wait at various observation points. The Colonel has never felt comfortable among Chinese. The vegetable grower was trying to be obsequious with his illustrious visitor, but all Orientals know that where fear exists there is no room for wis-dom. Wave after wave of cares and jealousies. All the sleepers, who were no longer sleeping, were listening through the open window. He said good-bye, tossing green banknotes at the feet of the old man of the wheel. It was a few minutes before midnight. He wanted his bodyguards to walk apart from him, so he couldn't smell the sweat of their armpits. Open country and moon. He saw the dome of the convent of the Sisters of Our Lady of Mercy, where eleven peons, who represented twelve nuclear families, were sleeping on the ground in huts built over the catacombs left by the Jesuits. Renters of the church's lands, kitchen porters, fuel gatherers, water carriers, shepherds, laborers. Eleven peons and their families, to do it all. And all for their food and a little clothing, plus a few centavos for salt, matches, tobacco, kerosene, and sugar. One man's evil makes evil for many others. Ding, dong, ding, dong. The bell sounds quietly, dispiritedly, as if gathering the dreams of the toller. An Indian. The sacristan, who because he is the most pious, tomorrow will be the priest. Zenón Borda was the former priest's name, but he died. His bed is a niche in the catacombs. Oh, dear Jesus. Borda was not a native. He was a Peruvian, and he'd arrived one day in a circus with llamas. He married a tiny Maya girl so pretty he called her Puñuy. Eyes open, thus they buried him in an earthen vessel. His only request was that they write this name on his mortuary receptacle. *Llullo sonccohuarmac.* Ignorant. *Soncco* and *yuya.* Heart, soul, thought. Ding, dong, ding, dong. *Puñuy.* Dream. *Huma.* Head. Zenón Borda knew very little about these things, but he believed in San Martín de Porres, which is not a bad thing when practicing the priesthood. His mother is living, and they employ her in the convent kitchen to scrub pots. She never speaks, but she thinks of the words her man said to her in a different language:

Llanquin	Sadness
Llanquini	Pain
Cheknikuy	Hatred
Pputy	Anguish
Manchay	Fear
Putirayay	Melancholy
Munay	LOVE
Llulluy	Tenderness

Oh, slaves, pre- and post-Columbian, in your lifetimes you have never known the word for happiness. Only the *soncco nanay*, sorrow. Quechua is a beautiful language. Ponchos and blankets woven from break of day. There are the Spanish looms. Corded wool and flannel. Dyes impossible to imitate. Postage stamps for kids' collections. Indian weaving for everyone. Later to be bought in shops along the Rue de la Paix and Fifth Avenue. Manuel Utazo Quispe, who has gone outside to relieve himself, swings the light of his lantern in the Colonel's face. God help me! He scrambles to pull up his trousers. Ding, dong, ding. The bell has no more to give. A great mercy. The Colonel picks up the lantern which has fallen to the ground and enters the first house. Ill and well, women and men, lie sleeping. Puñuy. Not even in their dreams do they see pretty figures. That's why they sleep with their forearms across their tightly shut eyes. It smells like dirty clothes. The Colonel turns away. Well, Colonel, sir, you caught us off guard. But we're just what you've seen. Money first, virtue later. Horacio was a pretty name. And why don't they rebel against those fine ladies? The Colonel glances toward the convent. One mother superior, twenty-two novitiates, and seventeen lay sisters, besides the oblates. A breeze rises from the small lake with its fat, forbidden carp and rafts of cattail reeds. The Colonel's mind is on sanitary stations. Bonifacio Maita also awakens; he needs to piss and he must also water the cattle. Later Asencio Báez emerges from another hut, on his way to the pasture. Someone hands them ladles of a smoking hot beverage. Who is that? It's La Minga, the idiot girl whose only service is to dole out the hot sugar water as everyone gets up. When does La Minga sleep? There's nothing in the world that woman loves more than noodles. A celebration. Something about a godchild, a godfather, or co-godfathers. It is still a long time before daybreak. The night is at its fullest, dominating everything. But suddenly a light flashes across the skies, as if to shatter the night into shards of pride. And the night bellows like a wounded wolf. The flock is returning.

Maita and Báez, in a dream, *puñuy*, had foreseen the storm. It's raining, Colonel. And La Minga had the hot sugar water ready. He doesn't need to promise. But the Colonel promises the three men he will have the filthy hovels torn down and new ones erected in their place. I will give you land and seed. That will be tomorrow. Tonight he needs that pestilent shelter to protect his boots from the rain. From time to time the night lights up like a guardroom. The Colonel conceals his fear. It is a different kind of fear. Not the *manchay* Zoilo's father had always known. It is fear that the bell will shatter and awaken the bats sleeping in the tower. Zolio sleeps. Everyone should awaken intermittently, at the tempo of the flashing light of the night, but they sleep. Only the Colonel and the Walkers, La Minga, and the three men staring at them in silence, are awake. The Colonel is thinking about Virginia. If only there were something to drink. Asencio Báez has a half bottle of pulque. There are glass jars that once contained instant coffee. The Colonel downs six ounces at a gulp. He would like to talk with someone who can read the blood of a slaughtered beast. They cover La Minga's eyes because she loves all living creatures. There is one huge sheep. The Colonel pays for it. Besides, it means that the following day there will be food for all. Eighty diners = an assembly. Bonifacio drools with pleasure. He has an enormous knife. The night rips open its entrails and screams like a madwoman without a moon. A sheep, good fat. Bonifacio slits its throat, slowly, so the blood will drip evenly. Asencio goes to look for Tula, who comes wearing only her petticoats. The animal is dying and its bleating awakens the shepherd. Very few are still asleep. What do you say? Tula seems not to have emerged from her dreams. Large, expressionless eyes staring at the red stain. Well, she says that things will change tomorrow. There are two faces on the same coin, my Colonel: three hundred-dollar pieces and a king's ducat. Only one has both heads and tails. The others have two faces. Ding, dong, ding, dong. Zoilo is rubbing his eyes in the bell-tower, as if the smell of the sheep's blood had reached him there. What about me? You, my Colonel, have the soles of your boots on the ground, and that signifies life, but that ground is the land men run from. And there will be dogs. There are dogs. Heaven! Oh, heaven! You are dressed in purple; where is the hidden, hissing serpent? Punishment is sought, and pardon feared. The sheep lies dead on the warm, steaming ground. Day is suckling at my breast. The children have already crept out to look for new potatoes and green peas along Huaylas Alley. The Colonel leaves, his nervous fingers playing with the riddle of the two-faced coin. Ding, dong, ding, dong. The chaplain covers his head with his pillow. But did you see the two faces, Tula? Yes, Tobías, for I am not blind to those things, as you know. The night is again mistress of the darkness. The city is lost in the humid silence after the rain. Virginia has bolted her door. The guard of Walkers changes, and the Colonel lies down to sleep on the leather couch in his office. Meritorious. Illustrious. Bizarre. Diplomas. Medals. The head of a stuffed puma. And the air and the sea outside, indifferent, panting, the gaping jaws of the universe; the universe above and the universe below belonging to a *pacha mama humaman hapik*—an idiot without memory. Well, take whatever you have, my friend, to get rid of the nausea.

Central America is a paper bird. Central America is satu-
rated with treaties, protocols, pacts, agreements, fiscal
immunities, deficits, credits, and especially, acronyms.
Dr. Lavalle is nervously pacing back and forth. The rendezvous is at ten, in Miracle Street. Through the window of his
office in the National Bank he can see where Miracle Street
begins. The man shaving ice from a block with a scraper is
concerned only with heaping the shaved ice into a paper cone
and pouring brightly colored syrups over those little mountains sparkling in the sun. Snow cones, tasty snow cones,
cocoa and mint! But Dr. Lavalle has something to do on that
street when the sun goes down, when the children are sleeping, when the snow-cone peddler is drinking up in beer with
salt what he earned during the day. Señor Lavalle's secretary is
a sharp operator. You're telling me? His name is Raúl Izaga
Méndez and he wears a *guayabera* shirt; he has slicked-down
hair and a thick mustache. He's getting rich. The National
Bank and the Ministry of the Economy are one and the same.
As well as the Ministry of Public Finance. Commerce and industry are merged under the Ministry of the Economy. Richer
from day to day. Raulito. Oily, with a ready smile. Pushy.
Why does Lavalle put up with him? Reasons. Ass kissing. The
government entrusts to him the study of the firm of Smithson
& Fry, Inc. And afterward, seeing to it that the external finan-
cial collaboration is profitable, that it increases, and is flexible.

143

. . . Señor Lavalle: the manager of Ferry Packing. *Hello!* By midmorning, a tranquilizer. Librium. The regulation on industrial development means a sacrifice for the exchequer. No, only during the month of April. Raulito is in the reception room talking with three men. They've come to request a fiscal exemption for their firm. They speak of the PNB and of the BCIE, as well as ALPRO. They also mention LAFTA and ICAP, which, in addition to what they have to say about the IDB and UNAM, constitutes a praiseworthy intent to economize on language. The Minister is waiting for you. I've already spoken with him. The Director, the Minister, has approved the statutes. Laterite minerals. INFONAC. Ten million marks from a firm from the Federal Republic of Germany is never hard to take. The title for the construction will need a little push from him. Men, human values, and the demographic explosion. Ah, don't tell me, my dear friend, don't tell me! Fifty-eight point one percent of the population is of working age. But who works here? There isn't enough work, and that's because there's no real balance between man and nature. But you'll see . . . and now, my God, now they're even taking advantage of the movement of the tides, and desalinating sea water, and with the prospect of great harvests from the sea—won't we have that balance? But, my dear fellow, what are you talking about? the economic stabilization of Central America. A basis for that. Well yes, well no. ICAP, CACM, ALPRO, IDB, the OAS, the BCIE, the ICAITI . . . the summit meeting in San Salvador . . . proclaimed objectives . . . free trade of rubber boots, embroidered dresses and ribbons, and tires . . . deodorants and toothpaste will be excluded from the 30-percent charge, the newly created tax resulting from regional unity. A population *de jure*. A population counted in a census. An indigenous, jungle-dwelling population not tabulated. We have the lowest percentage of wage earners, gentlemen. Our workers are self-employed. They're dying of hunger, it's true, but that happens in every country where the workers are self-employed. My plans for the immediate future are to create an

144

organism that will promote unity within the region.

Miracle Street faces Diagonal 3, and is the site of the new building of the Polytechnical School and the older building of the School of Pharmacy. It is our hope that the pound sterling will be subjected to greater pressures in the coming months. The Third World poses a problem. Bundle up 'gainst the win', friend. I use' ta have a li'l stand on Martí Street where I roasted peanuts. The thicket, old buddy, where we get the grass for tomorrow, yeah? The film over my eyes came on me like a flash. The tango, buddy, makes everythin' sound sad, so sad. Our country is equipped to export up to two million pounds of powdered milk to the other countries of the region. Our country has signed the first draft of the general treaty on economic integration. Come on, Lavalle, don't fuck around. You'd like nothing better than to drift with the current. So the boy wants to be a pharmacist? Well you see, my friend, that shed was constructed when everyone thought it was impossible to split the atom. The dean has perfected a baby bottle that resists boiling and sudden cooling. A baby bottle is a beautiful thing. Where is the Congress of this nation? It isn't necessary to wait for Congress to convene. At ten, on Miracle Street. Where did Trinidad de los Santos strike yesterday? And One-Eye? Where's One-Eye? The conditioned reflexes of the people. They associate the Colonel's voice with food. Citizens! The Colonel seems content this May afternoon. Right in reach of my hand a knife lies just beggin' me to pick a fight, but I don't grab it. Cozy down, dove, and perform Wilson's fourteen points. Ten o'clock, empty hour, a tiny hole in the zero. A bullet can enter through that tiny hole. Three thousand, four thousand, five thousand. And you, buddy, some of these greenbacks? Look what that makes you. Raulito counts. Five hundred for him, and four thousand five hundred for the Director. A good morning. A good day. While it lasts. . . . Hey, tell me, why Raulito? *He is somebody for you to reckon with.* Ah. Why were you named Director if you can't handle the position yourself? Either the whole five thousand clams for yourself, or I find it difficult to respect you, Lavalle. Whom are you looking for? Raulito. Whom were you asking for? Raulito. Who the fuck is Raulito? The man you work for, Señor Director, I mean, Señor Minister, I mean, Señor Lavalle. . . . And how did you clean out that wallet, Julito? I was hanging from the back of the car. There is a large clock on the School of Pharmacy. Seven-fifteen. Daytime. Still daytime. The French perfume firm of Dupois is interested in our coconut oil. Whose coconut? My coconut. Ah, that's different! Fifteen hundred, two thousand, twenty-five hundred. Raulito counts. Two hundred fifty for Raulito and the rest for the Director. Citizens! We're poor, but not that poor. The reward on the head of Trinidad de los Santos is raised to twenty thousand pesos. And on One-Eye to fifty thousand. A foreigner. Here lies without pain or glory an American Indian known only to God. He took two dichloride pills. Who?

How do I know! Not even God knew him. Visitors are not permitted. Eight-thirty. Lavalle leaves in his bulletproof car en route to his residence, along bus route 22. A porch with enormous coffin-shaped earthen urns. The Chinese gardener is watering the bougainvillea hedge. A shower, talcum, clean clothing, and a scotch and soda. Nine-thirty. Citizens! He descends the stairs, restraining his impatience. Twenty minutes to go. Miracle Street isn't far. In the hall, Georgiana, dressed in a green sari, is lying on an ottoman. So beautiful. A Japanese proverb says that a single word can warm three months of winter. Lavalle was in a hurry, and he was frightened. Another whiskey. The word, the word, old man. The most beautiful eyes in the world. Say just one word, one word, and she will close off the road to Miracle Street. But God saves the moon of the wolves. The clock on the School of Pharmacy, slightly fast, was striking ten, as if air were escaping through the tiny hole in the zero.

President a fortiori, Valentín Oruro. By what roads did the blood of Guanca and Gualpa, who honeycombed Potosí, reach the tropics? As it was dammed up within volcanic wombs, it became stained with green. St. Philip of Austria and the *cholo* Patiño, with his mixed blood. Oruro, *oruga*—caterpillar. Black *oruga*. White Oruro. And yellow Chiquita Banana. To each his own, right? Tel' me, Chiquita, does Miracle Street have an exit, or is it like the tit of the manatee, it doesn't bend, it doesn't nourish? Dr. Oruro was worried about that meeting at an hour when all good Christians are taking off their *chapines*. A *chapín* in Guatemala is something besides a clog with a cork sole. But Guatemala is a little to the left of this story. The same road, but on the edge of the Maya territory. So, wrap 'er up in a tamale, what the hell do I care. The shared misunderstandings relative to the conduct of industrial nations—Señor Christiansen from Norway is speaking—nations industrial of conduct the, etc., etc., in the matters of aid, commerce, and the export of technology to developing countries. The report was clear. In English. Translated from Norwegian. Don Valentín reads it and thinks it over. Hey, Chiquita, bring me the file on earnings and the current economic balance, and a whiskey. He believed he was a good president. With a headache. The psychiatrist will cure it, Don Valentín. The minute he tells Your Excellency that you have a presidential headache. My skull aches, but not my head, but that's because I'm a *cholo*, not white like you. Get out, you're a pain and I don't want any more of your lip. No, it isn't the same thing. I have a hunch, Chiquita. Holy smoke, you're a big fat coward. Miracle Street is open at both ends, and you don't find a moon like this just anywhere. They may have the factories and hospitals and amusement parks, but we've harnessed the moon shining over the pepper trees and ceibas. Drunk and hanged. I've been a good President, Chiquita. Maternity care, nutrition, schools, Common Market, tariffs, freedom of information. Yesterday they called him venal and he didn't even blink an eye. Me, venal? *Venum, vend,* sell. *I* sell myself? Nobody knows what's going on here. And nobody knows what it means to sell, or who's doing the selling. Mr. Shit Seller is the President of this country. Mr. Shit Seller is Colonel Arruza. I shit on his mother. I'll bet that what happened to Arnulfo Arias is what's going to happen to me. That's how it goes in the countries of the isthmus. Today I'm someone, tomorrow a colonel in the National Guard. Here all the gods ought to be named Borgia. Nine-fifteen. The sky is peaceful. The land says nothing. The sea belongs to the octopuses. Everyone should read Strümpell and poison his neighbor. Ground glass, needles, and arsenic in the morning coffee. I'd need a tacky lackey. Give me the valerian. I'll bring you crataegus. No, give me valerian. My diaphragm hurts. Chiquita Banana gives him the crataegus with his second drink. A beautiful tropical woman, full-bodied, and feeling the splendor of the sunset. The International Coffee Agreement is lying on the presidential table beside a small, steaming, savory-smelling cup. The country's London representative will talk about stabilizing the basic product. I've been a good President. Similar agreements for sugar and cocoa. The President sips his coffee. Valerian, crataegus, coffee, whiskey. Presidential headache. He will not wear a tuxedo. A *guayabera* shirt. Chiquita, look at me. They look at one another. He wants to read political betrayal in those moist eyes, but he sees only phalluses. Chiquita, I don't have time now. Wait up for me. We have something to do; Black River and Thirty-third. Why are you going to the rendezvous? You told me that Mr. Shit Seller's out to screw me. That's what Virginia-the-Cunt said. Look. We ought to have a child, or at least we ought to get married right away. The President is watching the flight of the scruffy buzzards that cleanse the city of all dead things. Sanitation Service. Oruro is near Potosí. Tin and silver. Where did your family come from, Señor President? He doesn't know, he is not absolutely certain, but he feels in his veins that icy wind they call the *tomahaui*. The General wants you on the telephone. The President speaks with his heart divided into four lodes—the Rica, the Centeno, the Del Estaño, and the Mendieta—and from time to time he exclaims, Why yes, General. Through the window he sees the branches of the pepper tree, a tree of great virtue, but he needs a swallow of his drink when he observes that two buzzards still wait in the green branches. Why yes, General. They will find the two cars on Bolívar Street, in front of the Rubén Theater. His heart grows calm. He feels the company of the valiant, like the time he walked the eighteen leagues from Madre de Dios to Panama. In a foreign country everything seems more distant and more lonely. There he had met Roque Guaina, also traveling on foot, beneath one of those trees that are large enough to shade more than a thousand men. Why yes, General. Roque was carrying a stick of lignum vitae. A holy stick, like iron, that he dips in the water. Afraid, with this? With his knife he had peeled the husk from a *suchicopal* and scrubbed his bare chest with the juice. Roque knew all the good things that trees provide to man. For the trip he was carrying various flasks filled with benzoin, courbaril, balsalm, pods of the drumstick tree, and oil of fir. At four o'clock he enticed a medium-sized iguana with tacamahac, and when it approached, he struck a sharp blow on the base of its skull. Why, yes, I'll go, General. Another whiskey. The buzzards were still there. He would have them killed, but then how would the streets be cleaned? They ate the iguana. Good memories from his youth, when all that he had achieved in life was a timekeeper's job in the American Zone. He studied at night to get his degree and return home. He carried his university books tied with a hemp cord. He drank more, and Chiquita warned him: Dear sweet boy, you're not going to a house party. Chiquita was always more or less right. He put on his straw hat, and his faithful servant called the guard. The President! No one ever knows from where those little peaks of conscience arise, like Mozo Hill, covered with brothels and palaces and convents. He kissed Chiquita with care. He loved her. They would have to get married. It wasn't phalluses now in those beautiful eyes, but marimba sticks. She was so delicious, so happy. Why are you crying, Chiquita? Chiquita's passionate kisses warmed slightly the cold veils of the *tomahaui* enveloping his soul. Roque wouldn't be afraid. The iguana was the one that was afraid. Chiquita, my love, don't listen to what nasty tongues say about you. You're my precious little girl; you are the only good thing the President has. They talked that way. Chiquita waved good-bye as she had done when she was a young girl waving good-bye to the guano boat going to the island of the birds. They had called her La Guanera until she came to the capital and was taken to the house of Madam Pipa Monte. Chiquita was so beautiful and so full of life that all the big shots fought to get her as their mistress. But Valentín Oruro took her to a little house on the outskirts of the city during his first term as President. Then into exile, and once returned, to a neighborhood high above a lake full of yachts. The odor of pomegranates spilled into the night. And the moon over the cedars and laurels. Chiquita will wait. She knows how to make paintings from the feathers of *tominejos*, hummingbirds as tiny as butterflies. She holds the many-colored feathers— from green to orange—in a pair of tweezers and glues them with cherry-tree gum to a coarse canvas. The national coat of arms. Beautiful shading outlines the symbols. In the background, a trio of dead birds, the same that Trinidad de los Santos used to hunt when he was a little shrimp hiding from

the peccaries, beasts with their navels on their backs. Roque
Guaina fell upon them and throttled the fetid gland, and then
cut their hocks while they were still alive to let the humors escape with the flow of blood. The remains were left for the
turkey buzzards, who are not frightened away by stench.
Twenty minutes to ten on the little diamond-encircled watch.
Chiquita Banana doesn't want to see what time it is, so she
removes it. *Swiss Made*. Chiquita would like to go back into
exile and marry the President. She imagines herself in that
apartment facing Central Park. The RCA Building to the left of
her heart. In the mornings she walked the poodle along maple-
shaded paths. What are you reading, Valentín? The former
President in his English cap, disguised against those who
didn't know him, reading old newspapers provided by an employee in the consulate. Raulito, now secretary to Dr. Lavalle,
Minister of the Economy and Director of the National Bank.
Find a place for him, Lavalle, he saved me a lot of trouble.
Raulito, the big operator. Chiquita glues the feathers. In New
York, Valentín read even the advertisements. Ornivaz Electric
dishwashers, on easy terms. Ben Franklin glasses glittering.
Look, Chiquita, look who's died. A druggist, an obscure man
who suddenly came clear in the exile's memory. Chiquita
orders the servant to come and frighten away the buzzards.
They stink. In New York there aren't any buzzards. Chiquita
prays that things will go badly on Miracle Street. A winter
overcoat and the cold air of the Hudson over the ships.
Chiquita remembers that March afternoon in the Cloisters,
standing in front of reclining pairs of stone monarchs brought
from Europe, when Valentín had taken her hand and said to
her: You and I will be like that, alive and dead. But in the
tropics everything is green, even the blood that comes from
afar, like that of Guanca and Gualpa, Indians with a hatred of
silver inside them. Even Villarroel would have turned green.
And the night is as beautiful as the day, and doesn't consult
the woman. But she knows when her husband is entering a
net, like a blind fish.

151

Waterloo-Palomitas. Palomitas, elevation 232, where they hanged Juan Cuevas at the end of the century, does not have the same elevation as the province of Brabant, 457 feet. If one places both maps over glass, the crosses of those killed at Waterloo appear above the circles representing volcanoes. In Europe the volcanoes are in the south. Lieutenant General Armenteros has spent a week trying to trap the bastards with Trinidad de los Santos in Marshal von Blücher's great strategic pocket. But moving Prussian dragoons is not the same thing as operating with two hundred forty badly equipped rural police. One-Eye, that devil, that damned and cuckolding One-Eye, is forcing National Hero Armenteros to ride the steed of defeat. The General has been drinking since morning with his aide, Commodore Narciso Pérez Almarche. Commodore, please impose Tipitz over Taxtlemilco. Don Narciso adjusted the maps. Is that right, General? It looks a little tipsy to me. You're telling me? They were even-up on drinks. There in that military staff room Armenteros felt capable of anything. Campaign telephones, the glass screen for his maps, paintings of famous battles, and portraits of the great military men of history: Napoleon, Murat, Alexander, Wellington, Blücher, Don John of Austria, Bolívar, and, in the middle, Armenteros, painted by the Belgian artist Fraset. Blue uniform, white cape, and helmet crowned with a heron plume. A horseman on a rearing roan, its nostrils dilated by the acrid gunpowder. Soldiers in the background, artillery, cavalry. Armenteros in Marengo or in Carabobo. A veritable army of lead soldiers on an enormous table, with papiermâché hills for the artillery and silver-paper rivers for the pontoniers. A library on military subjects. The bar with French brandy for highballs. An ottoman for the women patriots who came to surrender themselves to the Hero. The Commodore is thinking that tomorrow they will have to abandon this beautiful refuge if One-Eye isn't found. Blücher at Möchen, always Blücher, while One-Eye hurls insulting shouts from the heart of the volcanoes. Hand me *The Battle of the Nations*. Look in the index. Glowing cigars. Night is upon them, as someone once said. The Commodore turns on the lamps and answers the telephone. The President. Two poles of fear speaking. Joseph fled to France. In spite of the fact that his brother had crossed into Spain with two hundred and fifty thousand men. This the General tells the President, playing the braggart. He can only be in the breast of lava and placenta of fire. I believe that's best. We'll go together. On Bolívar Street. Meanwhile, the Commodore is writing a letter to his younger brothers and the uncle who lives with them. I can see you in my mind, my brothers. Narciso. If the General read that letter, he would call his aide disrespectful, daring, and brazen. He's swilled to the gills. He's sitting in a chair made of leather and cow's pelvis, trying to hold onto what is slipping away from him. Now he's talking with Oruro. He's saying he's not going to wear a uniform, but a *guayabera* shirt, a panama hat, and dark glasses. I know that Oruro can always avoid being recognized simply by removing his false teeth. Where could those two be going? They're hiding from something. Of course they're so accustomed to exile and jail that it's a night like any other for these beggars, what the hell. Today, presidents and generals, and tomorrow, Daytona Beach. He hangs up. Give me another highball. Land of volcanoes, of silences, and alcohol. The General gazes at the portraits hanging on the walls. God, what would those giants have done in a land like this? Less than a hour. The important thing was to get to Miracle Street. What was the Commodore saying to him? Oh, God, spare him from some Indian who kept butting his head against him. Bye, bye, General. An English attaché once told me during the war that you can't believe such things until you come to America. The General heard him but he wasn't listening. His portrait was there, facing Bonaparte's. Grab him by the lapels, and then butt that head. Why does the General suddenly ask such a foolish question? Narciso, tell me, can a guanaco be trusted when he's chewing coca? No, General, he spits hot and heavy, and can knock your eye right out of your head. The General has never owned a horse like the one he's riding in the portrait. The Belgian painter copied Peter the Great's horse. And Napoleon's spyglass. And Bismarck's helmet. What happens is that the guanaco is jealous of any two-footed animals that might steal away its little llama. Nobody understands America, do they, Commodore? From tip to toe, America is different. That's why Waterloo doesn't fit over the land of the volcanoes, or the pampas—we tried it there, too—or over the jungles of the Amazon, or the savannas, or the Andes, or the pasture land of the gringos. It doesn't fit. Just as the "Marseillaise" doesn't fit, or Parliament, or the Prussian eagle, or the ballet. We are ourselves, genuine, by dint of the blade and braggadocio. Condors instead of eagles. Tumult or total silence. The orgy of the carnival or the mourning of Lent. Beans and hog meat, pride and vileness. Is that true or not? I'm not saying anything, General. Well, you'd better say it isn't true, or I'll bury you up to your ass in shit. Tell me that America is marvelous, and that I'm a stinking pig. Say that? They were so drunk they could say anything to each other. Well yes, sir, you're nothing but a piece of shit, and that's what I was writing just now to my brothers and our uncle. Your uncle is a cockster, and besides, he's not your uncle, he's your father. You take that back, or this knife'll leave you a gelding. But neither of the two moves from his chair. The cow pelvises are steady. Shall we respect each other? Yes, let's. The General

154

struggles to his feet and tries to put on his *guayabera*. First he adjusts the straw hat. You weren't serious when you said that about my uncle, General? You really hurt me. It was the high-balls, my friend, you know that. How could a priest be your father? That can't be. The Commodore helps him into the starched shirt that smells like a bride's sheets. The General suddenly has a thought. Hey, old man, tell me: How do you kill a man without anyone finding out? You can do it cleanly with a little cut in the groin that leaves no trace of blood. Right here? Right here. And then you can carry him off, already dead, as if he were only drunk. The General has to leave. He doesn't need any company. You stay here, Commodore, with the little lead soldiers. And play some music for them. Where're you going, General? A military man must never fear death, Commodore. What're they going to do, shoot you? The General walked out to the street, his mouth strangely twisted. It was quarter to ten. The Commodore's uniform was filthy and wrinkled, with only three medals. He went to a glass cabi-net and removed one of the General's dress uniforms and put it on. It was a garden of medals. Spanish shako and saber. He shouted for Basilio, the aide, a bewildered Indian. He showed him how to operate the Polaroid. If you tell the General any-thing, I'll cut off your ears, understand? Now he had the pho-tograph for his young brothers. The Indian went out without saying a word. Now that His Excellency had left, he finished the letter. How do you like the snapshot? Someday you'll have the surprise of seeing me arrive on horseback, wearing this uniform. This country needs a real general who will take the responsibility for finishing off all the crooks and bastards. A general who doesn't play with little lead soldiers, or pretend to keep order in the country with the tactics they used at Wa-terloo. What our people need is a man backed by the army who could assume the presidential functions and make of this so-often oppressed nation a place where democracy and lib-erty—the two great American virtues—would reign forever.

At that point he fell asleep.

Ten o'clock.

Corner of Bolívar Street.

Lighted advertisements.

False teeth in a pocket.

A man wearing a *guayabera,* trying to look like Aristotle Onassis.

And One-Eye on Miracle Street, the heart of the volcano.

A turtle will leave the bay to swim fifteen hundred miles through the Caribbean without stopping—only for the pleasure of returning after three weeks to the starting place. How? Like Niña Huanca, it doesn't need a sextant or a map.

America!

God knows what the hell that is.

His name was Poppy Charente, he was a mute, of French origin, and he delivered the mail along the keys of the Texas Sound. The mute liked to maneuver his hovercraft at top speed, leaving a wake of whirlwinds and waves of foam. He cut so near *La Bellotte* that he almost threw Cortés, who was varnishing the masts, to the deck. That motherfucker! What did it matter to Poppy if someone insulted his mother? Besides being mute he was also deaf. They were anchored in the key, painting the hull, the gunwales, the forecastle—where the crew slept—and the quarterdeck, which housed Niña Huanca's mahogany and lignum-vitae suite. Scaffolding protruded from the portholes. Paint your ship, sailor, and rid her of the seaclap. Did you hear me? Paulito was absent, recovering in a hospital in Corpus Christi from an alligator bite. The bastard took off his foot. Poor creature didn't get much to eat there. What burns my ass is that anyone could be so fucking mean as to say a thing like that. Cortés had fallen. Laughter. What's the matter with the man? Nimes is too old to wield the paintbrush. Old, old, ooooold. Weis and Cortés are the ones who pull all the weight. Happy, because at sundown they'll be going to one of the twenty houses that make up the small settlement—the tavern, the tavern— where they'll glut themselves on alcohol and beans and rice and pork. And there are always girls, and they take on anything. Agustina, and the Linchpin, and the Maserati. With their straw mats and mirrors and towels, and washbasins and permanganate powders. Everything portable, beneath the white mangroves. And later, the two men wash the shared bad taste out of their mouths with the pulp of the extremely bitter fruit from the shrub. The parrots seem to laugh at all this. Nimes stays on the boat, or at the most, visits Niña Huanca in her house high on the hill, especially when he feels the desire to sit beside Juancita's grave. The mute conducts his business on the key in the time it takes to down the beer always offered him by the tavern owner, who is also in charge of the post office. Bag for bag, the beer, and good-bye. The wake of swirling wind. Motherfucker! Laughter rising from the scaffolding. From her window Niña Huanca has seen the mailman. Nipe is the name of the parrot she has owned since her father's death. Solitude on earth. Nimes had brought her the female parrot, accompanied by a scrawny male with a foul tongue. All the parrots on the key descended from that pair. Someone told Huancavélica that it would be good to call Nipe Eve, and the male Adam. But the feathered male screeched that his name was Singuerico, and no one ever moved him from it. Besides, he didn't live long. Huancavélica took Nipe with her when good weather settled in, although in the Caribbean no one gives a damn about that. After the death of Juancita, a Negress from Trinidad married to Arsenio, a tambourine player, came to take care of the house. Arsenio was a Brazilian with a pair of legs well suited to dancing the carioca and a finger that could evoke a thousand vibrations a second from the parchment of his tambourine. Teresinha danced too, wearing a brief skirt and a bandeau over her breasts. Sailors in all the ports of the Antilles roared when she sang of Bahia in her bad accent, "Meu limão, meu limoeiro, meu pé de jacarandá . . ." Black girl, black girl, shake your ass, dirty bitch! "Uma vez, tindo-le-le, outra vez, tindo-la-la." Teresinha and Arsenio. A Portuguese from Aruba killed Arsenio on All Saints' Day in 1952. And all because the Portuguese said something to Teresinha that offended the Brazilian's honor, and then Arsenio called him a sonofabitch, and the Portuguese buried his big blade in Arsenio, and Teresinha was left a widow, fat, and the owner of two tambourines. Until 1961 the woman from Trinidad wandered through the brothels of the Caribbean, from the best to the worst, as always happens, and when it came to the point that she had to compete with iguanas for her bed, someone told her to go to Huancavélica's key, where it was still possible to do business. Until Juancita's death Teresinha stole clients from the Linchpin and the Maserati. Agustina still hadn't hove into sight. Just before Juancita died, Teresinha came to look after her. The Dominican woman liked her. Let me comb that fucking hair. Your tongue's rougher than a file. What hair! Well, you can't do much with the *ciguapate* flower. Who told you that, tell me? My grandmother, and she knew what she was talking about; she had a Spanish father and an English mother. Black as pitch. Don't laugh, it makes you cough. To Teresinha, Niña Huanca was a goddess delivered by the sea every two or three months. Snail shells and nimbuses. Juancita died on an October afternoon; all that coughing. Before she died, she asked Niña Huanca to let Teresinha remain in charge of the house. From that moment the woman from Trinidad was the guardian for the whole port. A more faithful woman you've never seen. She wanted to kick out the prostitutes to clean up the key, but the tavern owner told her to go to hell. And the whores stayed. That would have been the last straw. Niña Huanca liked to wear a lace robe around the house. "Meu limão, meu limoeiro . . ." The second floor, with a terrace over the downstairs porch, contained a large living room, two bedrooms, and a bath. The walls of the living room were covered in a golden moiré. A piano, four enormous armchairs, and an ottoman. A fireplace, what for? Lamé curtains, three rugs. The chandelier was a beautifully proportioned spiderweb of crystal drops. A portrait of Matalax, the father. A niche for the Virgin of Montserrat. A beautiful painting of *La Bellotte* under full sail. What, what did you say, dear mistress? The archpriest damns the sea. What

archpriest? The Archpriest of the Indies. The madam who pro-
cured girls for the count who died in New Orleans read the
cards and she told me that someone's uniform shirt would
soon be wrinkled. Those people are like cows. I used to comb
her hair, too, after her bath. But she was so healthy it was em-
barrassing. You smell of leather harness. Do you want an explanation? The prisms of the chandelier glittered like sparks of
water. The mailman brought something. Probably a letter for
Paulito's sweetpea. It hurts you that your son doesn't write
you. It shouldn't. A gray hair. Her silvery chignon shone, stiff
and shimmering. The Trinidad woman's skin was the color of
seaweed. Agustina is dying to dip that dwarf's wick. Did you
ever, mistress, hear anything so degenerate? Nipe, perched on
Niña Huanca's right shoulder, says ass and bastard. The tavern owner calls from the garden that he has a letter from her
son. From her son! Niña Huanca asks for a rum and water
with lemon. She walks out on the terrace and falls onto the
canvas ottoman. A crescent moon already shines in the sky.
The laces of the robe fall away from her body. Her naked belly
is as smooth and beautiful as the sea. Teresinha sits near the
ottoman. "Meu limão, meu limoeiro . . ." Huancavélica reads
the undated letter.

Dear Niña Huanca:
    Shortly the cock will crow. A man will leave at dawn with
this letter and will deliver it to your man in Belize to forward
to you. I haven't slept for several nights. When I lie down to
sleep, I feel an anguish I can't identify; I don't know whether
it comes from the fear of finding myself alone, facing an undertaking that can change the course of the country, or
whether it's caused by premature remorse over what I plan to
do. It is difficult to explain. The fact is that I lie down only
during the day, and then with my eyes wide open. If it all
works out according to my plans, in two weeks I will have everything ready for the old man. It's a difficult operation to
change a tiger's game. They say the Walkers are keeping their

eyes on everyone, and that *he* never takes his eyes off the Walkers. My project involves none of the stupid ideas various people have considered in planning to overthrow him. It's very complex, the mechanism of the contrivance I've invented. So much so, that if I tried to explain it to anyone now, he would take me for one of those wild-eyed savants who go into the bathroom with a book and come out carrying the top of the toilet tank. Soon, through the newspapers, you will learn everything. I imagine that recently you have more than once come across the exploits (I, exploits?) of One-Eye in some newspaper or other. Apparently they believe I'm a Central American Robin Hood. What you can be sure of is that the old man would cut off his arm, lose his teeth, and pay a million dollars for the robin redbreast that's robbed him of tranquility in his country, and more, in his own home. It will please you to know that I've managed to filch his wife, and what's more, she's enthusiastically enlisted in my cause. The poor woman suffers from what the Americans call hot pants, and she's ready and willing to take on anyone down to the bootblack who shines the old man's boots. And our tropical Casanova swallows everything she serves up. Worse, he suffers like hell. He may be a bigshot outside the house, but at home he has to sleep in the chicken roost. In the year I've spent in these countries I've learned who's who in high society; it wasn't difficult to figure who's touchy and who stamps letters with chicken shit. They're all in my computer, going round and round. And fate depends on following what the machine decides without worrying that it's good for some but bad for others. The important thing is for it to be bad for the old man; as long as he gets screwed, it will be great for me. I know that later there will be some who throw revenge in my face. I, too, have considered that point, and have even gone so far as to consult a certain friend of mine in Germany. It's true that as I consulted him, events forced me to my own decision. Fortunately, I acted in time, because my friend's answer never came. By telling you this I'm not trying to exonerate myself from any guilt my acts may bring. The first thing one must do if he wants to understand another human being is to put himself in the other person's shoes. You know better than anyone, mother, how I've suffered. Don't you think I have the right to hate, considering that he denied me the beauty of its opposite? I know that many innocent people will fall before me. Did I not fall crushed beneath the feet of others? The Scripture teaches us that we must love our neighbor (our *near*-bor)—that is the most difficult act of all. What value is there in loving someone who is far away, someone we don't even know? Well then, I thought that in exchanging love for hatred, what then becomes difficult is to make the victim of our hatred someone who is far away, for hating our "near-bor" is very easy. My hatred of that old man forces me to be intractable with any other human, near or distant, who either opposes or facilitates my plans. One day you will understand this wordplay. Before I end this letter, I want to ask you a favor. Will you try to dock at Hersey in Belize within ten days? My men will return Sinfonías to you—it isn't he; it only looks like him—to bring back to Enriquillo. My men will arrive just before dawn, with further instructions, of course. A Cuban named Rufo will be leading them. Don't give them a peso. They're sonsofbitches. I want to get moving and get the whole thing over with. After all, it's about time. I send you all my love,

Your son,
Miguel Ángel

Huancavélica stood up and ordered Teresinha to use the mirror installed on the terrace to notify Nimes that the boss needed him. I see something in the glare of the sun, chief. It's Niña Huanca. Seahorses began to gallop over the crests of the waves, and the men sang, knowing that soon they'd be weighing anchor. Everything was in order for the following day. That night there would be a good dinner on land and a falling-down drunk, and all the rest. Hurry, get going, hop to it! Shouts of boisterous merriment rang out through the quiet night. There was music and the pleasures of the dance. Ooh, baby, I'm going to eat her up! Teresinha took out her tambourine and the dress that rippled in the air. Whooo-eee, brother, put down the roast pig and come look at this! "Meu limão, meu limoeiro . . ." A large table in the garden covered with a fiber mat. And on it, the suckling pig Nimes had roasted behind the corral. Platters with jalapeño peppers, beans, rice, yucca, and a huge salad of avocados and onions. And a relish of black pepper and chilies that had a kick stronger than the jalapeños. Happiness. None of them had a weak stomach or loose bowels, so the banquet was like a May Day. Punch bowls with sliced guava in syrup, custards, and hunks of coconut. Great baskets of fruit. And coffee steaming in an enormous iron kettle over live coals. The tavern-owner-and-postmaster went out three times to vomit only to return, pale and even more greedy. Cortés, never loosing his grasp on the Linchpin, claimed for the two of them the brains and tripe of the suckling pig, which no one wanted anyway. Paulito, using Agustina as a cushion, gobbled everything she tossed down him. Take off your brassiere so I can be more comfortable, and they laughed through missing teeth. Nimes ate very little but drank a lot. The Maserati was also drinking incontinently. Silent tears. I drink to see whether I can hear the sound of my family's prayers. The tavern owner and his woman, Mary Lou, heaped jalapeños on hunks of meat and took turns with a carafe of wine, which they drank from the bottle. Huancavélica was cradled in a hammock about fifty yards from the table. Her son's letter had saddened her. From time to time, Teresinha brought her a drink. Teresinha liked walking through that unruly sea of desires, her hair flowing free, her buttocks swinging, desires at her whim. What's the matter, little mistress? Did that letter from your son bring something bad? Memories of his father. Teresinha felt slightly dizzy, and lay down on one of the mangroves supporting the hammock. A beautiful night, isn't it? She was curious to know what kind of man her mistress had loved. A man who had captured for-

163

ever the love of a woman like Niña Huanca had to be something special. He passed by, unseeing, never realizing the harm he was doing. If you were a woman you fell before him, broken, the way the royal palms fall before the hurricane. That was when you began to want to dominate his power, capture him with the roots that held you exposed to the air. I, who know what men of all races know, never knew love until we lay together in pleasure, and once he left me, I never knew love again. He was coming along the bay at a gallop, pursued by enemies—he never had friends—and suddenly, as he rode by the drydock where my schooner was being caulked, he saw me . . . ! Holy Mary, it seems like I can see it too, dear mistress. He tore the bridle from his horse's mouth, walked toward me, and before his first kiss I already felt my still-unconceived son in my womb. As he clutched my waist, I saw in the garret of his eyes hundreds of his sons, living and dead. They were the sons he was later to give to women and to firing squads. I'm getting the hots, dear mistress. Well, go find someone to douse your flame. After what you've told me, not all the men of the key together could satisfy me. Laughter and cries from those at the table. He was like a wealthy Greek. Like a bull parading his balls in an exhibition. All the rest are nothing but full-size embryos, adult eggs, stumpy devils trying to hide the regalia of angels in the shadow of their buttocks. Night with an orbit larger than any other. That's why they talk such crap. Nothing will begin tomorrow. It all happened yesterday. Go, go. She had to write a letter before she left. Stumbling, she walked to the house, and beneath the portrait of the captain, she wrote:

My beloved son:

La Bellotte will be ready in Belize. I don't understand completely what you hint at in your letter. But you are filled with such hatred, my son, that I am afraid. There's a name on the tip of your tongue and you would like to grind it up and lose it in the torrents of your blood. Spit out that name, my son. That would be worth more than anything you plan to do. There is a different power for you on the wind. Greatness isn't limited to those who can weep before familiar tombs. Escape, run like a child without a past through forests where there are no mandrakes or yaguas. Ascend the river on a raft of peace; it will bear you against the current to places others could never reach. You must, my son, be more than the simple echo of a uterus. Tear from your heart the sad idea that you are the fruit of a woodland penis, and nothing more. There are many other things in a man's life. You must find them. This is the first time I have dared write this way. Perhaps no mother should speak in such a manner to her son, but . . . am I a mother or a boat captain?

Affectionately,

Niña Huanca

She could hear the sailors. The wind had borne away the misty breath of the water, and they could see Grand Cayman. They were sailing close to the wind. Cutting through opaline veins of water. Pass me the bottle. They had slackened the sails because the sky had turned completely purple. The hurricane was already beginning to nip at the stern. "Meu limão, meu limoeiro . . ." The women were yelling because Teresinha was trying to steal one of the men. The watermelon is best cut in the early morning, which is also best for matches between English gamecocks, but one sinks his teeth into the papaya in the nighttime, and it is best to cover the papaya with a mantle of anemones to prevent it from turning bitter. Once everyone was quiet, Cortés followed the Negress. The men were so drunk their trouser legs were damp. Easy does it, now, I'm about to capsize. I have the cuntshell of all the good winds. But Cortés lay stretched out in the middle of the road. It was almost dawn. Teresinha came to sleep in her mistress's room, a room like a golden cage, to dream the same dreams as

165

Niña Huanca. A bay, a horse, and a nameless, faceless man for Teresinha—a man who crushes women's flesh. And the Negress from Trinidad cried out softly, and whispered to herself: Arsenio, my love, don't stand in my way, and don't bug me! Go to hell, please!

The three men entered through the back gate of the walled house; a tall man was posted there who led them toward it. It was Rufo, the Cuban, a bad guy, if ever you've seen one. In the garden they saw the shadows of the other mercenaries from Belize, and glowing cigarettes. Rufo left the men in a large room with peeling stucco columns and a green crystal chandelier. In the center of the room, a table with glasses and bottles, and on the floor, a bucket of ice. Rufo invites them to help themselves. The three sit down as if in a fishbowl within reach of an infamous cat. But the cat leaves. Oruro has refurbished his gums, and again looks like himself. Lavalle feels as if someone has stuck a fishhook in his mouth. The General turns his eyes toward the enemy, like the bull of Crete. They do not speak. It is still early to climb into the same bed. The General roars, and drinks. Lavalle feels screams of fear in his lungs. He pours himself another whiskey. He's afraid he will say something about the socioeconomic balance, and that Armenteros will get into the act with his logistics, or Valentín with his constitutionalism. And the cat's paw poised on the edge of the fence. Where's the rest of the squad? He has to choke back his nausea. You were saying . . . ? No. The three look like patients sitting in a dentist's waiting room. Oruro pours himself a half glass of cognac. They appear to be resigned. They are all equals here. The only thing visible through the window is a black mass of trees. Ten-thirty. The

167

General feels a lump in his throat. His head aches. For an instant he believes he is going to die. They are the three factors determining the equation of that strange silence. He suddenly shouts. Pretty damn brave treetops! Oruro orders him to shut up. Lavalle wants to tell him he scorns him, but he too finds he needs to keep silent. Swaying balloons left from a bygone party make him seasick. He feels cold, and everything seems dark. The Borgias' ambush. Oruro belches. *Excuse me!* They continue to drink. The tropics are a sponge. Bismarck said it. Now he began to talk. Another sacred cow, Bismarck. Oruro falls upon an old sofa of worn silk. He is weeping loudly. Lavalle insults him. What are we doing here? Coward, coward, cream puff! Armenteros slaps both the President *and* Lavalle. I am a real man. Are you mad? Don't you realize they can hear you? The silence is worse than the voices. There are eyes in that silence. They clasp each other's hands. The light, what happened to the light? Eyes in the darkness. They press one another's hands, and all three weep, very quietly, so as not to startle the phantoms. I'm dying. Who's dying? Valentín, are you there? Tears fall on their hands. Could we just leave? And go where? And the shadows in the garden? Mercenaries. We'd be better off with the Colonel than with the unknown murderer who set this trap for us. They hear eleven o'clock strike. And with the last stroke, the light comes on again. Green light. What's wrong with Oruro? He's sleeping. Or dead. Valentín! Sleeping or dead, he's no use any more. The General is so drunk he says that One-Eye's one eye is staring at him as if it wanted to suck him into eternity, and that he doesn't give a damn. Lavalle confesses in a sweet voice that he's beginning to believe he never was anyone important. They too are going to sleep, or die, sweetly. At least at your burial, General, your horse will be present with all your decorations pinned on its trappings. Your horse will be there. And perhaps weep. It will weep. Lord, Lord, what will become of our poor country? It has to happen someday. Let us drink and await death together. The President has preceded us. They have poisoned him. Long live the President! Lavalle falls on his side upon a Pompeian bench. Green foam dribbles from his lips. Only the General is still standing. Everything is going black. . . . My sword . . . Give me my sword, shitasses! My spyglass! Do not restrain the vigor of my steed! The General tries to whistle, but his breath leaves green spittle on his limp, dyed mustaches. Gaucho! Ah, my faithful campaign companion. Carefully aimed birdshot explodes the balloons clinging to the ceiling. The General claps his hand to his chest. Mercenaries, you have burst the heart of the lion! He thinks he is dying. He can scarcely see the columns or the green light of the chandelier. He sighs, and begging mercy from the god of battles and heroes, he falls. The three men lying on the floor form the most elemental biophysical group we know: men joined together who believe themselves essentially divine and immortal. Those who control the power of the state, and who influence it in their own behalf and that of the groups with which they are allied, to the detriment of other groups. Everything depends on the universal vision the individual has of himself. And of the human race. And of the continent. And of the planet. And of the cosmos. They lie motionless, as if dead. But no blood seeps from the General's chest. Green saliva drools from Lavalle's mouth. Oruro's lips are swollen. No one looks at them because no one wants to. They will have to find new employment to provide for clothing, a sword, sending the son to the Polytech. In their dreams, remote from reality, motionless, without courage, the three follow the trail of the blond man up that stairway that never ends, that never branches. It leads, or can lead, to hell, or to the Milky Way. The bastard son precedes them along that stairway. It would be horrible if it weren't for the escalator. Thus God saves us. The journey will end in a jiffy. But not the agony, right? Someone is speaking, saying things no one understands. It is someone who belongs to the endogroup, but who is, nevertheless, giving orders to the ectogroup; he is dressed in green, with green foam, with green blood, with green light. Take this man to the

jail in Enriquillo. That is the order of this man—fuck him!—
who talks as if he had the echo of a hole in his face. Could it
be One-Eye? No need to tremble, dear Orurito, at this stage of
the journey. That one to the mines in Copiapó. Or if not there,
to the saltpeter mines in Iquique, damn him. And the General
to the island of Zante. The General wants to protest but his
tongue is paralyzed, and, what's worse, his ear is tuned fine,
his arms and legs like those of some doll sprawled in a corner
of an attic. He would at least like to make an obscene gesture,
but he can't. His fingers are like leftover noodles. Take those
two in an ambulance to Puerto Barrios. I want them on a ship
and out of the country tonight! No one will stop you at the
border. They've already been paid off. The *Ghiraldo II* leaves
early this morning for Valparaíso, and three hours later, the
Xanex for Piraeus. Give these letters to the captains. They
know what they're to do. The three men want to yell but the
yells don't come. And my mother will take this other parasite
to Enriquillo, or somewhere near there, for the police dogs to
sniff out. The men are carried away. Lavalle accepts both his
insensibility and his destiny. The only thing he would like to
do is ask Georgiana's forgiveness. She is the fountain and the
unborn child and the word that he seeks. Sleeping birds nest
in her throat. Amen. I shall say again with my silence, amen,
because I cannot imagine her tepid hallelujah. She is my
hearth, my self . . . and no telephone. How, then, can
Georgiana hear in this turning back in time? Perhaps her iron
lung has an ear sensitive to sobs of repentance. Georgiana! To
this late-born tenderness. Georgiana! To this desperate shout
that is leaving to drink and smoke in the taverns of Iquique.
North, Mr. North, dressed as Henry VIII, you will no longer
ride in the last car of the little train that hauls saltpeter. Saltpeter is no longer needed for the fields. The Brazilians make it
synthetically. Nitrate from Chile. Not needed any more. Balmaceda was right, but Copiapó is still where the gold grows.
You're telling me? But what can a lover do without a telephone? Listen, the motors of the refrigerator trucks. I would

170

say to you: Georgiana, I want to carry you in my arms down all the roads of the world, and a little Arab burro will trot behind us so you will have your life-giving machine on the slope where vagabonds pause to eat the grapes and bread of charity. And people will wonder: what is it the burro is carrying, the thing that shines in the sun and breathes like a beached dolphin? The motors start up. The General swears in the funnel of his voyager voice that he will paint all the walls of the horizon with blood. And he sees himself in the distance dressed as a marquise, a marquise who says she doesn't want to breathe any more. The General must hurry, hurry, to prevent that. Marquise! He will offer her the disguise of a princess. But he reads death in her eyes. What the fuck, marquise! But the marquise now has happy eyes, and she raises her skirts. Adultery, always adultery. The General is so embarrassed that he wants as quickly as possible to reach the boat that will carry him to Zante. With the morning breeze, the captains will gain half a day's sailing. Oruro, too, wants to reach port quickly. He feels a constitutional sadness and disillusion. Will it be a sailing ship? All that are left now are clippers carrying cinnamon and lemon. He remembers that in his garden he had a lemon tree whose flowers vibrated in the moonlight. Would this be a moonlit night? He wants to ask the truck driver skating along the yellow path whether he knows the root of the tropical *alibí*. He barely hears the truck driver say that his mother used to make an unguent with *alibí* that cured suppurating wounds. Where are all you strangers going tonight? Safe conduct. Pass. Everything is in order. But no, sir. Can't you see the President is inside here? Look carefully beneath those quartered steers. Godspeed. Now they will have to live without the things they have grown up with. Marquise! The lady no longer has the General's face; now the lady's features are enormous genital organs. Like those he had invented for the Museum of Historical Reproductions in Brasília. A ship's siren sounds its warning to leave. First the ship to Valparaíso. Adiós, comrade. It will be forever. Later the

171

ship for Piraeus will set sail. Adiós, General. In Zante there are good figs and olives. The National Hero is dead. May God rest his memory. This letter is from Miguel Ángel Matalax. Lower the stretcher. Gold or saltpeter. There is also synthetic gold. Economist. The squaring of the human conscience. And then, the General. A letter from One-Eye. And this little runt with a buttonhole for a tchampaka flower thought he could capture One-Eye? The laughter was of a kind borne only on the ocean breeze. At least on his catafalque, he would like to see himself in uniform. But destiny has clothed him in filthy overalls. *La Bellotte* is in Belize. How was my son? They lowered the residue of a President down the hatchway. The chief is great. The President's mouth feels as if it is bridled by a bit, muzzled like a dog's. No more discourses; no more constitutional reforms. But he remembers what he could have written tonight in his office after the aides-de-camp and the palace superintendent had gone. He would have written his theory concerning the outer sector, that is, the sector consisting of the groups that do not accept the status quo or are not even aware one exists; that is, delinquents, sexual perverts, homicidal maniacs, drug addicts and traffickers, as well as the advance- and rearguard elements that do not infringe upon the law because they live off it, promulgating it, applying it, or abolishing it. It had to happen someday. And the nightingale will continue to sing and the corn will continue to thrust its fine beard through the husk. Everything comes, brother, the good and the bad. Every god sooner or later has the floor chewed away beneath him. It's a short walk from Yucatán to Panuco. Not presidents, but kings like Montezuma and Cuauhtémoc, found themselves in hot water. Habeas corpus is a good thing in a land of convicts. But this isn't a land of convicts, sir. This is a land of conscription, proscription, and subornation, which is not the same thing. A land with a president and suborners, which is not the same thing as government by talented men like Grenville, Fox, Erskine, and Grey. The ship is making for the sea. He hears a woman's voice roaring like a puma. Shove off! The captain, with her parrot, Nipe, on her shoulder, stands at the helm. The sailors secure the sails to the yards and scramble up the rigging, preceded by macaques that leap from mast to mast until time for the boat to sail. What one hears on deck resembles a delicate *haiku*. It is the captain singing. A shaft of daylight peers through a rift in the curtain of dawn. Belay the foresail and let out the lugsail. Paulito is removing the President's shoes. And tickling the soles of his feet. But the toes beneath the socks do not react. Paulito laughs and sucks on the socks. The dwarf knows that this motionless man has signed decrees, has commuted death sentences. He has been an important person. One of the macaques has run below to the cabin and is sitting on Oruro's belly. It tears a button from his shirt. Sea air blows through the porthole. It smells of molasses and rum. The day a president smells the mists of the Potomac from the White House for the last time could not be more sad.

Paulito's bellows of laughter are echoed by the choruses of the monkeys.

A President moves toward exile.

At the hour when Indian children run to piss in the stable.

When the Walkers' eyes are heavy with sleep.

When the bell in the Church of the Assumption calls the first mass.

Get up, my son.

Just a minute more.

And dots of light over the banana trees.

One-Eye gave the order by radio, as always. They must be in Bohique early on the morning of the fifteenth, where once and for all they will cut off the retreat of the rural police. The plans were laid for them to continue to the capital and establish a revolutionary government. I'll make them drink out of cockbottles. A cockbottle is used for collecting a bed patient's urine. Shut up, you, we don't want them pelting us with shit. They were happily cleaning their weapons with rags torn from their women's petticoats. Rags that inflamed desire. Ohhhh, baby! The gringo priest had died, and now Trinidad had no one to talk with. Zósimo, too, was six feet under. But more than his swaggering lieutenant, he missed the priest murdered in an ambush. Trinidad still got pleasure from the excitement of the eve of a raid. His soldiers are now called locusts. The teeth of the wind. The Koran refers to hunger in a figurative sense. Trinidad de los Santos, in person, has spoken with One-Eye. El Chino is serving hot corn soup. Trinidad feels cold. From a pole parallel to the ground and supported by two forked branches hang the hindquarters of a zebu steer liberated from a farmer's pasture. The great bonfire sears blood and fat. The men are ready, hungry, waiting for Hilario Macabeo, who is roasting the meat, to give them the signal. They are singing and cleaning their weapons to keep from attacking the meat too soon. Gimme back the rosary of my dear mother, aren't you ashame' to keep everythin', and then run off with another mother? You're one bad woman. Woman, woman, woman, ay, ay, ay, ay! Promote the growth of herds, says a placard half-visible in the light of the bonfire. Retaliation. Raids organized while fire trucks race from one place to another. The government forces have already come out in pursuit of the guerrillas while the reserves guard the railroads. Armenteros's plan. One-Eye said that's what he would do. And he's going to walk into the trap at Bohique. They've also heard that the General has given orders to cast lots and shoot one out of every five men. One out of every five. The guerrillas know it, and laugh, revealing filed teeth, oh, yeah? Five out of every one, not one out of every five. How can they do that, buddy? How about kinfolk, pal? Or don't they count? They laugh, but without real pleasure. Trinidad de los Santos is more serious than ever. By lot. Is that what "your lot in life" means? Trinidad prefers to start a lawsuit, even if it's allowed to die down immediately afterward. The law must never be a game. He shares his thoughts with no one. He's as solitary as a buzzard. The meat! Trinidad didn't taste his morsel. But his men—six hundred and seventy-eight, counting the cook—whip out their knives to cut off the best portions. And hunkering down they eat, each with his salt pouch ready. Salt for beer, for tequila, for meat, for everything. They had some artillery, good supplies, and each man had at least one rifle. Tomorrow they'll rake the government army with their fire. One-Eye has ordered them to keep the boys happy, with a good ration of alcohol in their bellies. And pulque, in small casks, passes from hand to hand. Pass me some, brother. Salt, salt for everything. Bloody, greasy lips. Less than a league away there's a sugar refinery, with a rum distillery nearby. Silverio and the second Macabeo load their saddlebags with meat and climb on the mule. See you later. A happy road, with meat and pulque, going, and on the return, meat, and raw rum—look at the size of them barrels, brother—for everyone. And a grand binge before the big day. Don't put me too near the rutabaga, frien', I got my religion.

You mean, buddy, you can bugger on horseback? And they laugh like crazy as the little mule trots through the empty night. Trinidad de los Santos is making his accounting of the men he has lost to date. Two hundred and eighty-seven, counting dead and wounded. He also lost the three old Vickers cannons with which he'd begun the campaign against Arruza. But God always gives what the Devil takes away, and now he has exactly six hundred and seventy-eight guerrillas—from middling to good—a dozen bazookas, twenty Polish machine guns, and about a thousand Czech guns. At Cerro Tablado the cannons had fallen into the ravine, even though they were mountain pieces. Those who were in charge of the cannons were *not* mountain born; they were plainsmen and coast dwellers. He has the names of all the battles written down in the notebook the priest gave him. Viera fell in Cauquenes, as well as another ten. His own companions killed Botaja after he'd broken both his shinbones. In the capital, Zósimo and twenty-three others. In Cangrejeras, they'd surrounded José Cárceles—the big-shit warden at the jail—and the sentries and hanged them by their private parts. After that, the rattrap they'd fallen into as the gringo priest was coming to meet them. That was the worst. The handwriting is that of Juan de Dios Cesarina. The worst isn't the writing, it's the numbers. Two hundred and thirty-two fell there. Only about eighty managed to escape. So what? Within three weeks all those camped tonight in La Hoza de Cavancha had joined him. Trinidad de los Santos had named several towns before marching on. Ciudad de Castro, Villa Cienfuegos, Guevara Alta. After the mayors crawled out of their hiding places, they would change the names back: Ciudad de San Miguel de la Encina, Villarroel, and Carmen Alto. That's life, I tell you. The pretty banana girl came singing down the hill in San Bertoldo. Bananas, the ripe banana is the bes'. On bad days, Trinidad's heart is heavy with mourning. He feels as if a roll of damp black crepe is coiling inside him, suffocating him. Pathway of hope, I have waited for you all my life, and you're going to be late now that home is so near. His father lay drunk on the newly turned dirt. He remembers the first time he drank a soft drink. It was the day Don Gaspar gave him a copper coin for carrying a message to the woman who sold roses in the plaza. It was tamarind flavor. He could still taste it. There are some things that never fade away, not even after one has drunk other things more clearly seen and harsher to the palate. Rivers of the raw rum that produces small explosions as it trickles down the craw. Always awaiting the pathway of hope. Mamá died and then one night his father threw himself into the ravine, believing he was a royal eagle. His classmates in Brother Anselmo's little parochial school called Trinidad de los Santos their chief. What else can a man be once he's drunk a tamarind soda? As a youth he almost married his neighbor Adosinda, who owned three hogs and a shed, besides the house and seven acres of good land. But Adosinda would have made him pay dear for that property. He preferred the young *cholita* who was willing to follow him barefoot, lugging the kids down many roads. They lived a few years covering their tracks. The roads that do not lead to a man's house are highways, not roads. There was no house. The house of the in-laws was no longer theirs; Trinidad had no taste for it except as a refuge for his family when the bad winds blew. Follow me, my *cholita*, and there, at some bend in the road, you will give birth. And so it was. Trinidad knew how to prepare savory meals. He made a hollow in the ground and lighted a fire. He placed stones over the flames. Upon the stones, beans, potatoes, and other tropical foods. Then, earth. One day everything would once again be as it had been, the straw mats unrolled on the ground and the sarape hanging from a nail at night, which is as God commands. Now, his *cholita* sells fruit at the railroad station at Tumillaca and the little ones help her peddle it in the coaches. One day Trinidad decided that his family should live far from where they were known, and he left them at the same elevation as the train, two miles from the border. Trinidad de los Santos has friends on the other side who would help the *cholita* if something should happen to the guerrilla. The little train on the border is always coming and going, with a half dozen rural police riding in the locomotive. Don Waldo Sirvant had been the stationmaster until he lost the position on suspicion of questionable sympathies. The new stationmaster is a man who has a quarrel with what he calls portable revolution. One day, Don Antoñito, they're going to get you, his good woman, La Pisagua, warns him. But it's the rural police that Don Antoñito indulges. What he doesn't know is that not even the fifteen hundred soldiers of the line guarding the territory from Taltal to San Alejo de Yausa could have saved him from Trinidad de los Santos if it hadn't been for the fact that his *cholita* and kids were to be kept away from trouble. Why call them *montaneros* as if they were gauchos? Why? Why do they fight against the government? Barefoot bastards, don't have any horses, and they're damn near starving. Bastards, that's what they are. And thieves and plunderers and murderers. Look, sir, it isn't a good idea to talk about any man that way. But Don Antoñito didn't curb his tongue. As far as I'm concerned, they're the teeth of the wind, or locusts, as the Koran says, that's what the stationmaster called the guerrillas. Shhh, quiet, even the wind has a sharp ear. Don Antoñito continued to scowl disapprovingly at everyone waiting on the platform. Most of them artisans and day laborers. Until the night Trinidad found himself camped only fifteen leagues from Tumillaca, the night the stationmaster was stopped cold in the middle of a telegram with his jugular vein slit open. His woman discovered him at midnight when she came to bring his coffee. She walked out to the platform carrying his cap by the visor, and quietly announced to those sleeping on their mats awaiting the early morning train: They've slaughtered my Don Antoñito like a pig. Dear God. And no one said a word. They all closed their eyes, and each imagined the death he would have dealt him. About two-thirty, when the rum from the distillery arrived at Trinidad's camp, there was a great hullabaloo; they jeered at those who had made the trip on the mule and now couldn't get off the ground after rolling off their mount. Hey, Macabeo, some stray bullet must have got your brother. Soon the other men were in the same condition. Only Trinidad stayed sober. Not even those on guard stayed clear of the kick of the rum. Huyeeee! Fewer and fewer still had the strength to pass the gourd. Eh, buddy! What kind of man are you? They couldn't even have swallowed water. By three o'clock in the morning you could have captured the whole camp without lifting a finger. Which is what happened at ten minutes to four. When even Trinidad de los Santos's eyes were shut tight. Forty jeeps rolled down the hill, motors killed, brakes off, lights extinguished. Beside each driver, a machine gun manned by two soldiers. One-Eye had showed compassion when he ordered them to close the door of waking with alcohol. Almost in silence rubber tires rolled through the grass. The order was given at exactly three-fifty-two, just when the moon set. Trinidad de los Santos heard metallic sounds. At first he thought it must be the volcano, but that was because he had opened only one eye. By the time he opened the other, it was too late. Simultaneously, eighty headlights flared over figures slipping from sleep to death. Get them drunk, you know? Trinidad shouted orders no one heard, not even the sentries, who were as drunk as the rest. They had to fire to get those who were to die up on their feet. Captain Tovar gave the order, and the machine gunner in the command jeep fired on Trinidad de los Santos. He fell as if he had been struck by a sledge hammer. Then the sentries opened their frightened eyes, but only for an instant, because cars seven, eleven, and twenty-four closed them forever. Hands up, the Colonel's paying for this round, as well as the last. Crouching under cover of thickets, the besieged looked for ways to flee. The machine guns were silent. Shouts of warning and desperation. It was as bright as the festival of Corpus Christi. More than six hundred men stood frozen, creating giants from their own shadows. At that moment General Armenteros's jeep skirted one flank; the command pennant fluttering at its side. Aaaaaatennn . . . chun! Beside the hero, a new aide-de-camp. The aides always change. It depends on the chief. The guerrillas understood that nothing was to be gained from running. Trinidad was dead. If they surrendered, they might find a way out. Hilario Macabeo dropped his gun and walked toward the jeeps. Put down your weapons so the General can see you, and follow him, twenty abreast. There are times it is easier to understand arrogance than submission. An officer walked between the headlights to receive the General's orders. History is full of nights like this. The night of St. Bartholomew, Chiclayo, Oruro, St. Gregory. Law and order. The philosophy of right. Fortunately, the General doesn't order any women and children shot, because there are only men in the ambush of the night of San Blas. This saint must be singled out in world history. Only men. The General gave the order to the officer as soon as the first three rows of twenty were formed. Fire! Forty machine guns can saw down a three-acre forest of eucalyptus trees in twenty minutes. In six minutes they sawed in half the trunks rooted in mothers and fathers; those waiting for any wavering. Fire! It was said in correct and proper Spanish. The officer heard it as Spanish with the accent of the sponge coast. The General received the order by radio, in Spanish learned with only one eye. Godspeed, General, and may those who have just died forgive you. How does your finger feel, buddy, after squeezing the trigger? Forty index fingers bent forever like a worm on a fishhook. They loaded the lifeless body of Trinidad de los Santos onto a truck that had followed the General's jeep. He was no longer missing. It would be like delivering the paws of the wolf. By radio the General announced to One-Eye that there were no more guerrillas left in the country and that the following morning he would enter the capital carrying the body of Trinidad de los Santos. One-Eye called the political editor of the newspaper *Patria* and gave him the news. They reset the first edition. Trinidad de los Santos dead. General

Armenteros, National Hero, wipes out Trinidad and the six hundred and seventy-eight men of his guerrilla gang in a masterly encircling operation at Hoza de Cavancha, near Bohique. It is the night of San Blas, and the day about to dawn over the city, the country, and the sea. Fatherland, oh, Fatherland, with the death of Trinidad de los Santos! The Walkers came to Colonel Arruza's quarters to give him the news. He didn't bathe naked on the beach that morning, or awaken Virginia with a kiss. He had to call the Secretary of Information so the radio and television stations could immediately announce that by midmorning General Armenteros would be entering the city along Diagonal and Twenty-third, carrying the body of Trinidad de los Santos. It is hoped that everyone in that vicinity will come to cheer the Hero's passage through the streets of the capital. By the time the city began to smell roasting coffee, the news was everywhere.

And the two, the living and the dead, passed between small flags waved by the children from the public schools.

Women wept. Women weep over anything.

Men whose trunks were not sawed in half, sturdy as the royal palms in the parks, watch the retinue pass by, saying little.

President Oruro commented in the palace: "I want never again to hear of these sad and meaningless insurrections. And in the event that it does happen again, I want the extermination operation to be carried out without the government's knowledge." The President speaks like a man from Bogotá.

His Excellency Señor Valentín Oruro was so moved he forgot to embrace Armenteros.

During the afternoon, Red Cross trucks carried off the bodies of the guerrillas who'd been on their way to Bohique, once they'd had a drink 'er two, yaahhhhh.

Mangy buzzards in the heavens.

Fruit, fruit, guava and soursop, tasty and cheap! When they came to the border that afternoon of San Blas, the kids and the *cholita* didn't get off the train. They went to find refuge on the other side. Their weeping was hidden, well hidden, deep in their hearts, where the rural police would never discover it.

There are thirty thousand species of classified plants in America. And many more in regions of the continent still difficult to reach. At first glance it seems to be a land like any other, but it isn't. America is as different from Europe as a man from his neighbors. For example, in the depths of his being Colonel Arruza has more than three hundred kinds of good and bad reactions. Some resemble the reactions of other men—as the sage in the Alps resembles that in the Andes. One reaction, however, has specific and well-defined characteristics. Why does he smile when others are weeping? Why does he feel a strange uneasiness when everything is clear and resplendent on the national scene? Oruro has called him this morning to consult with him on the decree confiscating properties of more than ten thousand acres for division among the peasants. The idea came from the Minister of the Interior, Zorobabel Lazcano. The President explained to him that there was some slight opposition on the part of the Minister of Justice, Lauro Arístides Barbosa, as well as Lavalle's previously known reservations, but the law will go to the parliament with all the weight of the executive behind it. The Colonel also spoke with Claudio Hinojosa Hernández, President of the Chamber of Deputies; everything will be in order so the decree can become law.

Thirty-six votes in opposition, and a hundred and nine for the majority. Following the massacre of the rebel group, the country has need of a radically left-wing law. The newspapers have already begun the campaign eulogizing the intrepid efforts of the government to establish economic stability in the agricultural sector. Spirits are inflamed when two days later, as he is leaving the ministry, Zorobabel Lazcano falls victim to assassination. Sweet tuberose, ripe mangoes, coconut candies. *Patria* headlined the death of the Friend of the Indian. Weeping, the widow says that Zorito—as she called him in private—always referred to them as *his* Indians. Zorobabel leaves seven books on the aborigine of this beautiful land, before and after Columbus. *Studies on Our Ethnography, The Peonage of the Native Indian, The Class Structure of the National Indian, Anthropology of the Contemporary Maya, Toward a Structured Rural Reform, Matriarchy and Virginity in Tebilango, Economic and Social Integration of the Native.* This last work, in press. The murder is one further reason for the Chamber of Deputies to speed up discussion of the law on compulsory expropriation. The day they bury the Brother of the Indians—so Lavalle himself referred to him in the funeral eulogy—the deputies who attended the burial, factions and party colors temporarily abandoned, returned as a group to the parliament, and when Don Claudio Hinojosa Hernández, opened the session in an emotional voice, the deputy from the left, Dr. Darío Rodríguez Barros, presented a motion calling for an immediate vote on what from that time would be known as the Zorobabel law. The result was one hundred and forty-three votes in favor, and two abstentions: that of Rodríguez Barros himself, and that of Lavalle, who thereby expressed his reservations about the third paragraph of Article Twenty-four. The common people know that Colonel Arruza is behind all of it—the good and the bad. You cannot deceive the people. Let *Patria* and *El País* say what they will. For if Arruza is behind the gun that has killed hundreds of citizens, he is also behind the pen that drew up the expropriation law, and the laws for the battle against illiteracy and for tariffs, and many other laws to improve the country. Furthermore, he always keeps a little strongbox

(that's what he calls it) from which he dispenses, with a prodi-
gal hand, moneys to meet special needs. Oh, how can I thank
you, Colonel, and may it be returned threefold. The people
like him, but nevertheless, his uneasiness scarcely allows him
a tranquil moment. Virginia is sleeping, her hands open,
warm and soft like the magnolias of her breasts. The Minister
of the Army and Navy has said of the first lady, in private,
that she seems to have recovered her hymen. Rear Admiral
Fowler, whose origin is Scottish, has always felt a profound
admiration for Virginia Pfandl Andrade. If it hadn't been for
Arruza, they would have been married in the Church of Santa
Coloma, which served as parish for the German's and the
Scot's haciendas. Fathers and children. Emigrants with two
generations on terra firma. Rural workers should have co-ops,
social institutions, associations for women and children, and
other community and local groups. So Zorobabel Lazcano had
believed. But he is dead. There are curious names in this geography. Another is Nephtalí. Name of orphans and poor.
One of those who aspire to be rich in order to wear patent-
leather shoes, and who long for winter in order to show off a
nutria coat, even if it means sizzling in the heat. In La Criolla,
Arruza was trying to blow away the straws of anguish moistly
clinging to his heart. God save me. Didn't everyone know he
was to be feared when his eyes were filled with revenge and
pulque? Someone had said, in the language of parliamentary
discourse, that he was wicked and sinister. Everyone knows
about the eyes of a man of mixed blood at the critical moment
of metamorphosis. I tell you, my friend, it bothers me so much
that I can hardly bear it. Some men even become criminal
judges, a very important charge, and they have to keep a cool
head. I am sad, my friend, so sad it seems I can almost see him
lying there dead among the candles. But then he laughed.
They were looking everywhere for One-Eye. They hadn't
posted a proclamation on every street corner, but everyone
knew they were looking for a certain One-Eye. Anyone missing an eye presented himself before the authorities to be iden-

tified and to establish that his conduct was beyond reproach. Someone threw a rock at me when I was a kid! Drink after drink was brought to the Colonel's table. The Walker named Drummond superintended their preparation—Chief Cup-bearer Walker—not because of any poison the bartender might purposely drop in, but to see that no spittle carelessly fell into the glass. You're telling me? It closes at two, at three, at whatever hour Arruza's uneasiness may have dissipated following massive transfusions of María la Sanguinaria. That bitch must be from group zero. The bartender had to grit his teeth to keep from insulting her fucking mother. Queen Mary and Raleigh. Give me a cigarette, you stupid shitass. Raleigh. A coupon on every package. What gift could she give him? The Colonel smokes without pleasure. No taste. But he exhales smoke through his nostrils. A telephone! Feliciano Correa is the pudgy Walker who plugs in and serves up the apparatus. Armenteros's number. 64 53 82. Parley or not? General . . . Colonel . . . Why're you talking so funny, man? My teeth are soak-ing, Colonel. Talk, Bloody Mary, talk, talk. What the shit is the filthy swine saying? The General isn't listening. In his imagi-nation Phineas Armenteros is lying on Lavinia's breasts and feeling the pain of losing the pleasure of surprising her in flagrant adultery. With whom? Who would the lucky one be? General . . . Colonel . . . What about One-Eye? Phineas Ar-menteros could forgive everything except being deceived by the son of Melina. What the hell! Goddammit, don't you hear me? Oh, yes, One-Eye! Do you think that six hundred and seventy-seven men, *and* Trinidad de los Santos, are a small matter? One-Eye is the one that matters. Lavinia is afflicted with a full-blown sexual appetite. She likes young men. Phineas is trying to remember all the Greek adolescents in the vicinity of the port. The ones on Clay, Crossman, Iberville, and Wells streets. Phineas's judgment is colored by his own weaknesses. General . . . Colonel . . . Well, I want to tell you, Colonel, that I think One-Eye is a matter for the police, not the army. My men aren't in any mood to be chasing after lawbreakers, you hear me? The Colonel can't believe it's Armenteros speaking. Say that again, tin medals! And listens as it is repeated three times. What the fuck! Another Bloody Mary. Lavinia, Lavinia! We'll buy a little house and our own sponge beds in Tarpon Springs. The Colonel throws the telephone to the floor. He has waited several minutes for an explanation and heard nothing but sighs. Bring me another telephone. Virginia. She isn't home, Colonel. He'd left her sleeping like a dead woman. He could have strangled her, but hadn't. The bartender has a face like Iago. What are you laughing at, stupid? He could easily have killed her in one of those moments when love is hysterical with hatred. He leaps up and staggers out to the street. He is followed by two dogs and his Walkers. The siren on his automobile shatters the city's sleep. The poor whores live to the north. The rich whores to the south. To the east are rows of small huts purveying sweet-potato candies, chitlins, and gambling. And to the west lie the jail and the barracks. Any of the houses could be the brothel where Virginia is being pronged. Open up! Men in undershorts, or naked, their ecstasy interrupted in its flower. There's no one here but the Indian girls, Colonel, and clients. No one-eyed man. Open up! Oh, my God! Open up . . . open up . . . open up . . . ! Dogs are barking. Five o'clock in the morning finds the Colonel in the middle of the municipal park beside the peacocks' cage, after yelling at the doors of more than thirty brothels and cheap hotels. Mixed jealousy and hatred; Virginia is surely playing the mare to some other stud. He can smell the coming day in every plant. He's tired. He'd like to have a cup of coffee with Oruro. Tomorrow he'll make that bastard of a General remember his manners. The President goes to bed with the dawn, when the carts of fruits and vegetables are beginning to arrive in the market plaza. Peddlers are clustered around the little old woman preparing coffee over glowing coals of dried manure. The chiaroscuro enhances the Colonel's anonymity. He skirts the cathedral steps, with their usual sprinkling of beggars. The great nail-studded doors will open when the bells sound the first mass. The Colonel surreptitiously crosses himself. He walks through Sin Alley toward Constitution Square, where the Presidential Palace is located. Officer of the guard! Heel clicks, salutes. The President is not, shall we say, feeling well. In his cell in Enriquillo, Sinfonías had become accustomed to reading very late and to getting up in the middle of the morning. Just because he's President he's not going to change his habits now. That leaves only Lavalle. It's the last hope of a sad day now being nibbled at by another, newer, one. Lavalle lives in Santa Catalina, a residential district with its own branch of Lord & Taylor. Lavalle has two Great Danes that bark at the Colonel's two dogs. They sniff each other's anuses. The Colonel doesn't find this strange. Lavalle is jogging around the garden in his sweatsuit. It's the hour for his calisthenics. The Colonel is too exhausted to start a conversation. He falls into a hammock. Spine sagging, he sleeps. When he awakens, he sees Georgiana. Entombed in her iron lung, she is as immobile as a sphinx. Lavalle's wife has returned. There is a murmur of aristocratic birds in the trees. I watched you sleep. Lavalle isn't here.

You were sleeping as if for a few hours you had decided to commit suicide. I was afraid to go home and find my house empty. We always come back, Colonel. Or almost always; we get lonely after the other man leaves. A servant brings coffee. The Colonel drinks three cups. We were happy, in our way, when she was going her way and I, mine. What could I do? Can you imagine a man named Arruza accepting the plural in place of the singular? Have you heard of One-Eye, Georgiana?

Georgiana looks at her hands.

A river flows between them.

People don't know.

Don't think.

As if guavas had eyes, that's the way the quetzal with the filthy feathers was examined that morning. There was a flavor of brown sugar and cinnamon in every hello and in all the godspeeds. They speak of the goose's keen sense of direction, but the people, too, know when they get up which way the wind is blowing. Good morning, friend, leave the flowerpots tipped so they'll fall on the bastard. Can you go to the market? Why yes, of course. If you bring me a tender little pig's heart, I'll thank you for it. Watch that I don't get it muddled. You, muddled? Be right back. Godspeed! Rubén, the one from León, with his cortege of lances and standards. They all pass by, good fortune, even those studied in Oxford, with their own statue and its ever-present dove. But León is not from this land. Because he has adolescent eczema, it seems the same thing, but it isn't. Here the oranges are called *chinas*, like pretty young girls. And a mulatto can shoot down a senator's rising star simply by watching to see how his shoes get muddied. It has ever been thus, and it seems as if everything is continuing normally until such time as the truth is known. It is a form of *relax*, as they say in the north. *Take it easy*. The *relajo*, as the Cubans call it, is a loosening of a man's moral galluses or suspenders. And he's ordering me out of the country, Captain! Are you sure he said that? General Armenteros called Captain Israel Melo, and shouted: He's ordering me out of the country! That is what by midmorning was being tested in every smile. What's happened, friend? What happened is what's happening, this is no land of chattering parrots. They laugh with a laughter that tries to be fresh. Did you hear me, blood? Highballs slide from one end of bars to the other. And in the waiting, the dice dance without respect to kings or queens. Nobody works today, it's Wednesday. What's so special about Wednesday? It's the day of the god Woden, and Woden's a translation from *dies Mercurii*. Here everything is commercial. They make commerce out of everything. And Mercury is the god. They place women in the position of Mercury to help them give birth. And one thing that's for sure is that it's the cosmic dust found between Mercury and the sun that gives the bananas that special flavor. And what if it were Tuesday, the day of the Teutonic god identified with Mars? Then it would be *dies Martis,* the day of the war god. What war, you bastard? To the man just arriving they tell the story of Monday, the moon day. What're you going to have to drink? Anything with a kick. The bars take orders for food. No one should go home to lunch when the country is on the brink of a crisis. Biscuits, hard-boiled eggs, tamales, shrimp and pork enchiladas—don't get that mixed up, bartender—avocado salad and waffles. The radio is turned on. Nothing from the announcers. Patriotic music. Soap operas are being shown on television, but they may be interrupted at any moment to announce that a hole has been drilled in the heart of stone. Or, "He's ordering me out of the country" might mean that, too. Or before Melo arrives, you might hear the sound of a shot. Balmaceda and Vargas did that. National leaders, all with different styles, different actions. The television program has been interrupted three times. Circumstances beyond our control. Don't leave me now. Not even Catareo is moving from the spot. Finally, some news on the radio. Bartolomé is pitching a no-hitter in the Caribbean League. Another star lured away by the Yankees. Attention, attention, General Armenteros, the National Hero, is speaking. Captain Israel Melo y Ortiz, carrying out my instructions went this morning at nine-eighteen A.M. to the residence of Colonel Arruza carrying an ultimatum from the nation's armed forces. The document granted Señor Arruza four hours to leave the country or, failing that, to surrender himself for expeditious trial for treason, extortion of the legitimate powers established by the Constitution of 1940, usurpation of power, subornation and mass perjury, depletion of the public treasury, murder and concealment of the body, etc. The head of the Colonel's guard, Major Rengifo, along with all his men, has placed himself on the side of our cause, and he accompanied Captain Melo as he entered Colonel Arruza's office to inform him that his only alternative was to accept what the country so generously offered, a helicopter and four hours to pack his personal belongings. The Colonel has accepted the ultimatum, and preparations are now being made for his exile. Yahooooo! Time to pay up . . . bartender! People in the streets, shouting and embracing one another with hysterical laughter and tears. Nineteen years of dictatorship liquidated with a simple signature. It costs so little to be happy, buddy? It's difficult to believe, with posters bearing the handsome figure of the Colonel still present on every wall and street corner. Women always have the most nerve. One woman rips the paper face, another, the uniform. And the Colonel displays his mortar and adobe guts. Oh, God, this is as great a moment as Independence! Chitlins and pork and biscuits, with plenty of tortillas for everyone. Where did they come from? Who the hell knows? And oceans of beer and pulque and rum and pisco and tequila. Salt, brother. I called him a fucking sonofabitch. . . . Hahahahaha! I called him a sonofabitch. . . . Gimme another snort of that *chicha*, buddy. If you don't believe it . . . Careful, here comes the Colonel! You don't scare my ass with that crap. If he shows up here I'll murder 'im! Hahahaha! They sing the anthem. Two helicopters fly over very low, skimming the terraces, and men flock out of the bars to raise clenched fists to the sky. Call him a sonofabitch now that he can't hear you over the engines. Knives appear and ventilate bellies filled with alcohol and chili pepper. Is that the first death? Who knows what's going on in the country, in all the little towns. They say there are several dead by the middle of the afternoon. But those bastards don't count. It will rain tomorrow and the water will carry everything away down the drains. They ripped open each other's bellies to see who hated the old cuckold the most. You're telling me? A lot happened in four hours. There in the late afternoon they began to load trunks and suitcases up the ramp of the helicopter. Blood, blood! No one wants to be the first to make a fool of himself. Blood, for what? The Colonel climbs into the helicopter with his hands in his pockets, so he won't have to shake anybody's hand. He stares at the Judases, and his smile is an Indian's smile, a smile learned from having seen it so often. And just when they're about to close the door of the helicopter, he hands a letter to Rengifo. You'll see, they'll spoil everything I've done, Major. You'll see. It's just a question of time. The letter is for the President. And he is borne off into the air, alone, without Virginia. Men like him always have a room reserved in some Hilton.

Most excellent señor:

This letter may lead you to believe that you find yourself the head of a state different from the one I ran for twenty years. Before October 3, 1949, all there was of what I leave behind me was a geographic name people believed to be a sovereign country, and all the symbols that accompanied our Independence. Possibly in these moments you and the gang of bums backing you will kid yourselves that you are speaking in behalf of our people. Seventy-five point four percent of our people are Indians, or people of mixed blood who can't count and don't count to us. The rest of us are sons or grandsons of people who came from some other land and who try to make the world believe we would give our lives for the Maya culture. The truth is that all we do is rustle human cattle. Using the symbols of Independence, and all that shit, we've arranged things so that others cut our bananas, and our cane, and harvest our coffee. And 11.6 percent of us lead a comfortable life. There was nothing nineteen years ago, there is nothing now that I am leaving and there will be nothing in the future, until this land is again the land it was before Columbus. What I want to make clear to you in these hours of defections and back-door heroism is that the only free man in this country is leaving; legally selected by me and recognized by all the rest of you. I say this loud and clear, I was IT in this beautiful and unfortunate land—and all of you were putty in my hands. Have no illusions, you didn't take me by surprise. I'm not leaving because you were cleverer than I was. To polish off all the ringleaders, this time around, I would simply have invited them to my house for dinner. The next day, there would be new lackeys. I'm leaving now because the woman I love betrayed me. Yes, just like in the tangos. Damn her to bloody hell! But this isn't a simple betrayal of the cunt, no, it is a basic betrayal. You and your friends can't understand what it means to plummet into empty space because the floor has been sawed out from under you in your own home. But I don't give a damn. The only thing a man like me had missed was the pleasure of feeling himself betrayed. Someone predicted to me that one day one of the many sons I had sowed through the world would come to betray me. The only thing I regret is that I didn't punch a hole in the face of the medallion. If you have courage, circulate this letter as an official document in *El Listín*. Good-bye, then, and enjoy it there in your cypress-barred prison. I believe I've earned my retirement and my freedom. I can buy everything I like to eat in New York, at Casa Moneo. Everything else is a question of imagination. Bourbon heals anything but a hernia. As I fly for the last time over these lands, I will see the coconut and coffee and chicle and cane fields and banana, all draped in Indian mourning. So it was in the beginning, and make no mistake, you'll never change it. A tree casts only as much shade as it has leaves, let the economists say what they want. The fruit of the tree belongs to everyone. This was the state established by Mother

Nature and, to a degree, I accepted her mandate. I wanted power and I had it. Though it may sound strange, I tried to divide the fruit among everyone. I must give you one last confidence. I laugh at the constitution and state. Yes, I have to laugh at all the shit that serves only to try man's patience. I used every last thing men created to enslave themselves. To enslave a man who enslaves others is no crime. The world will have to put on a new face. The hippies or the Indians, perhaps the Chinese, or even the Negroes, must undertake that task. Someday we shall talk about these and other things in your exile; that, too, will come in time. It's lovely to talk about one's past mistakes beneath a foreign palm tree. We'll be seeing one another, soon.

Colonel Arruza

Children want to sleep through even the most solemn patriotic commemorations. Only the grownups stay awake, recounting their exploits and their Pittsburghs. They change the names. Even the man selling sweet-potato candies wants to be a hero. As night arrives, General Armenteros again appears on the screen. With him are the President and his cabinet. I am here to inform the people that as long as I live, no military man will ever become President. I am asking President Oruro—and I cannot refrain from calling him the exemplar of patriots—to make a sacrifice at this moment of joy and supreme decision. We shall need him until the time we hold free elections, the twenty-third of next month. For a people born in the womb of Mother Liberty there is nothing like the word election. Men weep. There is little alcohol left in the cantinas. As they rock their children, women sigh. Sleep, my son, sleep, your father is with the men in the cantina, and won't be home tonight. Will he come home tomorrow, mommy? On the radio they've reported that there were several deaths today: September 3. Dates, dates. There's talk of a convention of the Liberal Party, with Don Mateíto presiding. But Don Mateíto died in 1953, my friend. Well, his son, then. Jackal face? So you don't like his looks, my friend. Don Mateíto, Jr., has a right na-ice smile. What the shit you talkin' about? You're a foreigner. I'm a *tico*. And since when is a Costa Rican a foreigner in a sister country of the isthmus? My country and yours are the two wings of the same bird. The same garbage, my friend, the very same. And so it begins. And one more man will not live to see the conclusion of the national fiesta. While our bird flew away in a helicopter. What difference does it make whether it was Sikorsky or La Cierva or Brennan who invented the escape vehicle? Those three cocks are damn well dead. What matters is that our prey escaped us while they were holding smelling salts to our noses. A whiff of ammonia'll take care of that hangover. The blades flatten the Walkers' dignity—dignity until yesterday—and they hit the ground. They bury their miserable bulldog faces in cow dung. Dogs for another master they'll be, won't they, Your Worship? Rengifo wants to be considered a national hero, and makes the rounds of all the bars, after describing the Colonel's last minutes to the country over television. Rengifo has a split ear, like the pirates of Tortugas Bay. Rengifo was first a bouncer in Las Vegas. It wasn't in Nevada, however, that he lost his earlobe. That happened in Goa, another place where they play rough. Keep your nose out of this business, understand? A Malayan knows about pounding ears. He says his earlobe is in the Arabian Sea. Go to hell! From Goa to Daman, from Daman to Diu. Not true, Portuguese. And the Portuguese responded in his tongue: Those fuckers from Cambay would eat out your ass. Doesn't matter. The world is round, and he came to Central America through the canal. And drinks and sweats and tries to smile when someone touches him familiarly on the shoulder.

He left, yes sir; it was go or be killed. And since they had to kill someone, they cut Rengifo's heart in two, there when the day began to dawn.

Filled with emotion, they sing. Fatherland. You're an Indian; don't deny it. Look at your teeth in the mirror, and you'll see they shine like a shark's. The Indian smiles, and shines the man's shoes. What day is today? What night? The day of Mercury. The day of commerce. Tomorrow will be the day of Jupiter. He had the best of the world: the air and the sky. The shoeshine boy doesn't care what day it is or what time, or about any gods that come from far away. Ix Chel, Itzamná, those are the gods. And Jesus God. The katuns computed dates up to fifteen hundred and sixty. After that, buddy, I don't want to hear, I don't remember. They count two hundred and sixty days, depending on the short or the long count. Twenty days for each month, and thirteen months. Why talk to me 'bout Thursday or Sunday? I count from one to twenty, beginning with udder and ending with king. What do you call the day? Well, I call it *kin*. And he continues to polish the shoes. Shoeshine, some call it. Pitcher, vixen, monkey, jaguar, serpent, earthquake, storm cloud. One dreams, one tries to pick the good numbers, and then plays a few pesos. When do you play twelve? When I get drunk and fall downstairs. Always whatever's natural. Always, boss.

The last thing the Colonel saw from the air, like Jupiter, Zeus, father and lover of the same cunt, was the purple peruke of the volcano. And it saddened him because you can't buy a volcano at Casa Moneo, like you can hearts of palm or jalapeño peppers. Coffee, sir? The servant is smiling, or weeping. He's an Indian. It would be sweet if the volcano would swallow the two-headed bird. The Indian could easily kill him. Yes, bring me coffee. Colonel, sir, I feel bad about it. And in silence he goes astern to the kitchenette. He stands there. The last light falls on his khaki uniform. He resembles the sphinx of Zsantl. The Colonel almost screams. For a moment he believes the servant is a chicle tree they're carrying to the Kingdom of Wrigley. If he were someone important, he would shout. He would hang the first bastard gringo from a ceiba tree for the sins of his father. But he isn't "someone" any more. He feels like crying. Sir. Get the fuck out of here. He slowly sips the coffee. The purple of God is fading into the distance behind him.

And below, the sea is tucking itself into foamy sheets to sleep. Good night.

A different country.

A different soil.

Passport?

He has none. A number. Laissez-passer.

A functionary of another foreign ministry accompanies him to the airplane for Miami.

He has to wait for his luggage to be transferred. The Indian stands close beside the Colonel. What's your name? Macario Maravé. Do you have a wife? They call her Eleana. How many kids? Six, at least. The Colonel has not been able to make the entire country happy, but this one Indian and his family can still be happy. He takes out a sheaf of American bills, he cuts them in half—always halved bills in America—and whispers a few words in Maravé's ear. The Indian smiles and kisses the hands of the traveler who now walks lightly toward the steps of the plane for Miami.

No one empties his rifle at the receding figure.

The day of Jupiter begins.

n the first century of our era (anno Domini) there were two hundred and fifty million inhabitants in the world. How did they count them? There were people living in Morros, but Cabral was still to come. Amazonia knew nothing of Orellana, nor the Tagalogs of Legazpi, the Indians of the Hudson knew nothing of that company apportioning dividends in England, and the Negroes of Ujiji had never seen a man like Livingstone. If this is true, then in any Brazilian or Spanish American or Caribbean hut, in any igloo or tent, the heart of an unknown and hungry man may be hidden, closely watched by the scribes who interpret the law, by the tax collector who nibbles at guts already squeezed dry, by the sentinel of order, or by the veterinarian who will shave the hair of his sideburns as they pull his useless teeth. Mountains to flee to. That's all I want, buddy, nothing more. I'd like to go to a land where man has never set foot. You still have the Moon; or go to Mars, old man, on the next rocket. America, Africa, Oceania, Asia, they've all still got virgin land. You're pretty out-of-date, brother. There's nothing virgin left on Earth, the horizons of illusion must be shattered, that's why we have the big operators, the guys always chasing after your sister. Once someone tried to be indigenous and unique. Be versatile. Dr. Colmenares made it very clear in the symposium. Progress, gentlemen, is born of hybridization. *Mula, mulae.* And wrap 'er up in a tamale, what the hell do I care. To walk through the jungle alone is to disintegrate, cousin, at a time when everything is moving toward integration. Of course ther're so many who walk that path that you can figure they're not alone any more. Or are they? A guerrilla? No, my friend, That doesn't do any good. You join and they hunt you. The best thing is solitary revolution. What happens is that you become a phanerogam, "one having visible reproductive parts," and there you are with your balls hanging out. The unseen revolution. The yes-man on one hand, and fires on the campus in the late afternoon. Without realizing it—it's 1968—twenty years ago revolutionaries were hatching in the wombs of millions of mothers, fattened on pasteurized milk and proteins from spring lamb. Mothers don't believe it. I carried Karl Marx in my belly. We have to learn from the rich classes of the industrialized countries, my friend. But what are you after with all your philosophy? The jungle has only one color at night, and cries of animal weeping. Over this rough ground one might reach the city of the sun, led by the voice of Campanella. And settle there? You don't have to settle down because you live in America. The fathers of Belarmino also have their city of the sun, south of the Inca empire. Have you seen Don Camilo Torres? I don't know, is he the one who looked like a dead man, sir? If the church is a long way from town, Camilo, the ghost of Padre Camilo, searches for the town and asks a man chewing, and expectorating black spit: How may I serve Your Mercy, my brother? *Mensaje* is a popular journal because the man who looks after the chicks doesn't know how to read. Have you seen a tall man wearing glasses, named Veckmans? No, sir, but my mother says that someone kissed her hand on the path from the cane field. Well, yes, perhaps that was the very man, demonstrating his love for a different neighbor. In the tavern they didn't know him and served him a mixture of beans and rice and green bananas. And he ate it, smiling, because the others were eating it. Wisdom comes with the years. And egotism. The man who isn't a revolutionary when he's twenty is an idiot. But he's also an idiot if he's still a revolutionary at fifty. Someone already said that, love. The man who's tired of chronic opportunists—when he's between twenty and fifty—moves to a flat mountain covered with thickets of broom that sweep away his grudges. Do you think you invented revolution, wise guy? But there's always someone who believes he's looking for something different, and that children can be born with their boots on and never have to suffer scarlet fever. What's your name? My name doesn't matter, or what I've studied. Where did you go to school, man? After all's said and done, you don't know anything anyway. Look, it's worth a lot to have read the modern writers who used to gather in Auer's Keller in Buenos Aires. Yeah? Who'll be a modernist tomorrow? The bartender has crossed eyes, and at night he dreams of dogs with diabolical powers. What the fuck, doesn't anybody talk around here? With rods of sun the heat seals the lips of yesterday's insurgents. Silent lips that open only for beer and salt. You sweat so much here you have to ease the kidneys. The protruding bellies of a few and the flaccid figures of the rest are imposed on the dank shadow of the cantina. A peons' tavern. My heart is bursting, brothers, and bleeding for you. He could have added, you fucking sonofabitching brothers, and nothing would have happened. He would *like* to say fucking sonofabitch, but the cross-eyed bartender seems to be listening a little too closely. A bartender with a big knife and gold teeth, a friend to the rural police. My God, nobody cares that the Colonel has been out of the country for a month and that they're holding elections for the Senate. It never occurs to him to say that things are going to the dogs, buddy, and that they're ruining everything. The man who's going to be a senator of the Republic has ears behind every ceiba tree, and drinking his health in pulque and making him a big shot is better than ending up in jail. Why do flames come in the night while some sleep? With the light, angels' heads appeared suddenly, wearing Spanish shakos and sporting limp mustaches, angels flying like those on their way to collect souls from purgatory. The country is worse off. The country is better off, don't talk horseshit. Depends on how you look at it. I guess so, yes. The radio and television carry speeches and harangues from the capital. Our best example is Japan. From raw silk—before the Meiji—in a hundred years they progressed to hovercraft. Goddammit! Work, effort, rice, fish. Doesn't it shame you that Japan has three hundred and forty-six universities and we have only three, staffed by moth-eaten professors who teach Roman law, Maya paleontology, and American constitutionalism, and all that crap? The black ships of Commodore Perry also visited our shores, and so what, so what, so what? Oruro is speaking, and Armenteros and Lavalle and a new and dazzling national figure: Miguel Ángel Matalax, born in Tlextanango. His baptismal certificate is in the parish church of San Gedeón. Camilo Torres passed through without reading it. The parish priest confirmed the newborn, the godfathers, and the holy water. The assistant parish priest is Don Miguel María del Carpio y Hannin. On all the walls, the candidate for senator has plastered his mug over the rags of a former Colonel. Who remembers? Who're you votin' for, Ruperto? Ay, pal. Did you just fall out of the mango tree, or've you been in the mud for a long time? Those who walk the roads alone with a secret and genuine revolution in their bedrolls, dare to suggest certain things at night in the *pulquerías* badly illuminated by kerosene lamps. They say that man is the be-all and the end-all, they drink a drink and lower their eyes, coughing quietly. There's a light at the end of the tunnel, and a man who does ugly things when he pisses. A lamp beneath which one awaits a little girl with percale sadness. Tango of Troilus. Modernists? Hey, redfoot, move over, you're makin' waves. And El Corro's father. What about him? Dealing with people that stare but don't talk, a man can't whet his ideas. Instead, the rebel feels like a Manila gamecock. Like Japan in the era of raw silk. Thus is history written. The caste of warriors, and those of farmers and of scribes. This is where I get off, brother. All this adds up to an impoverished agrarian state. A state sustained by bone and callus. And the Pfandls, the Veguillas, the Ramírez-Vásquezes, the Sterling-Díazes, the United Fruit, the Gómez Tuñóns and the Goldsteins? Those guys pluck the low-hanging mangoes, sweetheart. But how do you bring in the people who watch from beneath wide-brimmed sombreros, saying nothing? If you try it, comrade, you'll be sticking your finger in the fan, and that hurts. I believe in int'gration, yes sir, and int'gration—I dunno quite what that is—but int'gration's got to be damn good for Central America. The Tico-ricans, Nicaraguans, the Traco-durans, Chapi-malans . . . Ah yes, boss, my sons'll live to see it! Senator Matalax makes his debut, as senator, in the bed of Virginia Pfandl Andrade de Arruza. He has had so much to drink that for the first time her flesh makes him laugh, and he makes jokes, polishing his fingernails on the best-known pubic hair in the region. A senator with a glass eye. And one eye filled with the kind of tenderness with which a Jew inspects clothing destined for Arab refugees from Palestine. Why are you laughing, tell me, why are you laughing? And she sits astride him and bites his shoulders and neck. Is there anything funnier than a jealous woman with her rump in the air? Sure, buddy, you say that 'cause you're not the one underneath. Bésame, bésame mucho, como si fuera esta noche la última vez. Hahahaha! We're going to be like Japan. The senator laughs at the shit they're broadcasting over the radio to the whole country. You hear me? This man laughs about everything. He shouldn't. Now that he's senator he ought to feel the gravity of the public charge. Major General Anastasio Somoza Debayle—hell, the newspapers say it—the last President of a family that ruled the destinies of Nicaragua for thirty years is not a happy man. He feels frustrated—don't laugh—and all Nicaragua and Central America is aware of that frustration. Then what's a loafer, a newcomer, a one-eyed man who's only been senator since four o'clock, laughing about? Of course it's not a question of the same country or of the same genes. What's happening is that Major General Anastasio Somoza Debayle is aware of the sentiments of his people. That's why he isn't laughing. They said in Matagalpa that he had just read the same speech he delivered one year before in the same hotel, and his eyes had filled with tears because he'd been unable to effect the promises he made then. Oh, poor dear, and not even Doña Hope could comfort him! And still, Senator Miguel Ángel Matalax, with a mountain of beautiful and gracile flesh seated on his prick, is laughing like a maniac. I assure you, doctor, there isn't much more to see in this country. Pretty daring. He missed the meeting of presidents in El Salvador, In July 1968. He missed the whole thing, and he's laughing. Johnson was there. Viva! Viva! Viva! Viva! Food was served to everyone, with *mole* sauce. Food and drink for all the employees of Central America, God save us. And afterward, Major General Anastasio Somoza Debayle bade farewell to five thousand bureaucrats—among them Don Eladio Carmona y Díaz, who functioned as wet nurse in the Municipal Maternity Hospital—and although there were many sharks left, the public exchequer was considerably lighter on that count. The shark being a creature of the ocean depths whose danger is equaled only by that of the barracuda. By analogy, in certain regions of America, every employee of the government is considered to be a shark. Others invited to the banquet in El Salvador were farmers owning more than seven hundred fifty acres of land (arable or untilled); cattlemen with more than five hundred head (bovine or equine); and military men with the rank of general—or others who without having achieved said rank were (at the moment), or had been, presidents of republics, heads of state, or ministers. It was beautiful to see how it all came off, wasn't it? Still, in the midst of such pomp and cordiality, one man had the nerve to say that Central American countries were *unable to sell their cottonseed for processing into oil at profitable prices.* Did you hear that? The first ladies were competing with the second ladies to see who could smell the prettiest. Our women are pure turtle poopoo, comrade, but the others were just as bad when it came to showing off their bodies and swirling around in yards of cloth. The people like that stuff. Bigshot or littleshot, everyone threw himself into the revelry, and the binge lasted three weeks. And no one had a gripe that afternoon nor did the secret police get out of hand. We're going to imitate Japan! An industrious people, they even manufacture pearls. Man should be king, epilogue, and harmony. Why don't you shut up, stupid? I still have it, friend. Affairs of the body and of integration. King, epilogue, and harmony. An interesting allusion when it comes to winning the will of God. And Camilo Torres knew it. And also Richard Godfrey of Massachusetts. For those two, both here and there, it was the common people that alleviated the pain of living. Or, over here and over there, as they say on the other side of the Atlantic. The mountains are the same, but there are always men of bad blood hanging around no matter where you set up your little shop. I don't give a damn about the genetics of rice. I want rice, rice. I don't give a damn whether that fly-covered cow's lung hanging on the hook came from a cow that grazed on experimental pasture land and chewed a cud of balanced forage. What I want is the lung. Japan, Japan. Rice with hull and all. The gringo calls it a paddy. Sorghum, yams, and cassava. And dried beans, friend, with the corn. And what's that? Sesame seed. Give me Spanish oil. That ain't for you, it costs too much. Cottonseed or peanut or sunflower oil for you. In Auer's Keller café he met a certain Dr. Guevara. My God, my God, why hast Thou forsaken me? It's been drought for everyone, from Jesus Christ right up to the present day. They fall like cane flattened by the wind in fields filled with ocelots and carnivorous piranhas. I want about a pound of that butter that doesn't melt. Men fear piranhas. This country is proud of having been among the first ten to sign the Universal Declaration of Human Rights. Article Twenty-two. And a little barley. Goddammit, read Article Twenty-two. Like Japan. Almond and cherry blossoms. We have those here. Are you going to tell me we don't? They smell so sweet in the still of the night. The night is so beautiful it makes you want to bathe in it after you've made love. The two young Indian girls—Soledad and Lupeana—remain faithful to their mistress's infidelity. Daiquiris and chicken legs on damp sheets. Mistress, do you want your rebozo? The moon spills into the valley of a few bright clouds. Do you love me, Matalax? In bed in these countries, they use the family name. The new senator is tempted to laugh. He always answers a question with a different question, in the manner of Ollendorff. I wonder where *La Bellotte* is? She's a frigate or a corvette or a brigantine with a chronometer cradled in green velvet in a mahogany box swinging in a cardan joint. Is she a frigate or a corvette or a brigantine? It's a world that smells of molasses and rum. The mahogany box that houses the apparatus that measures time, and the ship that watches over the queen bee. How is the little old lady? The little old lady? You call the tide, the spume, the resting place of whales a little old lady? She is the sea. She! As the fig tree of Ceylon is her body. Do you know her? And only with mandrake algae could a lover buy the kiss she bestows after making love. Because love is the most important part of her, not that pollen distilled on the underarms of machos. On the underarms and groin. If I told you whom she always loved, you wouldn't believe it. She, the light of the sea, wanted to hold him once again in her arms before she died. That's why I let him leave alive. My husband? The Colonel. He could have gone to the meeting in El Salvador, but he didn't want to. I went, his wife, surrounded by Walkers. I didn't know you then. And who's better? Tell me the truth. He or I? Why do you want to know? Ollendorff method. The wind is important to me. She is the sea: sea and spume. I am the earth. My father lives from the land. Pineapples and bananas and coffee. Who are you, Matalax? Who are *you*, madam? The Indian girls, curled up in the shadow, clap their hands over their mouths to contain their giggles. So formal. So familiar. I am the wind. I was engendered beside the bay by a horseman who never dismounted. Have you ever been to Mount Hermon? You always say that word. The night dares caress Virginia's breasts. A desire cries out in her that had been sleeping. The senator's brain waves begin to change. Virginia is naked, clothed only in a rebozo and an emerald necklace. The alpha rhythm is functioning. He has perceived her cry. Once again in the night he looks at her, and feels revulsion. Hermon is a sacred mountain—sacrosanct for lovers—that permits an iron lung to float above its peaks. And it will disintegrate in the cataracts of those condemned before their time. Those who died without getting to eat their cow's lung. Why do you suddenly despise me? Alpha rhythms, receding. Earlier, you laughed. Well, you laugh, or you cry, or you feel a burning in your gums. What does it matter? I won't tell you the name. It's like the name of a geographical region in the Caucasus and in America. He wants to irritate her. This stinking whore is not paralyzed like Georgiana. Georgiana will not inherit land, although her father and her husband and all the men who adore her on bended knee own land, but rather, because she won't want it. She's different. She despises jeeps and Piper Cubs and cassava. Miguel Ángel Matalax is the son of the sea and an equestrian colonel—a sonofabitch to the ends of the earth (or perhaps not quite that far)—but the truth is that he feels the nausea produced by exchanging hours of hunger for a flask of French perfume. This woman is naked. He would have had to remove Georgiana's clothing himself. Virginia accepts his blows in silence. The Indian girls sit frozen, like the statues of El Petén. The three remaining Walkers hear nothing, or if they hear anything, they believe it's a new way to begin lovemaking. The mastiffs try to rouse from their drowsiness to bark. But what she awaited was not to come. You don't love me any more, you don't love me any more, Matalax. What does it matter if she screams? Tomorrow he'll kick her out of the house. It's his house. Colonel-son. And see who'll dispute it. As he walks by the tiger that dismembered Don Cletito, Miguel Ángel hears through the bars something like a poetic sigh. The senator walks rapidly toward the city. He's in a hurry to see himself in the morning newspapers. The ink is still damp on San Bernardino. *Patria* has already printed his story. *La Tribuna, El Listín,* and *La Gaceta* will each praise him in a slightly different form. Alvarito Luengo Viú, the senator's press secretary, goes from one editorial room to the next, correcting proof. The statesman, the patriot, the man, the writer, the traveler. Biographical sketches in four different versions. Born in Tlextanango February 23, 1940. Son of humble farmers. The eldest of eight children. He began working in the fields when he was three, to help his father. In 1943 the family moves to San Fermín de Aja. The house of Celedonia el Quintero is buried during the earthquake of 1945. The only one removed alive from the ruins is Miguel Ángel. Orphanages and public charity until in 1946 an American engineer and his wife take him under their wing. They send him to school in the United States. He studies law at Harvard, and afterward, social sciences in Maguncia. He travels around the world. He loses an eye in Gaza as a United Nations observer. He teaches in several African and Latin American universities. He volunteers to work in the Red Cross to carry food and medicine to Biafra. But his greatest ambition is to return to his native country to free it from the man who has oppressed it for almost twenty years. Tirelessly, he studies national problems through the constant information he receives from the clandestine group that unhesitatingly accepts him from the first as its leader. The photographic documention is convincing. In Gaza. The small plaza of Tlextanango with the house where he was born. The ruins of San Fermín de Aja. The Alpuentes, who remember the Quintero boy. They're not sure what his name was. The baptismal certificate. His class at Harvard. Walking beside the Rhine with a professor from the University of Mainz. What ever became of him? Giving instructions to Trinidad de los Santos. The main street of many little towns is named Trinidad de los Santos. And also the Plaza de las

Armas in the capital. Plaza de las Armas de Trinidad de los Santos. So they can say we have good people here. It is written. Tomorrow, someday, the copy of *Patria* will be strung on hemp cords to aid passersby who relieve themselves, but today it is in the cafés and barbershops announcing to the nation that the new senator well deserves the popular vote he received. There he goes down Third and Diagonal in an open car. A blond hero. The glass eye is the center of public curiosity. A beautiful red eye, a clot of sacrifice for humanity. The heathens love triumphal parades. Viva! Viva! But these people are silent, watching coldly. Dr. Colmenares's theory of hybrids is applicable to progress, not to reversion. *Mula, mulae.* Virginia is not at the hero's side. A hero must never exhibit his mistress, no matter how high her station. The hero must be free. North Americans always surround their national figures with wife and children. Ay, dear wife, from the warm land one travels to the cold, where the apple grows, dear heart, that we have never known. The Senate is the source of first ministers, as El Petén is the source of three short but navigable rivers. So where are we, friends: is Señor Matalax from the warm country or the cold? He's from where the jungle begins. From the place where so many foreigners hide; like the one who says he has to talk—no shit, mind you—with the kind of man who looks you straight in the eye from beneath his wide-brimmed sombrero; he sits in the *pulquerías* and taverns always holding a filthy and empty glass. The radio and television no longer report anything about constitutional guarantees or revolution. Agricultural diversification. We must imitate Japan. Arruza is now a black line drawn through a name in the nation's history. The posters bearing his likeness are stained by the torrential rains that cause the rivers to rise from their banks. And the wind to gallop like a maddened stallion over the gigantic lips of the volcanoes. A different likeness is on the street corners. A blond young man with a different profile. One of our blonds. Half-gringo, half-local. Deep down, all the half-breeds feel proud of the lie. There is a kind of wild whistle in the throats of the women along Diagonal as they pronounce the new name.

Have you seen a foreigner named Camilo? Just now I saw him cross the sidewalk. He had a little hole in his heart, but he was walking just fine. Godspeed!

MRCA PSN 22
TX   232415/9   MAINZ   29/28 9 1830
M. MATALAX
BOX 324
BELIZE (B.H.)
PROFESSOR EERKENS GRAVELY ILL WISHES TO KNOW WHETHER
YOU ARE GUILTY DEATH HEROIC GUERRILLA TRINIDAD DE LOS
SANTOS STOP ANSWER CABLEGRAM STOP GREETINGS   ORMAYER

MRCA   POSN 12
TX 149706/7 MAINZ 19/18   15   0015
M. MATALAX
BOX 324
BELIZE (B.H.)
PROFESSOR EERKENS DIED MIDNIGHT STOP SENDING MAIL
MESSAGE DICTATED FOR YOU STOP   ORMAYER

They delivered the two cables and the letter at the same time.
Miguel Ángel Matalax was a senator of the Republic.

Mainz, November 14, 1968

Unfortunate friend:

When but a few hours remain before a man is to
deliver up his soul to his Creator, he cannot squander
his time quoting the most pertinent passages of all the things
he has read. Nevertheless, my friend and amanuensis, the
very kind Professor Ormayer, will record here a phrase from
the great Ovid. *Si fuit errandum, causas habet error honestas.*
You know Latin. If I erred in sending you to that beautiful
land, my intention and my motivation were honest. Your silence following receipt of my telegram confirms that the error
was grave, grave to the point of having given birth to a crime.
God forgive my stupid naïveté! For months, filled with enthu-
siasm, we planned together an undertaking that only you
could carry out. Only you, a young man from Central America,

so often wounded to the depths of your soul, only you were in a position to lead the poor of your country, the downtrodden, those who come into the world only to remain suspended in that abyss that leads to pain and death. You were the captain needed by our Central American brothers, as we affectionately called them. In the twilight of my years I saw in you one who could realize the great ideals of my youth. I would have liked to be a Fray Bartolomé de Las Casas, or a Fray Junípero Serra. More than anything, with all my soul and strength, I wish I could have followed the footsteps of the former. You know that I have the work *De justis belli causis apud indos* with me; it has always been with me, it will always be with me. It is our most beautiful treatise on what human compassion should be toward the conquered, the defenseless, the poor both in spirit and in material goods. No sooner had I consecrated myself to the ministry than I asked to be sent to American lands. Apparently my superiors considered that my talent—how soon my talent, how quickly everything, will be gone!—was destined for affairs more important than that of sharing, and attempting to remedy, the pain of the afflicted. They believed that the fundamental service to God was that a council determine what He might tolerate in the light of new technical and scientific advances. And I was the one destined to probe the possible, the feasible, and the probable, within that great and divine wisdom. With such an enormous task before me how could it have been possible, feasible, or probable for me to cross the Atlantic? I shall die without every having seen those beautiful American lands. As recompense, my name figures in many Christian books and documents that, if I am to believe what others say, contribute in some way toward introducing a breath of fresh air into the rarefied atmosphere of hermetically closed and sealed sacristy attics where are zealously guarded the antiquities and memories of other times. If I also erred in that, *in Domino confido*. In sum, only you could undertake my dream of the Indies. And you have destroyed my dream. The man I met in the library with the drowsy attendants was a murderer. That is, he became a murderer; I do not know whether in championing good or in opposing evil. The fact is that you asked for a place at the meager table of the humble, but you did not break the bread they offered you, instead, you broke the neck of those who struggled to seek more land on which the poor could sow their wheat. I have heard from the lips of Ormayer what the newspapers reported. You are responsible for the slaughter of San Blas. Point by point, Miguel Ángel Matalax, alias One-Eye, planned every detail of a terrible massacre. I could not believe it. That is why I inquired by telegraph—I could not lose a single minute—and asked you to tell me the truth. Your silence of several days confirms that the newspaper reported the truth. In the blood of more than five hundred men you have drowned one of the most modest and precious crusades for liberty in the history of oppressed mankind. But hear me well, Matalax, hear my voiceless words, buried in the tomb before they reach their full strength. Trinidad de los Santos and his guerrillas will live forever, while you, even breathing, will be dead, and in your death you will hear throughout the beating hearts of those you killed. Don't you realize that they—our brothers the Indians, as we called them—are the image and the cry of millions and millions of beings who claim recognition of their dignity as men? You told me in your last letter that they are creatures whose backs are turned. Of course they were turned as you and your unworthy companions encircled them in stealth. Their backs were turned to betrayal, to perfidy, to infamy. Their backs were to you, but their faces were turned toward the Creator. In Him there is no evil or hatred. Trinidad de los Santos and his men are now in His dominions of love. And if God grants me his pardon, I hope very soon to be with them. It will be beautiful to walk the infinite untracked path that leads to the dwelling place of the blessed. Father Godfrey will be chatting with one and another as I arrive, barefoot, for so I have asked to be buried. Find the way of God, sir, it is all good times here.

Poor creatures who finally can hold out their hands without fear.

WILHELM EERKENS

Note from Professor Ormayer: Professor Eerkens dictated the preceding lines. He died at four minutes after twelve midnight, two months after his seventieth birthday. Although Professor Eerkens was not a Catholic, he was shrouded in the white habit of the order of the Dominicans (the same in which Fray Bartolomé de Las Casas waged his battles) and, beneath his bare feet, fulfilling his desires, we placed the ancient volume *De justis belli causis apud indos.* We buried him on the sixteenth day of November at four o'clock in the afternoon in the Cemetery of the Incarnation. I myself spoke the last words before his interment. God grant the eternal blessing of his true peace to Doctor Eerkens, to Trinidad de los Santos, and to the millions who preceded and will follow them in the struggle for freedom! Amen!

PROFESSOR ORMAYER

Macario Maravé—Maca his neighbors called him—recognized the buzzards from Copán by their flight. A Polish photographer who had changed his name from Janposki to Giravolta, and who took photographs of the tourists at the Maya ruins, taught Maca that buzzards fly the same no matter where they come from, but that the wise man is distinguished from the fool by the fact that the former never cites his sources. In Santa Rosa de Copán there were a few ancient buses that carried passengers to the Square of the Hieroglyphics. Macario had left his uniform in San Pedro Sula, and when the helicopter returned to its base, it went without the man who had not been embarrassed to serve coffee to an ex-dictator. Tegucigalpa, San Pedro Sula, Santa Rosa de Copán. Land of *catrachos*, Hondurans, people who were strangers to him even though they understood one another's tongue. He traveled on foot, by night, suspicious, with a pile of cropped bills beneath his wide-brimmed hat. The reward of opportune pity. A cup of coffee. A kind glance. Beneath his sombrero he carried half of a new life. Macario Maravé, the Indian who had enlisted to see whether he could make captain without doing too much damage. Some said that Maca was a good man and could deceive a rattlesnake with his sheep's skin and his tiger's heart, but the truth was that the rattlesnakes could have eaten him up during any lazy siesta in the hayfield. He was carrying the halves of enough bills to buy a small ranch and a

214

herd. A house of locust wood with a flat tiled roof. He didn't want it along the Higuito Kelis or on the Sumpul, although the water from those rivers would irrigate the tobacco. He wasn't a tobacco planter. He didn't even smoke. What interested him were horses; he'd begin with a stud from Mexico, where there are plenty of good horses. He had the soul of a foreman. But you can't be a good foreman in a foreign country. He felt about as big as a thrush in Honduras. That's the reason he wanted to go back to his own country—oh, for a good binge and a warm heart!—but he was a deserter; they'd be searching for him, and besides, they'd look beneath his sombrero. Just to be sure, he spent his afternoons in the Square of Sacrifices near Giravolta's photographic equipment, considering the pros and cons. Spongy moss and iguanas peered from the cracks of the ruins. In the distance, turtles and armadillos glittered in the sun. Don't you want me to take a photograph for your sweet little mother? For three lempiras I fix you three copies. Eh, unnerstan', eh? Every day the Pole ate a greasy sausage with an overpowering odor of garlic. And black bread his wife baked for him. Raquel is a magnificent cook. She don't eat meat because she can still smell the smoke of the dead in her nostrils. Raquel's father was beadle in the Conservatory of Warsaw. Eh, unnerstan', eh? Finally Macario had his picture taken and paid his three lempiras. His face was sad in the photo. Much sadder without a uniform. The Pole belched frequently and Macario had to move away. So, your people think you are serious because your face is sad. That is not what makes serious, my frien'. The Jew always laughs. Don't worry. Eh, unnerstan', eh? If you give me a lempira, I will give you an advice. A Jew's advice is a good thing, my friend. Look, Giravolta don't talk shit. You have something beneath that hat and it ain't intelligence and it ain't a *carajo*, as you people say. Go back to your land, bury the half of what you are carrying and deliver the other half. Eh, unnerstan', eh? And who should I give it to? Well, who do you think, wretched little fella? You're as bad off as a ghetto Jew. You want we should be partners? So tell me the story and tell me how much money you have with you. It took three days for the Indian to open up. More than three thousand three hundred dollars in good currency from Macario's country. Where is the other half, wretched bastard? Four more days and three nights passed before the Indian Maca decided to show his piece of paper to the photographer with chestnut-brown fingertips and yellowish saliva in the corners of his lips. Giravolta had invited him to his house to taste the blintzes filled with pot cheese and marmalade that Raquel prepared. Giravolta kept trying to meet Maca's eyes. Eh? Eh? Eh? And to soften Macario's hard heart he told him of the martyrdom of Raquel's father. Raquel had breasts swollen with unborn children. A sad gaze, dissolved in kosher tenderness. Raquel is always weeping, even though her eyes are dry. She weeps because she cannot go back to Warsaw, eh, unnerstan', eh? Not while there are memories. And I say to her: The memories will disappear only with death, wife. And Raquel, she says there they will be more distant, unnerstan'? She has a sister and three nieces and nephews. One day her mother threw herself in the Vistula. Or she fell. She was a half-blind, fat-bellied old bitch. Raquel don't like I should call her mother a bitch. The father is ashes of fire, not of earth as he should be. You don't believe, me, wretch. Macario lay sleeping and Giravolta watched over his sleep. Several times he attempted to remove the sombrero, but Macario opened his eyes the moment the Jew's hand came near. Suspicious man, I wanted to see if you have any fever. In the mornings the house smelled of strong coffee and the honey of tortes Raquel baked for the guest. She had learned from her mother. That's the way we Jews are. Everything is tradition, everything we own, follow me? Eat. Eat some more. You like it, eh, you like it? Take off your hat at the table. You don't take it off, eh, suspicious? Money cut in half is good for nothing, Macario. The man who gave it to you that way is an evil man. You give gifts or you don't give gifts, but you don't cut them in half. If I say to you: My brother, here is my wife. Sleep with her. It is a supposition, eh, unnerstan', eh? That don't mean you have to sleep. No. I give her to you for pleasure. And that night Macario slept with her and enjoyed her, but without removing his sombrero. And the next morning Raquel looked at her belly in the mirror to see if it had grown. Before she prepared the tortes for breakfast she drew a circle around her navel with salt and milk. That morning she sang in the kitchen. The Old Testament says: "And he died in a good old age, full of days, riches, and honor." Giravolta listened to her sing. She was kneading the yeast and the wheat flour, she, his wife, she, Raquel. The husband entered the bedroom. Macario lay naked on the bed, his sombrero on his head, his eyes open. And so? Why don't you cover your member, you wretch? You have come to bring disgrace to this house with your silence. Eh, unnerstan', eh? Raquel is singing. What have you done to her with that sinful, uncircumcised radish, eh, what have you done to her? I'll hold my tongue, wretch, because the Talmud says that the first to hold his tongue in a dispute is the one who comes from a good family. And they sat without speaking all the morning, even through breakfast and lunch. Raquel sighed deeply, and also ate in silence. Your assurance asks for further assurance, bad woman! It was a cry torn from Giravolta's heart. He left the house; he ran through the streets. He ran out into the country to seek the river where he could wash his chest and stomach. He lay on his belly by the shore of the Higuito Kelis for more than an hour, weeping his misfortune. When he returned, the house was dark. He had to wait in the kitchen until his wife was finished in Macario's bedroom. He drank through the night, sipping from a bottle of pisco. Raquel appeared at the first light of dawn, fastening her bathrobe. She handed her husband a piece of paper and scolded him for having drunk all night. You cannot dress a nekkid man, Raquel, nor shoe a trotting horse, wife. His tongue was foolish. Bring me my coffee, wife, and give me my spectacles. She went into the kitchen to touch her belly and prepare the coffee. Giravolta spoke in Yiddish when he was alone. She returned from the kitchen, said that her son would be called Aaron, and again left the room. The photographer mumbled a few words as he tried to put on the spectacles Raquel had left for him on the table. Old whore, old whore. He will not be called Aaron, no, old whore, no, eh, unnerstan', eh? You are not going to take the money and the son and force me to name him after your father. No. He will have the name of my father. Joachim. Too much humility is pride, Raquel. Foolish tongue, bright eyes. The paper said: "My faithful Simeón: you will give the bearer of these bills the remaining halves, on the condition that he comes to you to report that he has killed One-Eye—and that it is true. Arruza." Giravolta's head cleared even before Raquel brought his coffee. Lay out my new suit and tie, wife. Raquel entered her husband's bedroom and the photographer entered the room where a naked Macario lay sleeping, sombrero in place. In spite of his jubilation, Giravolta felt revulsion, and he covered the soldier's penis with a wet towel. Macario opened his eyes. I know everything, eh, unnerstan', eh wretch? I have read this paper. And that was all your secret? Big deal! For one thousand eight hundred and fifty-seven dollars I have sold my honor, but I shall be a man again. Do you know what one thousand eight hundred and fifty-seven dollars are? Then Macario dressed, and they talked all the morning and part of the afternoon. The tortes were even more savory than those of the previous day. My son will be named Aaron. Shut up, wife! The first thing Macario had to explain was who One-Eye was. One-Eye was the one who had killed Trinidad de los Santos. I read in the newspaper that he is a senator now. And you feel uneasy because of that? A senator has his heart in the same place as any other man. Raquel burst out crying, remembering Kennedy. Tomorrow at dawn he would leave on the bus. Just you? Yes, my frien', just me, with four bills only to show to that Simeón, and in the meantime you stay here tossing in the hay with my wife. I will carry the bills and the scrap of paper, and when I return, we will settle our accounts. During dinner he learned everything that had happened in the other country. That night Raquel slept with her husband, and at the break of day Giravolta prepared to leave. Remember always our proverb, Raquel. Never forget to be suspicious. And with heavy heart, he left the house. It was raining lightly and rainbows played in the air of the new day. It was the first time he had been separated from Raquel. Together, in 1938, they had crossed through Germany, Belgium, and France when Giravolta sensed that things would be very bad for the Jews. In Marseilles they had embarked on a Dutch cargo ship bound for America. But cargo ships never know where they will end up. The couple was left in the port of La Ceiba on the same day the Germans and Russians signed the nonaggression pact. And there they remained. Later, Tegucigalpa. And from there to Santa Rosa de Copán. The bus faded into the night after a day of chickens, pigs, and parrots. Market day. With a flourish, at two in the morning, the bus drew to a stop at the terminal, no more than a little roofed room with a bench where a Chinese, an Indian couple, and a plump fellow who looked like a Cuban refugee, were sleeping. A room divider with a little window for selling tickets, a set of scales, and several bundles. A strong odor of fat and indigestion, and a clock. That was the terminal. Simeón is a Jewish name. A typical name of the tribe of Judah. Giravolta pointed his nose into the night and began to walk, sniffing at every street corner. At seven in the morning he knocked on a door. Simeón was not surprised to see a fellow Jew. Together they breakfasted on several greasy dishes served by a half-Indian servant girl named Encarnita, who also did pretty things in her master's bed. Simeón was a Lithuanian, and in spite of the tropical heat he always wore a wool cap like those worn by reindeer herders. In the room where they spent the greater part of the time Simeón Koopman (three times in his life he'd changed his name and his age) kept several precision instruments, among them a microscope, in addition to a radio station for talking with friends in other parts of the world. Of all those details what most attracted Giravolta's attention was the enormous safe embedded in the wall. After they had eaten breakfast, Giravolta took out Colonel Arruza's note and without loosening his hold on it showed it to Simeón. Simeón read it carefully and held a great magnifying glass to the signature. Then the two Jews stared at each other for almost an hour, scrutinizing even the pores of the nose and the glitter of the eyes. So? Simeón opened the safe and placed on the desk the missing halves of Macario's bills. Giravolta unbuttoned his jacket and drew out the four halves the Indian Maca had given him. Simeón studied them with that enormous magnifying glass of a Bulgarian forger. Hmmmmm! Then they sat staring a while, and during that interval Encarnita served them coffee three times, and brandy from Tel Aviv. And when it was almost noon, Simeón ordered his mistress to remove her panties, and she obeyed and went into the bedroom. Then the patriarch placed the bills in the safe and was out of the office for more than forty minutes. When he returned, he said: It is not good that one man keep the things that belong to two. And Giravolta nodded and felt a sense of relief in his heart. For a moment he thought he would be invited according the laws of hospitality, but Simeón said nothing of the sort. Encarnita crossed through the office to get more coffee and more brandy from Tel Aviv. For three hours they drank and spoke in sentences from the Talmud and in proverbs both knew well from their racial tradition. "Fighting with their hands and praying to God in their hearts." Yes. 1 Macc. 15:27. Honesty is pride. Yes. It is, yes, you know it is, brother. The truth is the daughter of God. What is mine is mine; what is my brother's is his and mine. True, but the girl will serve you coffee, nothing more, you hear? Yes, but that is like carrying oil to the city of olives. Amen. Your friend has a friend and the friend of your friend has a friend. It is so. And why did the friend of my friend, who is you, not come to take coffee? Because he holds the other halves of the things. Then you will do it? Giravolta hesitated. Simeón rose and said to his guest. Go to see her.

Who is "her" ? Woman, the seat of all pleasure and evil. Her name is Virginia. Ben Syra said: The day is short and the labor long. One-Eye has ceased to love her. There is another woman. Have you ever seen inside the heart of one of these women? The camel who would have horns loses his ears. Encarnita served dinner, and they drank a carafe of wine. When Encarnita served custard and slices of guava, Simeón ordered her to display her buttocks to the guest. She obeyed, and Giravolta did not turn pale or make rude remarks or raise an eyebrow. Then, although they had drunk a great deal, Simeón in a falsetto voice sang a psalm from the Torah. In a beautiful baritone, Giravolta chorused the melody. For an hour the only sound was that of the flies. Encarnita! She came from the kitchen with more coffee and brandy. Simeón threw a cup of steaming coffee in Giravolta's face. Giravolta made no rude remarks and did not clench his fist. He wiped his face with a checkered kerchief. You want the money so much, brother? Yes. Why? I want to return. To Poland? No, not while the bad memories are there. Where, then? To Israel. Then, hands clasped, the two Jews wept. Arruza was my friend. Remember that a man forewarned is a man forearmed. One-Eye knows that she is jealous and that she will kill him if she can. You know? Tears still flowed in those so happy moments. Forgive me, forgive me, my brother. I wanted to test you. You will fulfill the mission of my friend. This very night. If you do it, I will give you more money than is duly owed you. I, from my pocket. A good cub need never be a raceless bastard. Encarnita went to bed and for two hours Simeón told his guest the private story of the public life of the country during the last two years. Then, thoroughly drunk, they fell asleep on the rug. But Giravolta was not that drunk. He arose with stealth and opened the safe whose combination he had retained in his photographer's memory. Then he went down to the cellar and told Encarnita that her master was permitting him to pleasure himself awhile. And so he did. And then left the house on tiptoe. A cluster of people with hens and pigs stood at the door of the terminal. Giravolta bought his ticket and settled into his seat in the bus.

The bus left at two-thirty A.M., en route to Tegucigalpa.

Tamales, hot tamales!

Coffee, cuppa' coffee, cigars!

Giravolta's heart was full. Money, and no killing. That was his philosophy. That same morning he would close up his house. Raquel, she, his wife, honorable as ever. Macario Maravé thrown out. Half and half with the money. One thousand eight hundred and fifty-seven dollars. Enough for a voyage to Israel, where they could begin a new life. And without killing. His name again. Joseph Janposki and Raquel, citizens of the promised land: "the joy of the whole earth is Mount Zion" (Ps. 48:2).

A man does not love a woman simply because her heart reposes in a beautiful bust. Commodore Narciso Pérez Almarche was discussing such things in General Armenteros's military laboratory. Of course, this Armenteros, a man without vanity and with altered drinking habits, resembled a barrack-room shit more than a hotshot general. Keeping his eye on him, keeping his cup always filled, and waiting patiently was the extent of his adjutant's duties. And talking and talking persuasive, balanced reason. There are two natural currents, General; one flows from the soul and one from the body, and the two never meet. Sooner or later every man's eyes will be consumed by the earth, General. Phineas was thinking at that moment of Lavinia's two rivers, no weeping willows on the shore, no royal carp, no children swimming naked in no man's water like deer surprised in a thaw. The legend says, General, that in the Gulf of Fonseca three Maya sirens sing elegies to the cabin boys on the banana boats. Phineas had no feeling for the Caribbean. His sea was the Mediterranean, but you don't just say that flat out unless you want to insult the mother of the man you're talking with. It's the largest salmon that burst their gills swimming upstream, or wriggling a place in the sandbar, and it's the adults with loose, ruined scales that persist on carrying the fruits of the land deep into the sea. Gulf of Fonseca, ay, brother, no man's gulf, mouth that doesn't eat, mouth that vomits. Right, Porfirio? Raulito is delivering a speech at the Rotary Club on the theme of "Health, Labor, and Productivity." Raulito is laying the groundwork. So intelligent, so handsome. The purchase of consumer goods in foreign markets rose to fifty-one million dollars this year. The ladies believe that Raulito is too radical, but he is *so* handsome. That fact has caused the stimulus for growth in exports to expand beyond internal economic limits, either because of payments to commercial agents outside the country, or because of a rise in exports. Lavalle, where is Lavalle? You almost never see him any more. He used to be so ambitious, so aggressive (in terms of enterprise), so much the executive, such a golfer, so courageous, and now he's always buried in the Ministry of the Economy, drinking, and smoking stinking cigarettes. Doesn't that seem strange to you, General? To Phineas nothing seems strange. He's thinking about what he would have done if Lavinia had run away with another man. While she could still walk, Georgiana had left on her own two feet, General. Now they've carted her away stuck in her tube. And the Commodore keeps a close watch on his boss, as if trying to discover something. Sometimes he thinks it's not the same man. Lavalle, a wet rag, walks out into the passageway to look for the bathroom. An empty ministry in a serene night. "Victory, let us sing victory, now I'm in glory, my woman done left me." It isn't true. He's soaking, drenched in alcohol and tears. That's why he's got to piss. And why not do the other? There's paper on the floor. *Patria.* He reads, his undershorts below his knees. To commemorate the festivities of the New Year, the Minister of the Economy and Director of the National Bank and Señora de Lavalle (née Georgiana Alberta Lynch) in their residence, El Paraíso—extremely cozy— gave a supper party in expression of their good wishes for this still-young year for a select group of intimate friends including, of course, His Excellency the President of this nation and his lady, Señora Esmeraldita Guiráldez de Oruro; Lieutenant General Armenteros—our Hero, as he is affectionately called in all parts of the nation—and Senator Miguel Ángel Matalax, who arrived in the company of the elegant daughter of our great landowner Pfandl. It is said that the soiree was to some degree the result of a conquest by a mischievous cupid and of a contract Virginia and Miguel Ángel are soon to sign. Dinner included meat pies, a special delicacy from Caracas, and *dulce de lechosa* custard (which is what they call our *dulce de leche* in the land of Bolívar) to honor two distinguished guests visiting the Lavalles: Doris and John MacDonald of Shell, a most delightful English couple passing through our country on their way between Maracaibo and the hearts of dear friends. Yes, General, the Central American Court ruled that the Gulf of Fonseca is a historic bay possessing the characteristics of a landlocked sea. And they say that shysters don't know how to write literature, eh, General? Raulito also has his doubts about whether Lavalle is the genuine article. It's true his wife ran away from him after she returned. That one can't stay put even paralyzed, right, Juan Diego? He isn't the same man, no. But he is. Raulito's eyes scrutinize every movement made by the Minister and Director of the National Bank. In general terms, the fiscal situation can be characterized within a frame of reference in which tax receipts tend to rise rapidly, while expenditures rise at a slower rate owing to the stagnation of funds for capital formation. Ah, what a guy! The foremost leaders of the nation—and their ladies—began to notice that Raulito knew a great deal more about economics than Lavalle, and more than all the previous experts in the field. Oruro should know that. What does Chiquita Banana, that is, Esmeraldita, say? We must convince her. The tea, the party, the charity fair. We would have bigger markets and better prices for our coffee if Raulito were in charge. At the shower, Esmeraldita came close to announcing Valentín's decision. Engineer Marco Aurelio López Andrés and his wife (née María Carolina Muñoz) are thrilled with the little bundle the stork brought them; the baby was baptized yesterday at her parents' residence. The nation's first lady was present at Carolina's party. The fact is that Sinfonías couldn't deny Esmeraldita anything.

You can't make up for so many years in Enriquillo, mister, except, perhaps, by a lot of banging. First the captain, and then this lady who seems to me was never kept happy. But Lavalle of the Ministry and National Bank was flying as if he had never been much of a flyer. When Matalax ran away with Georgiana it broke the nerve of Martin, not Ernesto, Lavalle. Taking the number of a current bank account in Switzerland with him, he went into exile to seek himself in the geography of the world. Raulito, Minister of the Economy and Director of the National Bank, you see, General! Phineas isn't thinking of that. He too has his plans. One day he'll escape when the army isn't looking, and by some route or other the wind will carry him to New Orleans, no matter how it pains those buzzards. The entrepreneurial class of our country—ladies and gentlemen—still maintain their particular code of expectations and conduct. Whether or not beneath the umbrella of the official party, both business and businessmen have ample opportunity for direct access to the highest political circles. A new voice is heard in the streets. A student. His name is Martínez. A loaf of bread is not a loaf of bread, it is four loaves when divided among four men. Kill him, kill him! Raulito laughs at such nonsense. A loaf of bread is a loaf of bread whether it's divided into fourths or into eighths. If Martínez is going to be so fucking stupid, he doesn't deserve to die. For Martínez the Maya sirens of the Gulf of Fonseca don't exist, because he's decided to eat the banana, not exploit it. Rifle in hand, cartridge belts crossed over his chest, he walks the same nameless paths walked by Trinidad de los Santos. The buoys of the three countries bordering the sea would have given him the green light, but Martínez prefers this land that swallows civilizations and cities in apocalyptic disasters to the sea that leads only—or so it seems to him—to the docks of the United Fruit Company. General Armenteros, find that man for me, and hang him. Says who? President's order. Sinfonías's order. The President couldn't have said that. The President is reading the *Chen-kieu yi-hiue* (The Study of Needles and Cauterizing

Made Easy), a text based on the Sung classics, composed by Li Cheu-sien in 1798. Just like in Enriquillo. If the jailer were there, he would tell him that acupuncture is the best way to cure a sick man. But it's the *coitus interruptus* of the Taoists that most interests the President, not Martínez with his rifle and cartridge belts. Sexual practice with Doña Esmeraldita, Oriental style, is augmenting Sinfonías's spiritual and bodily powers. Why don't *you* go find him, Don Narciso? I'm tired of playing the hero. All I want to do is to drink and be left in peace. He was so drunk that the Commodore was able to write his family. Soon I shall be the leader of this country. Get your things ready, my dear ones. There is always a touch of tenderness in the Commodore's letters. He is promoted to colonel, and Armenteros turns the military operations against Martínez and his guerrilla band over to him. Soon he'll be shouting from a jeep. Not even God dumps crap on Colonel Pérez Almarche, you hear me, Lieutenant? Not even God! And he pulled up the breeches of his new uniform. He was soon noted for drinking gin from his campaign helmet. Not even God! Now there was no One-Eye to give orders over the radio. One-Eye? He isn't here, he had to go, he was forced to leave, he isn't here. He slipped through Virginia's fingers down a thread of water between Punta Casignina and Punta Amapola. He fled before he was shot dead by three Walkers one gardenia-perfumed night. A senator has been lost. Have you searched for him, lady, along that league of seashore? They laugh. She knows they laugh. That's why she's losing the screws that fasten reason to the hub of events, of things. She feels them falling as she walks through the streets asking whether they've captured a banana boat carrying one eye too many or one eye too few. Never pairs. A senator has been lost. My love—the one-eyed man, the fag, the philanderer—isn't in the city, he isn't in the bed, he isn't in the sheep-gut prophylactic. The siren Ugu allowed the octupses to eat her tail to ensure that Aziel, the guardian of the treasures of Hell, would look to the west. Oh, Cassil, Cassil, angel of solitude and tears. What time is it? Why do you want to know, lustful, lustful, lustful, woman? My head aches. I've lost another screw. And it hurts here, too. He is a doctor from the British-American Hospital who looks like Kildare. Where does it hurt? Right here, beneath my breasts. Rose-colored. If you want to touch them, you must ask permission of Colonel Arruza. Oh, it hurts! I want to abort something that has its claws buried in me. Like a needle from a ground pine. He left, doctor, before I could see him dead. I'm losing my memory. If you ask me what country we're in, I wouldn't know whether it's Guatemala, or El Salvador, Honduras, Nicaragua, Costa Rica, or Panama. Her eyes have changed color. They had been so beautiful—German eyes with tropical sparks—beautiful. As she lost her memory, which they threw into the receptacle for waste and surgical dressings, the sparks died out and Virginia's eyes turned to nothing.

Eternity is procreation. That's all, brother, and the same is true for man and for cattle, for wild animals and for the lowly pig. We're here because two people were joined together in bed, and here we will be for our sons and grandsons. And so on and so on, unto infinity. Who are they? They're others. Why don't you look at them? Because I don't have eyes in the back of my head, or ears either. The other man's back is turned, too. I suppose. We've been standing this way for hundreds of years. But the country belongs to both of us. A man has to talk to be understood. I talk with my kind, and he with his. Sure, we talk. But different, man. A tapir ran by, fleeing from the smell of fire. Wild game is carried to market after it's roasted. Tapirs with fat turned to cracklings, and pacas, deer, wild pigs, and even lizards and iguanas. Savory meat wrapped in banana leaves. The boys raid the dens at dawn. Traps that shatter the paws of animals in flight, and wattles of greenwood poles, with bonfires beneath for the roasting. When a man's going to market, he goes sober. On the way back, he has a quick one in every cantina. That's the way it is for whites, and for those of other colors, too, my love. They call the new guerrilla leader Cara de Agua. Some day he'll wake up hanging from a wild-plum tree. Francisco Maxal is his real name. Maxal means whipped, or beaten. God knows why Francisco carries a name like that in the eternity of his presence here. He has three kids, who're named Maxal too, although in the villages they've begun to call all of them little Cara de Aguas. A fine name. The grandpa is still alive. He's a justice, a very old man. The father, too, was an agent in the Indian judicial system. Francisco studied introduction to Spanish literature in the capital. When he was older, he worked as a guide and interpreter for Indians who came to file suits in the nation's tribunals. Be seated. The lawyer says be seated. And the Indian sat when Cara de Agua translated the order into Quiche. So he spent several years selling wild game, guiding the lost, and interpreting claims and disputes before judges with severe faces. Difficult to explain all that. What is the claimant's name? He doesn't want to give his name here, or his age, or anything. He must leave a bond of fifty pesos for his paper with the official stamp, and tell him not to be stupid about this, you hear? One day the word spread that Cara de Agua had taken up arms. Who knows whether he'll have any success. The proof of the pudding's in the eating. The very first thing he did was to hide his children where no one would recognize them, and his grandfather, too, who wasn't any good any more, even for administering justice in the community. The one with cloven hooves got his wife one night, and carried her away. They didn't lose much. The word is that she's giving the come-on to everyone; what she liked best was cantinas. Now in fancy new clothes she's putting on that she's the wife of Cara de Agua. Since she said she'd shared a cot with Maxal, even Colonel Narciso interrogated her, but soon everyone realized there was little water in that spring. In the rude palm-thatched hut Cara de Agua always slept with another woman. March and April are bad months to go into the mountains. The rains were slightly late that year, but when it rained, it poured buckets. Maxal had been planning things for a long time. He began with three men. At the end of the rainy season he had fifty. Heroes and antiheroes. Some were one— some, the other. No man's land. Have you seen Maxal's party? Robbers, nothing but robbers, have you seen them, you no-good shitpot? Well, no, sir. I ain't seen them, but let me tell you you're not the man to shit on me. Oh, no? You're going to feel the leather, boy, for being so fresh and rude. But occasionally the four directions were confused, as in Boliva. It's a goddamn crock to believe a man has eyes and mouth in the back of his head. Karlitos Marx. So who's that? And it's a bad thing to let your beard grow in a land of smooth-shaven men, understand? Yeah, it's a hard row to hoe, this life, macho. But macho like a wild boar. Wanna cuppa' coffee? That's how men talk, face to face, with their cups of coffee between them. But it only happens between men on one side or between men on the other side. Never between the two sides. You ought to know, brother, who Señor Marx is. Not a gringo. Don't you even know who the President is? Oh yes, oh yes, I know who the President is, yes. Heroes and antiheroes don't mean a thing when it comes to eating the fruit of the coffee plant. And the coffee planter's in Switzerland enjoying the rewards of other men's sweat. What's left for you is the pulp of the gourd, brother. And the gourd itself for gathering the cassava, which is good to eat cooked with a little meat. But, goddammit, don't you know who Karlitos Marx is? It's bad enough you don't know Señor Marx, but what I can't forgive is the fact that you don't know the President's name is Juan Elgidio Báez. It isn't Oruro any more, not any more. Oruro belongs to yesterday. And Don Juan Elgidio belongs to the day before yesterday. But the day before yesterday always comes around again. Arruza is sowing in some other country. The Lord gave him to us, and the Lord took him away. Blessed be His holy name! Don Narciso's a general now. The Constitution of 1940 returned Báez. He has a baby boy named Lincoln. Báez promoted Don Narciso. General Armenteros disappeared one night. The witches of Zante came to fetch him. To show him Lavinia in another man's arms. As many as drops of water are the betrayals of woman. Pompano stuffed with black grapes is served to Phineas to check his appetites, a Pan hiding half in rockrose, half in mid-air. And one day there was only one of them. And Lavinia never noticed the difference. Could a man ask for greater happiness? Woman, rub your hands with pine rosin and serve me wine from Samos, letting it trickle through your fingers. So he sits facing the Mediterranean of America, awaiting the ship on which Ulysses will return, drinking until he's senseless. Someday his kidneys won't function, but death will take of Phineas only what hasn't functioned. Cara de Agua, too, asks: Which way do you go? But they change the points of the compass on him. Not out of evil, no; it all depends on where you're sitting. Join Francisco Maxal's guerrillas and end oppression. Fifty-three, fifty-seven. It's bad when you have to steal cattle for meat. A man's back doesn't see, or hear, or speak. Cara de Agua looks at the ceiba trees filled with black birds. But it's on the bark of the *huacallis* that he leaves the signs of his passing. Revolution. Cara de Agua. He's satisfied because in San José de Salvatierra they made General Narciso dance. And cut off the heads of eleven of his rural police. Fifty-six, fifty-five, forty-four. A few more, a few less. The important thing is for a man to have dignity without the fat that spoils everything, you understand? They are alone, alone. Yes, but they share their solitude with the sky and the volcanoes. Still, others believe that they're not alone; after all, the machinist has his machine and the paralytic his social security card. There's a number on the back of the machine, and the machinist's overalls also have a number. Everything in order. Everything has a number. IBM. Indians constitute 75 percent of the population of this country. Pure-blooded Indians, beardless, quiet Indians who one day—you'll see—will cry out. Why don't you turn around, mister, and look at them with your own eyes? Your back is blind, mister. Just turn around. And in the middle, the silence, no man's land, the ceibas and the *huacallis*. The heroes and the antiheroes running from one side to another, on burros, on foot, or in a jeep with a banner. And fingers pointing in every direction. I think he went that way. North, south, east, west. Yesterday it was Trinidad de los Santos. Also Zósimo. And Godfrey. And Martínez. Thousands. And before them there had been others. As others stood in the second ring of backs, Arruza, Oruro, Báez, Oruro, Báez, Armenteros, others, others. And other constitutions. But the trees are and will always be eternity, like flesh—whether of cattle or of man—and like the sea and its fishes, hurricanes: everything that procreates. The stars are eternal and they don't procreate. Who the fuck told you that, doctor? The IBM of the Ministry of Social Planning? Bodies and antibodies. Heroes and antiheroes, no matter what the man says who believes he can arrange everything as easily as making the V-for-victory sign. Man is free only when no one wants to sell him or give him freedom. Cuppa coffee, mister? A long, long wait with your eyes glued on the clock in the National Bank Building. Cuba was called the cork island because it didn't sink. And this country's just like that, man, pure cork. They come and they go, and—what happened? They rise and they fall, only they remain lame all their lives. Where did you see him? Right here in the cinchona patch. Was anyone wounded? One of 'em was rotten with gangrene. The worst of it is that the rural police know that Cara de Agua has his witch doctor with him. That means they won't be able to kill him if his god-in-the-flesh is protecting him. These days you can't take out your peter just anywhere and have a good piss. The troops'll whistle a bullet past you. The troops or the guerrillas, for there are some of both around here. You're telling me? Things are so bad around here, brother, you can't tell which way the wind's blowing. What about him? Watch out for the quiet ones. Cara de Agua had the reputation of not having much to say. But Don Narciso was a big talker and anything he said you could hear loud and clear. Hang those two men! Someone had already told him that if a leader wants to stay in command, he'd better learn to keep a cool head. And those four men, give them five times five lashes. I don't want to see that look of treason in their eyes again. Twenty-five welts on your back are hard to take, but backs don't see or hear or cry out. Where'd you say Maxal's gang went? Fingers pointing west. Useless search, as useless as if it had been carried out by the mounted troop, a bunch of shitasses with pretensions of being a presidential bodyguard. Soldiers with soles on their shoes. Not worth a damn, brother. You give 'em a blanket to sleep out in the mountains and they pick balls off of the cloth to plug their ears, you know? Soldiers from the capital, good for making little Concha fall in love with them, and then for eating the candied coconut the mother-in-law prepares for them. Good God in heaven! And then they're the ones who say, well look, with just a tiny exception my mother-in-law's meek as a lamb. Ah, let me spit on that corpse! Sell me two handfuls of corn and my daughter'll pay for it when she visits me. Sun pouring into the sewing room. A quiet, clear afternoon. Why must there be revolution when everything is so orderly and peaceful? The doctor drinks his apple pop and palpates the abdomen of the pregnant woman. Could you, just while you're here, check my belly, too? It swells and swells, but as far as I know I'm not pregnant. What could it be? The doctor doesn't diagnose the tumor. Better she be deceived by the barefoot witch doctor. He will touch her belly with hands anointed in ancestral magic: burred nettles, blood of the first menstrual flow, and armadillo claws. Who is that trotting along the crown of the mountains? Whose silhouette is that deified by horse and sun? It must be One-Eye. They still believe in One-Eye in these parts. One-Eye is worth more than all the guerrillas—the ones who came before and the ones we have now—and worth more than all the governors and military men. One-Eye burst on the horizon one dawn like a character from Valhalla, and one afternoon he disappeared, just like that, carrying his love over his shoulders. In his passage through this country he slew the dragon and then renounced it all, when he could have been emperor of Central America. Trinidad and Lavalle and Oruro and Cara de Agua are all bastards, one no different from another. One-Eye is the man who could turn around all the men who stand with their backs turned. But he slipped through our fingers like the proverbial golden goose. Good things stay with us only as long as we deserve them. Tavern talk. Emotions stirred by pulque and other lesser drinks better left unmentioned. His daughter and that man's over there, though still young kids (I mean young ladies like Doris Day), would gladly have given Don Miguel Ángel everything they had, because men like him don't fall in your lap every day. You sound like a queer, to me, mister. If you weren't so plastered I'd like to discuss this with you in the corral. It's nothing, nothing; conversations of booze and cigars. Don Juan Elgidio speaks to the country on the radio. We are able to report to you that in no other part of Central America has a more intensive, more serious, or more promising campaign been made on the cattle front than that being realized by my government. Suffice it to say that since I returned and once again assumed the presidency of the Republic, at my administrative order steps have been taken to import one thousand two hundred registered bulls. And I am sure that in all this time all the countries of Latin America combined—with the exception of Cuba, for which we have no figures—have not, proportionately, imported half the number of stud bulls we will import in a few months' time. But to what end have we currently been directing the efforts of the nation? The greatest effort, citizens, is being directed toward the construction of hydraulic projects. I assure you that all the countries of Latin America combined—I repeat, we lack figures from Cuba—do not, proportionately, have plans for hydraulic projects like those my government is studying to put into immediate execution. Furthermore, our efforts will begin to reverse our wasteful economy, with highways, roads, railways; with everything necessary to make us feel confident that we shall once again be as prosperous as in the days before the arrival of Columbus. Take off your hat, badass, you're talking to the President! You're abusing your democratic privileges. So come on, where is he! Shadows of heroes announced with cries of jubilation. Dark shapes of salivating antiheroes. Who's shouting? No one, no one. Actually, there's nothing but silence. Who's spitting? It's the salted fish making my mouth water. Adiós, adiós, little Elvira. Grandpa is an old man staring at the dust of the road as if searching for tracks of lost caimans. Godspeed, Captain. The voice always sounds as if it were concealed. Have you seen Maxal, old man? Grandpa Lucio shakes his head without raising his eyes from the dust where he sees an ant carrying a seed on its back. The jeep stirs the quiet of the road. Why? The horseman of the dusk rides the crests of the mountains. It must be One-Eye. People believe in him. They're dumb clods. One day he'll come here to the plain and ford the shallows of the river. That man had something I'd never seen before in this part of the world. But he went away because we don't deserve him. He went away because there's too much pride in our silence. You talk a lot of shit for a lawyer. As for me, I think the man left because he'd done his job. And what about us? We're pigs, buddy, who keep waiting for them to increase the gross national product. You're a stupid idiot, and if it weren't for the fact that I'm about to have a drink, I'd bust ya one in the snout, hear me? Cantina conversation. In his hut, Cara de Agua whispers things in his *cholita*'s ear. The imperialists are trying to conquer our people by starvation, but they won't get their way this time. Yes, my love. They've founded their businesses on the backs of the weak, the passive, the traitors, and the cowards, but I, Micaelita, I can count on the brave men, the decent men, the good men, hear me . . . hear me . . . hear me?

La *Bellotte* sailed from Caicos on the ninth of April, the day of her birthday. In the logbook Huancavélica noted the festive day with the monogram McM, the mark of McManus, the designer and builder of that beautiful, recently caulked, marine creature. She set sail with banners flying, face bright, body graceful, hair flowing—spars and masts, lines and sails—smiling at the sea. April 9, 1910, is a date recalled in English shipyards as readily as September 26, 1934. A beautiful figure, *La Bellotte*'s. One-eightieth the size of the *Queen Mary*, but at least as pretty. An old lady with fine skin and healthy innards. Like the captain. How old is Niña Huanca? She doesn't put them on or take them off. Fewer than the schooner, of course. More than curious adolescent girls. It was three days before she saw the silhouette of Matthew Town on Great Inagua in the Bahamas. They went there to take on salt, a cargo the captain didn't much like because it leaves the hold tainted for other more delicate merchandise, or ruins the composition of powder, even when it's hermetically sealed in barrels. Paulito climbed the masts with the same agility as before he lost his foot. Nimes had made him a foot of tanned sheephide and wood that the dwarf wore only when he was on leave in port. They docked near the salt-loading docks. Nimes and Huancavélica did not go ashore. The mate was beginning to feel too old. He wanted to retire to the key. He'd talked it over with the captain so many times it was taken for granted. The next trip would be the last. But when the moment came to stay behind beneath the mangroves, he began to feel a kind of prickling in his hands, and he was the first on board. The next trip will be the last, I swear, and that time there won't be any prickling, not anything. The dwarf, Weis, and Cortés spent the night on shore. Very early the next morning the police delivered them in a paddy wagon. They were so drunk they could barely say their names. Paulito had lost his wooden foot. The captain paid ten pounds so they wouldn't have to appear in court. Habeas corpus has been sacred in English law since 1679, and although it works to the benefit of the man who's been arrested, it's often a bother, especially when a ship has to sail. A bribe is a prudent recourse on such occasions. Nimes brought some hammocks on deck, and the three men slept off their drunk until the sun bore down upon them. Then Huancavélica gave the order to apply the Natalwaks Statutes, still current in embarcation contracts on some keel ships happily plying the Caribbean. Cortés and Weis were hanged by their feet for three hours. Since Paulito had but one foot, he was hanged by his hands for four hours, since that position is more easily tolerated. That's what's prescribed by the statutes written by the Angolan freed slave who became leader of the buccaneers. Every half hour, Nimes threw a bucket of water over their naked torsos. Once their punishment was completed, they ate with good appetite and without rancor lay down to sleep until the stevedores notified them they were ready to load on the sacks of salt. April 16, without further calamities, they left Matthew Town en route to Montego Bay. There they rid themselves of the hellishly stinking salt and loaded on all the barrels of raw Jamaican rum *La Bellotte* could hold.

They set their sails to take advantage of the even, steady wind that blew the entire four hundred miles of the voyage. Two days' run saved. Ramoncito, the son of Don William García, the consignatory, delivered the port and customs documents to the captain and two letters: one from Pinkerton's,

Inc., and the other from Georgiana Lavalle. The unloading and loading took place in less than five hours, and after filling the tanks with water and fuel, at a little after nine, they once again set out to sea to get the advantage of a fine night breeze allowing them to sail before the wind.

April 19.

La Bellotte, like new, haughty, enchanting the moon with her fine bearing. We're headed toward Grand Cayman. A Brandenburg concerto on the radio. The two letters on my table, the rum right beside them. Had I been born a boy, I'd like to have been a composer. Everything's backward. My soul is sad. I must need the "Magnificat." It would be good for me to cry, but I don't know how. Weis weeps easily. And Paulito sighs like a little old woman. A letter from Pinkerton's agency. New York. 100 Church Street. I ought to throw it in the sea. Always new turf on the cemetery of the sea, its tombs lying open like nuptial beds. Silk pajamas, silken gowns, with flowers on both sides. Laces that adorn the air. And in the depths of the ocean, the only dead that move; the only dead that maintain some life. If my ship should founder here in Bartlett Deep, the Gulf current would carry me north to the coasts of Florida, Georgia, the two Carolinas, Virginia, Maryland, Delaware, New Jersey, New York (I must open the letter from Pinkerton's), New England, Nova Scotia, Iceland, Ireland, Spain, Portugal, the Sargasso Sea, and once again, the Caribbean. To die, to live, to encounter. Nimes is at the helm because no one can hold the course before the wind as well as he. Soon the old man will leave us. He wants to end his days on the key, near his Juancita. I don't know why. The dead are never joined in the earth. Beneath the earth, everything is permanently still. My parents are separated by a handspan. It's more than a continent between them. Amen. The maritime museum in New Orleans wants to buy *La Bellotte* from me. I have confidence in the winds that this beautiful siren will not end in a place like that. She's still too young—as we reckon the ages of ships, dogs, and elephants—to submit to the enemy. She is ten years older than I—the age of parrots, ceiba trees, and turtles—and I plan to die with her, on her, the two of us embracing before the final mystery. A beautiful cemetery the sea. Always changing. The letter from Pinkerton's:

New York, March 10, 1969

Dear Señora Matalax:

We hope that this letter reaches you, wherever you may be. We are submitting the report, to the present time, of the activities of Señor Arruza from October 23, 1968, when we received your request for an investigation:

Señor Arruza stayed at the Hotel Sheraton in Miami until October 29, on which date he traveled to New York on a Greyhound bus.

Señor Arruza attracted no notice in Miami or on his trip north. During the months of November and December Señor Arruza stayed at the Mayflower Hotel (61st Street and Central Park West). He rose early, had breakfast in a drugstore on the south corner of that intersection, and afterward walked through Central Park to the Metropolitan Museum. He had lunch in the museum cafeteria and at about two in the afternoon walked down Fifth Avenue to the Frick Gallery. Some days he walked down Madison Avenue. At three-thirty he visited the monkey house in the zoo, then returned to his hotel. He never bought a newspaper, and he never spoke with anyone. The hotel receptionist exchanged routine conversation with Señor Arruza when she handed him his mail or his weekly statement. Señor Arruza did not ask for any radio or television set to be installed in his room. After resting until seven-thirty, Señor Arruza left the hotel and, always on foot, walked daily to the Rainbow Room, a restaurant located on the roof of the RCA Building, in Rockefeller Center, and there he spent two hours eating, drinking copiously, and contemplating the city by night. On three occasions he went to the theater. Twice a week he visited a call girl, a woman with whom one makes an appointment by telephone. His correspondence was limited always to statements from his banks in New York and Berne. On December 28, Señor Arruza contacted a real estate agent, a Mr. Thompson, of Brown, Tauberman & Thompson. On the 30th, by automobile, he accompanied Mr. Thompson to East Hampton, Long Island. He was shown a mansion with a walled garden near St. Matthew's Episcopal Church. January 2 he signed the bill of sale, delivering a check for $356,000 in payment. On the 3rd he left the Mayflower and moved to the estate. In the bill of sale were included two automobiles, a yacht outfitted for deep-sea fishing, plus all furnishings, curtains, carpets, china, crystal, etc. An employment agency provided Señor Arruza with a chauffeur, a cook, a gardener, a valet, and two maids. The house has a dock in the rear where the boat is anchored. The chauffeur is responsible for the fishing gear and engine. Every day Señor Arruza goes out fishing, completely alone. Until today, March 10, Señor Arruza has not shown the least interest in anything happening outside his estate. Saturdays and Sundays his call girl comes to visit him. Her name is Miss Dianne Hayward. Please inform whether you desire us to continue our investigation. The agency's fees to date are $1,234: payment can be made to any bank in the United States.

Sincerely,
F. H. Bond
Assistant Manager

The philanderer, the braggart, the cock with seven combs and clear eyes, had been tamed, what the hell do you think of that! Rum tastes dry in the mouth when the Devil gets the last laugh.

April 20.

Almost night. We entered Georgetown under little sail because the wind's been blowing like fury. The crew went ashore. They left me here alone with Nipe. Nimes went too, to visit a half sister on Grand Cayman. The others went to the tavern run by Prazeres, a half Indian from Guyana who distills his own liquor, and who, they say, has the hottest girls in the whole Caribbean. I know they're trash with teeth they can put in and take out. I told the boys to have a great dinner for me, because no one knows how to fry oysters, de-licious, and cook turkey with *mole* sauce like Prazeres's woman. Red Beaujolais wine, deep red, to ease the sadness. The postmark on Georgiana Lavalle's letter says Paris 75, 5e Arrondissement, Paris 75. And a second postmark on the red and blue border:

Paris, April 7, 1969. Since yesterday I've been going around and around with this envelope, as if it were a roulette wheel. Dinner. I'll eat on deck. Nipe is my dinner companion. She likes to peck at the plates and stick her beak in the wine, which, naturally, is excellent. Nipe clutches food in her claw and lifts it to her beak. She looks like a person. Lights are shining on the scales of the Cayman. A third dinner guest is with us. Her name is Ella Wheeler Wilcox. I like her poems. "Laugh, and the world laughs with you." Nipe has climbed on my right shoulder, cracking the hull of a sunflower seed. "Weep, and you weep alone." Nipe flies to the top of the mast as if aware of Ella Wheeler Wilcox's lament, or mine, which is slowly rising in me. "For the sad old earth must borrow its mirth." Lend me your mirth, earth. Profound silence all about. Perhaps in Prazeres's tavern they are sharing a little laughter, at a good price. Nipe returns and lifts a clawful of seeds. "But has trouble enough of its own." Poor earth, Ella Wheeler Wilcox, poor earth that denied you mirth in 1915. It had enough of its own problems then. The First World War. Then Abyssinia, the Second World War, Korea, the Middle East, Vietnam. Earth, sea, air, life, wine, death. 5e Arrondissement. On a map of Paris I see that there are many familiar landmarks in its boundaries. St. Germain, D'Orsay, St. Pères. Georgiana is living with Miguel Ángel in one of these places. Perhaps I should visit Paris someday. I too deserve an honorable old age.

Paris, April 6, 1969

Señora:

Have you ever heard of me? My name is Georgiana. A beautiful name for a useless creature. So useless that I wasn't able to intervene between your son and the Seine. In the mirror of my iron lung I watched him walk away. This morning an inspector from the prefecture came to visit me. He showed me a photograph. It was Miguel Ángel lying on a table in the morgue. He will be buried tomorrow in Pantin. I shall follow the funeral coach in an ambulance. Then what shall I do? I don't know. Your son had beautiful hands. They will never caress me again. Your son left no letter, and no last wishes. He jumped into the Seine from the Pont Neuf. I am sorry to have to write you this.

Affectionately,

GEORGIANA

Nipe did not descend from the mast. For what? She knew only a half-dozen words and they were all dirty. Huancavélica went below to her stateroom. She had to sleep. The following day, very early, they had to take on a cargo of sisal. The night was warm, one couldn't help but feel it. She woke very late the next morning. Paulito brought her strong coffee. They were sailing now toward the northwest, the bow pointing toward the Yucatán Channel which they would cross the following day between four and five in the afternoon. Let out the lugsail and start up the engine! The captain was on deck. Secure the cable and haul in the sail. Don't you see that the wind is showing its horns? Portside a land breeze was carrying the odor of bird's nests and corn. It was time. Well, what the hell, boys? Pray: if it's too rough we can go back. But now it doesn't matter. We go at it for all it's worth, come what may—whooeeee—for here no man turns back, you hear me? The captain, her hair flowing—coals and ashes burning from within—scrambled about the ship like the others, securing *La Bellotte*'s rigging, for she was beginning to shudder under the assault of a fierce knife-edged wind. This one will blow away the gulls. Shut the hatches and commend our sins to God. Niña Huanca grabbed the wheel. Foam and wind blew over her. Haul in the sail, for here she comes to put us to the test. If she can. Because I'm blowing hot, too.

Goddammit, give me more engine, it'll take more than this to break me!

The daylight was swept away by the wind, not the night, and *La Bellotte* hurried to catch up with it, so as not to be caught blind at two in the afternoon.

New York, 1970